REDEMPTION WEATHER

ACES HIGH MC - CEDAR FALLS
BOOK 1

CHRISTINE MICHELLE

REDEMPTION WEATHER

ACES HIGH
I
MC
CEDAR FALLS, WV

CHRISTINE MICHELLE

Cover Design ©2025 Christine Michelle
2025 Paperback Edition
ISBN: 979-8-89706-015-3

ABOUT THE BOOK

When I married Walker Smithson, I thought it was the happiest day of my life.
My family was there, we had a bright future ahead of us, and the world was ours for the taking.
Then the storms started coming.
First, there was the one that took my family.
Then, there was the one that took my husband.
Moving to a new town, new state, and starting a new life was never on my agenda. I couldn't take the ghosts, both living and dead, that haunted my every waking moment in the town I'd grown up in.
I'd been wrong about my life before. Being wrong brought me to Cedar Falls, West Virginia and left me on the doorstep of the same motorcycle club that had failed me before. It took me to a place where my future was waiting for me.
You know what they say about smoke? Where it appears, flames aren't far behind. I wasn't ready for the scorching

passion that developed between us, but my Smoke withstood the storms and brought me through to the other side where the only mark left on me was the one that he burned into my heart.

TRIGGER WARNINGS

- Cheating (not by main character)
- Family Deaths
- Betrayal
- Strong language
- Violence
- Car accident
- Orphaned child
- Fertility struggles
- Adult Situations (the steamy parts)
- Mentions of drugs/alcohol

AHMC
CEDAR FALLS
1

Poppy & Smoke

1. THE STORM

JULY 12, 2015

W E H A D B E E N A R G U I N G A B I T M O R E T H A N U S U A L L A T E L Y , B U T H E had never failed to come home before.

I sat in my living room, body twisted so that my chin rested on the back of the couch and stared blankly out into the vast darkness beyond my house. Once in a while, a flash of lightning would allow me to see down the lonely stretch of gravel drive leading from the old farmhouse that I'd inherited from my parents. My field of vision almost expanded to the place where the drive would meet the road if it weren't being swallowed back into the darkness before my eyes could follow the path. The fast-paced, tink-tank sound of the rain hammering down on the tin roof that covered my large expanse of porch was normally something I found soothing and would lull me to sleep as it had since my childhood.

As an adult, the rapid-fire sound of unrelenting raindrops hammering into the tin roof held neither promise of sweet dreams nor any respite from the worries that invaded my mind. Walker and I hadn't left it at a good place that morning when he took off for parts unknown with his club brothers.

He'd been born into the life of the motorcycle club that he was now a full-patched member of. His momma, having been one of the club's sluts, and his daddy – only known for certain thanks to DNA testing – had been one of the club's brothers in the Aces High MC. They'd originally been with the Tallahassee Chapter down in Florida before Walker came to help start the new chapter in Sierra High, Georgia.

Walker had known his whole life that he'd become a part of the club, and just as soon as he was old enough, he'd prospected and bided his time until he got his wish. I came into the picture three years later, when he was 22 and I was only 19. We'd clicked from the first moment we met and we'd been damn near inseparable in the ten years since. The past eight years of which we had spent as a married couple.

Our problem was that we both wanted to start a family about five years back. We had been casual about trying for a baby in the first year, and serious as hell about it the second year, By the end of the fourth year, we had both grown frustrated for our own separate reasons. He didn't like having to save up on the baby batter for a week before I was ovulating. He really did not appreciate being called from work to come service me like a prized racing stud when the time was right.

I didn't enjoy the fact that he'd grown resentful of the ways the professionals had told us to increase our chances. My heart ached two days ago, when I'd been ovulating, and Walker flat out refused to stay home from a club run the guys were supposed to go on.

My dreams of holding a sweet little baby in my arms

were dimming; the ones of carrying one in my own belly were almost gone. It's true, I was only 29, and the doctors had confirmed my body was not the problem, so technically my dream should still be alive and well.

My husband was angry and resentful that his body was the issue, and he couldn't give us this thing we both wanted so badly. I was fully aware he'd given up on the prospect of expanding our family about a year back, despite the fact that I hadn't. I got mad at him for not following the doc's orders on how to keep his sperm count up. In recent months, he simply refused to show up at all, and that left us in a horrible place.

That was why I brought up other possibilities that morning. Our doctor explained that we would be fantastic candidates for IVF treatments. Walker scoffed at the idea saying he wasn't making a baby in a petri dish. He would not even discuss raising someone else's kid, through adoption, with me either. We'd both blown up and he'd left. It was just past two in the morning when I realized that for the first time in our marriage, Walker hadn't called, texted, or come home to try to fix things.

A boulder of anxiety sat in the pit of my stomach as I worried and fretted about whether to face his possible ire by calling his club brothers to make sure he was okay, or if I should just wait and hope all he was doing was blowing off steam with his guys.

The storm heaved angry moans as winds blew through creaking trees and determined bolts of lightning slammed down creating such a resounding cacophony of thunderous booms it left me with raised hairs on my body and more anxiety swelling deep inside me.

I texted him again. I never called late at night, in case he was riding and it distracted him. Not that I thought he'd be riding in this weather, since he took his bike and not his truck that morning. Besides, I'd already attempted to call earlier in the day, numerous times, and I had been sent straight to voicemail each and every time. That was a devastating blow in and of itself. Walker knew how important the day was to me. He knew I'd have a hard time, especially with another storm blowing through, yet he chose to remain silent.

> Poppy: Babe, please, let me know you're okay. Storm's bad out here.

I waited.

The storm beat down the land around my house. One particularly loud thunk told me a large branch must have fallen on the roof somewhere. I prayed there wouldn't be any damage, because I'd been saving money in case Walker agreed to the IVF, and I knew he'd see to a new roof on the house before agreeing to use the money for making a baby in a goddamn petri dish.

Thirty minutes since I'd sent the text, and the storm raged on around me. The constant tapping of the rain on the tin roof had become more of a frenzied maelstrom of unrelenting noise. Thunder clapped through the night every two minutes or less, and still all I heard was the silence from my phone. The boulder in my belly grew heavier. I relented and decided to text Snake who happened to be Walker's closest brother in the club.

> Poppy: He has never not come home, texted, or called by now. Please, just tell me he's somewhere safe and he's okay. I'm not asking for details. This storm is scary, big shit fell on the roof, and I'm worried he's out there in it on the bike since his truck is here.

Five minutes passed.

> Snake: He's fine. Hunkered down since he has his bike.

> Poppy: His phone broke?

I didn't send that last message. I knew better than to put our business out there to his brothers and get them involved even if I did also consider Snake to be my friend. Honestly, it didn't matter though, because I also knew that Walker had to communicate with Snake somehow, and he still hadn't contacted me. I finally let go of the pent-up emotions that had been building and let loose the deluge of tears that ran in hot, wet rivers down my cheeks to soak the front of my night shirt. It was Walker's t-shirt, the one that smelled the most like him.

Ten minutes of tears later.

> Snake: He let you know he's good yet?

> Poppy: No. Thanks for telling me.

It was almost three in the morning by the time that last text went out. The boulder of anxiety and worry, that he'd been hurt out there somewhere, was eased only to be replaced with the latest crack on my heart.

Staring into the darkness beyond my window, I couldn't help but feel the sky had opened up this turbulent mess of booming thunder, white-hot lightning, and swamping rains just for me. Shouldn't the world shake and cry for you when you realized your heart cracked so wide open that it feels impossible to ever recover? I already knew things were bad between us, but the storm, the night, the significance of everything culminating on this particular day seemed to cry out to me that my marriage had just come to terrible, inevitable, and sad ending.

My parents had been gone for six years, my little sister with them. They were taken in a car accident during a storm much like the one that raged outside my window. Lightning struck a tree just up ahead of my family when they were driving home. My dad swerved to miss the brunt of it when it split and fell. The slick roads and sloppy shoulder sent them down over the embankment and straight into the swollen river below. The car had rolled down 75 feet to the water and entered top down. They never stood a chance of making it through that.

Rain continued to trail down the windowpane in time with the tears that streaked their salty paths down my cheeks. Walker was out in this mess somewhere, and didn't bother to let me know he was safe. He had to remember that it was the anniversary of my family's accident, because he had been there with my older brother, Keith, and me when it all went down.

That's how I knew, deep in my gut, that we were finally over; because the man I'd loved all these years would never leave me to worry during a storm like this one. It said everything that he couldn't be bothered to contact me on this day, the anniversary of my family's deaths, during a storm so similar to the one that had taken them. The fact that he had left me to grieve alone and worry about him on top of that spoke volumes. His cell going straight to voicemail for me while Snake was able to get a hold of him was even more telling. Then there was the fact that Snake would have said: "He's here, don't worry," if he had been in sight somewhere.

Two headlights lit up the view outside my window. They were sitting high enough that I knew it was a truck coming up my drive. I thought about turning the porch light on for whoever it was, but then I remembered the power had gone out hours ago.

Walker hadn't brought the generator up to the house from the shed out back because he stormed out on the heels of our fight instead. I had candles, though I hadn't bothered to light any. There were flashlights stowed here and there around the house too, but I hadn't bothered to grab any of them. I didn't have it in me to get off the damn couch and out of the window. I watched as the shadowy figure navigated in the dark from the driveway to the porch. Then, I listened as the doorknob was tested with a jiggle, and once found unlocked, turned fully to admit the stranger into my house.

"Babe, you need to lock the fuckin' door." Snake hissed those words out irately before he attempted to scan the dark, shadowy room. "What the fuck? Poppy?" Concern laced his voice as he took in the scene. "How long has the power been out here, babe?"

"Don't know," I answered with a scratch in my voice from disuse, or possibly the emotion that had tainted it with a gravel-like quality I didn't like all that much. "Most of the night, I guess," I added apathetically.

"I know you have a generator, babe. Why don't I hear one running?"

"When I went to use it to plug the fridge in, it wasn't there. Still in the shed, where Walker left it this morning, I suppose. It's a might too heavy for me to drag up here now that the yard's a damn pond and with the winds the way they have been," I explained as I went back to staring out the window. Lightning lit up the sky, and therefore my face, since I was looking directly at it.

Snake sucked in a deep breath before cursing out, "Fucking hell!" A light from his phone shown as he angrily stabbed at the screen for a while. Then he tucked it away again before he spoke. "You mentioned something heavy fell on the roof? I came to check, doll. I can use my phone light, but if you have a flashlight that'd be better?"

"Should be one in the drawer there, behind you," I told him as I sort of half-assed pointed to the little desk that sat in the entry way of our house to catch all the crap from our life as we walked through the door. Mail, keys, and pieces of this and that littered the desk on any given day.

"Fuck!" I heard him exclaim a few minutes later, and when I went to investigate, I saw what had caused his reaction. The branch, or whatever had hit the roof with a loud thunk earlier, had done damage. Rainwater leaked in all over the bed in the master bedroom.

Maybe it was the weirdness of the night, the stress I'd been under, or perhaps I'd finally just snapped and gone plain crazy. When I saw how sad my carefully chosen duvet cover and shams looked, as a soggy mess under the steady trickle of water, I laughed. I laughed so hard Snake trained the flashlight in his hands on me.

"Babe?" he questioned gently.

Once I swallowed my laughter back down, I shrugged. "No one's using it anyway, why not?"

Why not, indeed?

Why not let the sky cry down on my sad marital bed, in my even more miserable house, and add more despair to the burden I already had to bear that night?

Why not?

"Poppy, let's get you back downstairs. I'll get the boys out first thing to help patch the roof when we can assess the damage in the light of day."

"Sure, why not?" I asked again knowing that nothing really mattered anymore. My husband couldn't give me a baby, and he hated me for that like it was my own fault. My husband didn't come home, didn't call, text, or care that six years ago that very day I lost most of my family to a similar storm. He didn't care I'd be worried.

He no longer cared if a tree crashed down on our roof, into the bedroom that seemed to be at the root of all our problems. I should have been sleeping peacefully in that bed when it happened instead of waiting up in the living room for a sign that he was safe and alive. He didn't care that the house now wept over our bed, the same way I wept – damn near nightly – over our tumultuous relationship. So, why the fuck not invite his brothers to assess damage to our roof when that should be his job?

"Poppy," Snake gently called my name again when he reached the bottom of the stairs a few moments after I meandered my way down in my fog of why nots.

"Hmm?" I made the questioning sound lightly as I took my position, cocked sideways on the couch with one foot under my butt, as I twisted to stare out into the stormy nothingness of the night once again.

"Poppy, are you doing all right, sweetheart?" he asked, voice soft and gentle like I was a stray dog he was trying to coax in for its own good.

My focus remained on the vast black emptiness outside before I closed my eyes, took in the slowing noise of the rain on the roof and the somewhat lighter whooshing of the wind through the trees. The rumbles of thunder were noticeably fewer and farther apart now, too. The storm was abating, and would leave fresh soaked land and swollen creeks and rivers in its wake, but what it couldn't take away or leave behind was my heartache or a cure for it.

"No, Snake, I'm..." The words I'd been about to say died on my lips as the low-riding headlights of a sports car pulled into my drive. The driver did not get out, and only paused long enough to allow for the bulky shape of a large man to unfold himself from the vehicle. He leaned in and words were obviously spoken. After he slammed the door shut, the car peeled out in reverse, backing down my drive at a dangerous clip considering the conditions. As it pulled onto the road, distant lightning lit the sky just enough for me to see that I knew that car, who was driving it, and none of it equated to good things in conjunction with the man who walked through my door being my husband.

That car belonged to a woman I had once called a friend, and her signature perfume wafted in on the wind before my husband could make it through the door and close it behind himself.

Snake stood as a shadowy figure near the stairs and shook his head, in what I could only assume was disappointment, at my husband. I almost wished for light, so I could see the emotion playing out on his face. Then again, I didn't think I could stomach seeing any more evidence of how, and with whom, my husband of eight years, my man of ten, had spent the night while I'd sat in our house with rivers of tears and a belly full of worries waiting to hear his voice or see his face again.

How did you walk away from the one person your heart had ever sung for? No matter that it had stopped singing, because it was still impossible to learn how to un-love someone you thought would be yours for a lifetime.

I didn't move from where I sat twisted on the couch. There was nothing left to move to.

"You're one stupid son of a bitch," I heard Snake hiss out on a whisper. The whispering wasn't exactly effective considering there were no ambient noises now that the storm had moved on and the destruction left in its wake waited quietly to be cleaned up and made new again.

"Poppy?" Walker called out to me. I didn't move, and didn't make a sound in response. "Why are you sitting in the damn dark, darlin'"

Walker hadn't called me darlin' in years, and the sudden resurgence of its use hurt worse than I could imagine. I was left to wonder if it was only because he'd used it on someone else that night. I sat there, unable to speak, because an odd numbness settled into my bones, shutting me down a little bit further with each moment of my life that ticked miserably by. At least, I couldn't until he attempted to move closer to me.

"Stop," I managed to choke out. "When we got together my best friend at the time made a play for you, and you swore to me that you would never come to me with another woman's perfume clinging to your skin again. I believed you did the right thing back then and fended her off like you told me."

I unfolded myself from the couch and looked at the shadows of the man I used to love, thinking it was probably for the best that shadows were all I could see. Then, as if I'd made God angry somehow, and the night was all about my punishment, the lights flicked once, twice, and settled back into their original on position.

Walker looked as though he'd been struck down by the shroud of anguish that clung to him as he took in my obviously emotional and disheveled state. I was certain I was nothing much to see. I'd dressed nice and applied my makeup carefully earlier, when I went to visit my family on the anniversary of their deaths, before another killing storm blew in. My husband had always gone with me before. This year I'd been alone. Six years to the day ago. I thought I lost everything. I found out, in the remnants of another storm, that I had one more thing to lose.

"Jesus, Poppy, it's not what you think. She was the only one that hadn't been drinking, and I needed a ride."

"Yeah?" I whispered. "I needed my husband. I needed the man who swore to love and protect me until death do us part, for better or worse, and all the other lies you told me." My voice never raised much above that whisper. "Today, of all days. Tonight, of all nights." I saw it dawn on his face as his brows crinkled up, nose scrunched, and then I watched his shoulders fall with the weight of what he'd done.

"I forgot," He spoke softly, words filled with remorse that meant nothing to me anymore.

"Went to the cemetery to see them by myself. First time. Barely made it back before the storm, because I waited so long for you to show up. You never answered my messages, picked up my calls... Power went out. You never brought up the generator, so I just sat here," I pointed to the spot on the couch I'd just vacated.

"I waited. I worried. Storm got worse. I texted again. Finally, checked with Snake to make sure you were breathing somewhere, so I could let the knots in my belly loose. A damn tree fell on the house. Roof's leaking on the bed we used to share."

My body vibrated with a glut of emotion that began to break through the momentary numbness I'd experienced at seeing who dropped my husband off in my driveway.

"You finally blow in after the cemetery, after the storm, after someone else came to check on me, and when you do, it was in the car of the woman whose friendship I obliterated for you. In the car of the woman whose scent is still clinging to you as you walk into my home." I stood there and watched him watching me while noting that Snake hadn't moved from the bottom step across the room yet. Both men stood still as statues as I ended my recap, but I wasn't done.

"I've loved you for ten years. I've loved you through losing my best friend because of you. I've loved you through losing my family. I've loved you through being hurt about not getting a baby right away. I loved you even when you gave up on trying to make a family with me. I loved you through you not being able to accept that your body was the reason, and I even loved you when you refused to listen to the simple things you could do to increase our chances." I took a deep breath before I continued because the next part hurt so much.

"I even loved you through our fight yesterday morning about trying IVF. But I cannot continue to love a man who doesn't want my love and can't – for whatever reason – give it back to me anymore. I thought I could continue to deal with it, but tonight proved I was wrong to think that. I was so wrong, and what we have can't be fixed, because I got your message loud and clear this time. It's unfixable."

"Poppy, please, don't jump to conclusions. I was at the clubhouse. Any of the guys could tell you that. She just happened to be there too," Walker stated.

I glanced beyond him to Snake and back to Walker. "She was the only one who could drive?" he nodded. "Then how'd

Snake get here? He doesn't seem drunk to me." Walker's shoulders stiffened.

"I wasn't ready to see you yet when he left. I hadn't planned on coming home tonight. I was gonna stay at the clubhouse to clear my head, but then Snake got here and texted that I better get my ass home any way possible. He made it a 9-1-1 text."

I scrutinized Walker with a head-to-toe once over that made me cringe. "You smell like another woman, your hair looks like someone's been running their hands through it, there's lipstick on your shirt and your neck, and you forgot the most important day of the year when I needed someone to hold my damn hand while I reflected on all that I've lost. And for all that I'll never have, because you gave up on making it happen for me."

Tears spilled fresh rivers down my cheeks as I stared at my husband. "You couldn't come home because you needed to clear your head about me trying to find a better way to have a family with you, and this is the state you come home in?

"Even when you forgot the importance of this day, I still sat there in the window, waiting, watching, hoping and praying you were okay. I've been praying you had club business that kept you. Praying you weren't dead like them. Not on a day like today. Not the day I lost everything else. Please, God, not again." My voice cracked as all my fears and pain poured out of me in those words. I swiped angrily at the tears on my face when I offered that piece of my heartache up to a man who clearly didn't deserve it any longer. The refrain that had been tripping through my thoughts all night set my emotions on fire once more.

"I think this'll be worse," I lamented. "This will break me even more because I ended up losing you finally. I'll still see you walking around town, though, and it won't just be a figment of my imagination like it was when I lost my family. You'll really be there, maybe walking down the street with my ex-best friend on your arm. Instead of trying to tell myself that you're dead and gone, like I did with the rest of my family, I'll just have to remind myself that you're no longer mine. No matter how broken that leaves me in the end, it's what I know will happen now."

"Poppy, no!" His voice sounded almost as broken as my heart.

"Can't fix this by myself," I pointed to him and the state he was in. "And I certainly can't fix what you'd rather ignore while you go seeking happiness elsewhere."

"Poppy," That time it registered that my name was somewhat slurred. I turned my back on him. "Get what you need to take to the clubhouse for now. I'm sure they can find room for you, since you planned to stay there anyway. We'll work everything else out later when you aren't drowning in everything you found entertaining tonight while I sat here heartsick and worried to death."

"Please, Poppy, don't do this." He cried. Literally, cried.

"No," I said as I glanced back over my shoulder.

"No, what?" he asked.

"No, I'm not the one who did this. We may have had our mutual issues to work out, but you're the one who dropped the ball on our lives yesterday in order to party. You're the one who only came home when your brother told you to. You're the one who sent me to voicemail, ignored my messages, and couldn't even let me know you were alive for the first time in ten years. You're also the one who came to our home looking freshly fucked, smelling like my ex-best friend, wearing lipstick that certainly isn't mine, and having her drop you off in *my* driveway."

I watched as he swiped at his mouth, thinking I'd meant that the lipstick was there when I had been referring to what I saw on his neck and shirt. "I meant what was on your shirt, but good to know she was on your lips, too. And that is why I am not the one doing this. You did this to us, and right now, I need you to leave. Get your things and go."

"Come on, man, let's go pack you a bag. You can crash at my place if you want to avoid the clubhouse."

"Seriously? You think it's cool she's kicking me out of my own house?" he asked Snake. I didn't bother correcting him that it was not his house as I had inherited it from my dead family – the one he'd forgotten all about today.

"Walk, listen brother, that woman – you got any love left for her in your heart – you'll do what she asked for now. She was broken tonight when I got here. You add to that misery for her right now, and you are not the man I thought I knew." Snake scoffed. "And I've already seen enough tonight to make me question that shit anyway."

"You believe I'd cheat on my wife?"

"I believe you're wearing enough evidence, and the way you chose to come here tells a story you aren't sober enough to deny right now. Let's get you a bag and get you gone so Poppy can get some rest, man. She had a rough fuck of a day, and then was up all night worried. That shit is no good, you give two shits about your woman, you come with me now and give this to her."

"Of course I care, she's my wife. My life," He corrected.

I wasn't sure my heart could crack into any more pieces until that moment. If only he'd treated me as if that's what I was.

2. THE AFTERMATH

I WOULD NOT HAVE BEEN ABLE TO SLEEP ON MY BED EVEN IF IT hadn't been soaked through by the rains last night. It would have smelled like him. Instead, I snagged a blanket out of the hall closet and wrapped up on the couch. I slept, briefly, but my ever-rampant thoughts continuously woke me.

What would I do now? I met and fell in love with Walker Smithson when I was just 19 years old. I'd had one other boyfriend before him, in high school, and that was it. Everyone I knew these days was tied to Walker and the club. Hell, even my older brother Keith was a member of the club, though he'd transferred to Cedar Falls, West Virginia to follow some girl there after our family died. He wanted me to go too, but I couldn't give up the house. He couldn't stay and see it, and the memories it held. I got that. We just dealt differently with the loss of our family. Now, I wondered if it wasn't time to let it all go and start fresh myself.

That thought became more and more the way I was leaning as I considered the fact that the only friends I had in this town anymore were associated with the club and being that he was the brother and I was just the old lady, I'd seen what would happen. I'd be the one ousted – as it should be – and while I understood the way their world operated, it would leave me even more alone than I already was. It might have been different if we'd managed to have kids together before we got to this point, because then I'd still be welcome around as the baby momma so long as I didn't cause any trouble for Walker and his boys, or any of his future women.

I sat thinking these thoughts, sipping my coffee in my broken house and dwelling on my broken relationship and the fact that I'd probably never have a chance at my own family now. That was a tough reality to swallow since it was the one thing I'd wanted more than anything since losing my parents and sister. I still yearned for babies. I yearned for a family of my own. I missed what I once had with my parents, my brother, and little sister. I still wanted to build that again for myself. I wanted to pass along my mother's recipes, my father's wisdom, and my sister's sense of humor to my children. I had planned to do all that with the man I loved. Now that he would be out of the picture, I wondered if I'd ever get a chance at any of it, and I hated him a little bit more for bringing even more loss to my life.

I heard the telltale sound of pipes blazing up the drive and saw Walker riding up on his Harley with a few pickup trucks trailing behind. Why I thought I would at least get a reprieve today was beyond me, but that's apparently what I got for thinking. I got surprised yet again.

Walker was first though the door while I continued to sit on my couch in nothing but an over-sized t-shirt and panties while I sipped my coffee. Walker's eyes flared at the sight of me so I wasn't surprised when the first sober words I heard from him in 24 hours were to order me around.

"Baby, you need to go get dressed. Guys are here to work on securing the roof."

"Okay," I stated as I sat my mug down on the coffee table. "That explains why the guys are here, why are you?"

He blinked at me. Once. Twice. And once more before he spoke again. "What do you mean, why am I here? I'm here to fix the leak with the guys and I fuckin' live here besides."

"Shit!" I heard Snake hiss out as he came charging through the front door. "Sorry, Pop. He doesn't remember a whole lot from last night."

I moved my eyes from a bewildered Walker to Snake then. "So, how did he explain to himself how he looked this morning?"

Snake winced. "He remembered, vaguely, being here. Figured it was you, I guess." Snake offered as Walker snapped his attention from me to Snake.

"What the fuck is that supposed to mean?" Walker sneered out.

"It means," Snake started, but I interrupted.

"Do you remember leaving here angry yesterday when I told you I wanted to have a conversation about giving IVF a try?"

"Yeah, and I thought I'd made it clear that shit don't fly with me," he stated coolly. It was clear he didn't remember anything I'd said last night, because no way he'd talk to me that way today if he knew I'd told him we were through last night.

"Walk," Snake hissed out, trying to contain his friend.

"Yeah," I murmured sadly. "You made that crystal clear when you walked out saying you had better shit to do with your time." I watched as Snake shook his head in what was clearly disappointment while Walker stood there getting worked up. "You remember much of your day after that?"

"What I did with my day isn't really relevant since I worked," he ground out.

"You had the day off yesterday," I reminded him.

He stared at me again like I was a stranger. "On a Friday? No, the fuck I did not." Walker glanced between Snake and me, and judging by our faces he realized he was missing something vital.

"Pay attention, because you miraculously managed to block out our heart to heart from early this morning," I told him. Then I proceeded to fill my husband in on how my day went, how my night progressed, how he came to be in our house between the hours of four and five in the morning, and how I asked him to pack a bag and stay gone awhile. I literally watched as his knees buckled and he went down to the floor, eventually managing to plop his ass down while he processed what I'd just summed up for him.

"I did not sleep with anyone else. I would not do that. I couldn't have," he was mumbling. Clunking sounds were coming from the roof above me which meant the other guys had went ahead and got to work on the branch embedded in there.

"Why didn't you fill him in?" I asked Snake.

"He wouldn't have believed me. I tried to tell him about who drove him home last night and he laughed and called me a liar. I'm really sorry, Poppy. I tried to get here before he did, but got held up by Prez this morning."

"That makes two of us, Snake," I muttered, because I was sorry to have to go over all this again, too.

"Poppy, we fought, but that's not the end." Walker finally told me. "I'm really sorry I lost my shit and forgot what yesterday was. I'm even more sorry – the likes of which you will never know – that I worried you like that. I swear baby, I never got your calls or messages. I would have been here. You say I got a ride from Tanya, but I swear I don't remember that at all. I would have never brought her to this house in any capacity. You have to believe me."

"I wish I could, but you did. Saw her car, with my own eyes, smelled her perfume all over you, and saw the lipstick on your shirt and neck. If not hers, it was some other woman's who was not me. None of it was good, Walk. All of it was heartbreaking which is why I really need you to go. I need space. You took yours yesterday and did what you did with it when the only thing I'd done to inflame your temper was ask to try one last thing in order to have a family with you. What you did, and didn't do in that time actually deserves my ire and since you got to do whatever you wanted when you needed space away from me..." I left the rest open ended until I saw he wasn't getting it. "You got your space free and clear, now I need mine. I need to sort myself; and I need to do it without you here."

"Poppy, we've managed to work through everything so far. Don't quit on me now," he protested.

I laughed.

"Really, Walk? Working through everything now encompasses you getting pissed at me for wanting to try every available option before I give up on having a baby forever? Not just getting pissed, but getting so angry that you walked out during storm prep on a day we were forecast to get a whopper of a nor'easter, the same day a similar storm took my family from me six years past, and you didn't give a goddamn. We all saw where your walk took you. It took you to the one woman who tried to ruin us in order to get you for herself in the very beginning of our relationship. Yeah, my cracking, dying heart last night really felt how we managed to work through everything when I was worried sick about you while you were busy cozying up to another woman enough to have just fucked hair and lipstick all over you when you finally showed up after receiving texts from your buddy. I won't even get into the fact that you miraculously received his texts, but none of the ones I sent you."

Walker pulled out his phone, and searched through it again looking completely puzzled. I held mine up with the string of texts I had sent him yesterday as proof. I watched his mouth drop open then as he glanced down at his phone and seemed to be putting two and two together.

"I won't even ask who had access to your phone yesterday, Walk, considering you don't even let me touch it." He swallowed thickly then.

I huffed out the deep breath I managed to pull in and then I looked my confused and despondent husband in the eye. "You need to leave. I need for you to go. You need to go and try to remember why you allowed some woman – who wasn't me – to be all over you at some point last night. Why some person obviously screened my calls for you, and you allowed that to happen too, because I know for a fact you never let anyone touch your phone. You need to figure out why you're so against trying to have a baby with me. You need to figure out why it was so easy to forget the worst day of my life yesterday, and you need time to consider that you made last night the second worst night of my entire life. And I need time to decide if I can move beyond any, or all, of that."

"Fuck!" He hissed out quietly.

"Fuck!" He yelled out the second time as he kicked off the floor and stood. Walker looked from me to Snake and back again. "Poppy, I have fucked up – a lot – but I have never, not for a single minute, stopped loving you. I need you to remember that." I took in his steely gray eyes with the faintest hint of blue to them that could be warm and loving when they locked with mine while we made love or could be cold and fierce when he was angered by something. His hair that needed a cut a couple weeks ago, and since he didn't get it had started curling a bit at the edges, was something else I would commit to memory with just my eyes, as I would never find myself running my fingers through it while we chatted in bed again.

The slight hint of stubble that graced his face and neck was something I had both loved and loathed over the years. Beard burn from stubble was always a hell of a lot worse than the time he'd grown out a full, well-trimmed beard. I had loved his beard. The guys had teased him about it, or some such, and he'd shaved it off never to grow it again. Who cared that I had liked it. Those large hands of his that went with his equally large framed body dragged through his hair in frustration as he catalogued me while I did the same. I would miss the comfort and safety I'd found inside those strong arms, beside that barrel of a chest, when I listened to his heart thump-thump, thump-thump, just beneath my ear as I leaned into him. I could hear the ghost of that sound now.

The ghost of that sound intermingled with a strangled version of my name from his lips as I turned and walked out of the living room and back into the kitchen where I didn't have to watch him walk out of our front door for the last time. It pained me to admit this to myself, but even if he hadn't had evidence of another woman on him when he came home last night, I had reached my breaking point. The fact that he was no longer interested in having a family with me – no matter how we had to go about that – and the fact that he had forgotten something so damn important to me, I had found the straw that always proverbially broke the camel's back. Only this time, that straw was breaking my already battered heart.

3. THE CHANGE

ONE THING BECAME PAINFULLY CLEAR OVER THE COURSE OF THE next two months, and that was the fact that I could not stay in Sierra High, Georgia one moment longer.

I could not face the aftermath of what those two terrible stormy nights had taken from me. First my parents and sister, then my husband, all were casualties of one storm or other. In their own ways they were all gone to me now. My heart was in tatters and despite the fact that Walker's last words to me had been, "Poppy, I have fucked up – a lot – but I have never, not for a single minute, stopped loving you. I need you to remember that." He hadn't really meant those words. He certainly hadn't been living by them during our separation. I knew this because he hadn't come for me. He hadn't called, messaged, written a letter, or attempted to contact me in any way, shape, or form since the day I told him to leave. I also heard the talk in town about how he wasn't exactly being chaste during our separation either.

Apparently, he'd given each and every one of the club whores a workout they wouldn't soon forget.

If that was love, I supposed I was better off without it. As expected, the friends I thought I once had were a rare sighting in these parts. They left me to my own devices and my own misery. The only person associated with the club who had been by to see me after the first month came and went was Snake. Every time he showed up his face seemed a little bleaker than the last time. My thoughts turned to him once more as I noticed his Harley creeping up the drive while I stuffed another piece of my old life into yet another box. Not unlike the emotions I'd boxed up and hidden deep, even from myself.

The door opened and the smile Snake had been wearing on his handsome face dropped off with his next step. "What are you doing?"

"What does it look like I'm doing?" I asked without a hint of emotion to my words while I sealed the box I was working on with packing tape and watched as Snake took in everything around him. It had been a week since his last visit here and as he was beginning to understand a lot could change in a week.

His eyes bulged at the sight before him. Boxes, packed ones, were everywhere. There weren't a lot of unpacked boxes left, because almost everything had been done. I'd worked the last day of my two week notice on the jobs I needed to give notice for the week before, and all of my other work was done remotely from home anyway so I'd had plenty of time to get shit done. Snake finished his scan of my empty – that is to say boxed up – house and he set panicked eyes back to mine just as quickly.

"Poppy, what the hell?" he asked again. "I was just here a week ago," he started. I waved his statement off.

"I've had the time, and it's time. I can't..." I glanced around the house I had grown up in, the house I now owned because of tragedy, and the house where I had been alone and swallowed up by memories for two whole months without so much as an apology from my husband. "There are too many ghosts here for me now," I stated simply.

He nodded his head sagely. "You find a place closer to town?" he asked as he swallowed thickly, knowing full well I hadn't, because if I had he would have heard about it by now through the wonderful southern grapevine. I just shook my head.

"Fuck, you two have the worst timing of any couple ever." His statement was laced with a goodly amount of frustration. I moved the box I'd just sealed up aside and stared at Snake, trying to puzzle out what that meant. I didn't have to make the attempt long, because Snake stalked over to me, kneeled down to my level, and lifted my chin with his fingers so that we were eye to eye and I wasn't missing a thing. "He's coming for you today. He had a plan, he's worked on it, and he's ready now."

I laughed.

Snake tipped back on his heels, shocked by my outburst.

"His last words to me were supposedly filled with hope, promise, and the fact that he had always loved me, Snake."

"I know, I was there for that," he reminded me while his brow was still furrowed with question.

"Uh-huh, and then nothing. Those were literally his last words to me." I stated simply as I moved slightly away from the man and pulled another folded box to me and started putting it together to hold the last of my things.

"Nothing?" Snake questioned as he watched me continue on with my chore.

"Nothing," I confirmed.

"I'm not getting you, babe."

I cast my gaze back in his direction then. "I mean, nothing. I haven't seen him once since then. I didn't hear from him once since then, not even to check on me, or to tell me that he was okay. Everyone else from the club stopped coming around or talking to me about a month back, and I figured it was because I was out completely now since I was no longer with Walker, but the conversations I overheard in the grocery store made that explanation a little more complicated." He just stared at me and waited for me to fill him in on those conversations. "Seems none of the women wanted to come around me because they were uncomfortable after having seen the way Walk was tearing through the club whores left, right, and center over the previous month." Snake's wince let me know there was merit to those conversations I'd heard.

"Poppy, I think he should be the one to explain, but he was working out whether or not he should let you go to be happy and find someone who could give you the family you want easier, or whether to fight and try again to give you what you want even though he didn't agree with how to do it."

"And the answer to his dilemma was found in club whore

pussy? We're still married, Snake. I asked for time apart to sort my feelings, and his response was to ignore me, our problems, our vows, and fuck everything with tits."

Snake dragged his hands down his face in frustration. "I didn't say he went about his time constructively."

"I haven't touched another man since my high school boyfriend before Walker ever came to town," I spoke on a sigh as I pulled the latest box closer to me. "We may have been separated, but we were still married, Snake. We were still under the vows of marriage, and I was still taking in his last words to me when he never came back, called, or did anything but let me find out from strangers, and former friends, that the reason he never came back, called, or anything was because he was too busy buried balls deep in other women. I have to say, as a way to show you love someone, that falls pretty damn flat."

"He wasn't with anyone the night of the storm. He'd passed out a bit on the ride home with Tanya. She pulled over, and made it look like what she made it look like to get under your skin. She admitted it to one of the girls."

"And instead of coming to me with this news he makes it true by fucking everyone else?" I asked again not getting angry just stating the facts. I had already done angry when I first heard the rumors, and as a result I had a few less things to pack up since they were smashed beyond all hope of fixing them.

Snake shook his head. "He was angry that he was living in the clubhouse, because you threw him out based on her lies instead of believing him that he wouldn't fuck around."

"But then he did, and that was only a small part of the

reason I threw him out, Snake. That night..." I felt the emotion I'd boxed up creeping back out at about the same time I heard another, familiar, set of pipes coming up the drive. "He broke me that night long before he showed up and I saw the evidence that had been planted on him," I explained.

"I know, Pop, I know." Snake finally muttered in a defeated tone. "Fuckin' idiot still doesn't realize what he was throwing away because of his pride," the man stated plainly as he stood up from where he had been kneeling beside me on the floor. "You want me to stick around for this? I have a feeling things are gonna blow when he sees the state of the house," Snake offered.

I just shrugged. "It doesn't really matter anymore. Nothing does," I told him, and he gave me a worried glance then as the front door opened, and the exuberant voice of Walker boomed out, "Poppy, baby, time to talk!" The words were coming out of his mouth as he pushed through the door. The exhilaration and exuberance left him as soon as the sight before him took hold.

"What in the fuck, Poppy?" he yelled then, anger turning his words red hot instead of glazed with the playful happy tone of moments before.

"Walker," I muttered as I finished putting the last book in the box I'd been packing and started taping it up. Walker came over to me, snatched the tape, and threw it across the room.

"What are you doing? What in the fuck are you doing?" he yelled, but more in a panicked tone than in anger at that point.

"Walker, have a seat, and..."

"On what?" he asked incredulously. "It's all gone." The last came out scratchy with emotion.

"It is," I agreed, only I was talking about more than the furniture and personal items. "Everything that belonged to you, I hauled out to the shed and locked up. I was going to arrange a day for you to come pick it up. I wasn't certain if you'd need to get a storage unit or if you already found a new place."

"Found a new place? Poppy, I wasn't even aware I should be looking for a new place," he explained, words still choked with the tears that shimmered in his eyes.

"Really?" I asked. "You broke our marriage vows and you thought you were coming back here to me?" I asked in a serious, if quiet tone.

"I did what?" he snapped back while turning an accusatory glare Snake's way.

"Don't look at your friend like that. He didn't tell me anything. I heard about it every time I had to go to town for groceries, to pay a bill, and while I was at work. It's why the clubwomen stopped being friends with me. They weren't comfortable talking to me while keeping your secret; only they were so keen to gossip about it in public that I heard it everywhere anyway. Heartbreak was bad enough to deal with. The loneliness of not having anyone, not one single person, care about me enough to check on me other than Snake since you've been gone was bad enough, but coupled with the humiliation that you were out there fucking every woman who would spread her legs for you..."

I shook my head as I felt my entire body starting to

quiver with the pent-up pain, anguish, and anger I thought I'd been boxing up alongside my possessions. I stared straight into his eyes then. "When I said no one came to check on me, that included you. Not one single phone call, text, or appearance in two months while I had to hear about what you'd been up to daily, and you strolled in here expecting things to be the same and to just fall into the place you finally decided you wanted?"

He swallowed hard. "Poppy, I..." he started, looked at the floor, then back to me before he tried again. I saw the moment he decided to spare himself and let his frustration loose on me. "You didn't believe me! You kicked me out because of some lie Tanya perpetrated again while I was passed out. I never slept with anyone, and you kicked me out for it. I was pissed."

"I didn't kick you out for that," I told him, my words quiet to his angered booming ones.

"You..." he started before my words sunk in. "You what?"

"I decided I needed space to think before you ever rolled into the drive with her. I was at the end of my rope, hanging precariously that morning when you walked out on a conversation that was important to me, before we could even have that conversation. Then you didn't show for the cemetery. Then it stormed and you never called or cared that I would be worried considering a similar storm had taken my family on the same day years before. That night broke me in a way you will never understand, because I realized that no one who loved me – truly loved me still like he once had – would put me through that on that night of all nights. You could have rolled in with Snake instead that night, and the result would have been the same. I would have still needed space."

"Poppy," he started, in a calmer voice.

"Your last words to me were to remember that you had never stopped loving me, but you did stop. You stopped before you spoke them, and you made it clear you had stopped with what you did during our time apart. You weren't showing me you still loved me over the past couple months. You were sleeping with other women. You weren't doing whatever it took to come home, because you were too busy utilizing your bed in the clubhouse. You didn't call, send messages, send letters, or come to me. You didn't check on me, not once to make sure I was okay."

"Snake kept me updated."

I laughed.

"Snake kept you updated? Snake wasn't trying to save our marriage. Hell, he acted more like a husband trying to make sure I was okay than you. He checked on me, made sure I was eating when I wasn't. He made sure I was sleeping, when I wasn't. He made sure I had ice cream stocked so that at least I could eat something while drowning in my own misery. That man – your friend – could have won me back with his behavior. Had you done any of those things yourself, you could have won me back. Instead, you continued to be a selfish bastard after me kicking you out for being a selfish bastard. You expected that being selfish and not giving a shit what was happening with me would win you my favor? You expected that I'd ever step foot in that clubhouse again knowing that you fucked every goddamn skank that walked through those doors? Just the thought that you would put me in a position to have to potentially run into one of the whores you were screwing while we were still married shows how little you cared. Did you really expect me to be sitting here waiting with breath held for you to come charging through the door once you got it all out of your system, even as you embarrassed and disrespected me?" I asked, legitimately wanting to know.

He said nothing, just hung his head in front of me. "You put all your effort into breaking everything further. I told you when we first got together that I would never be able to live with a man who could be with another woman while he was with me. I reiterated that message when we went through it with Tanya the first time. Separated and taking time to sort ourselves out didn't mean you had a free pass to easy pussy while I was sitting here devastated that the love of my life couldn't even pick up a fucking phone to see if I was okay. Hell, I couldn't even have managed to look at another man if he was throwing himself at me, let alone sleep with one, because my heart was too broken to breathe some days let alone hit that level of activity."

"Poppy, shit," he started then lifted his head so I could see the tears that were running freely down his face. "I don't know what's wrong with me lately."

"Well, that makes two of us," I informed him as I stood and moved to go across the room and collect the tape he'd thrown there. I ran my fingers across the hole he'd managed to put in the wall where it hit, and I just felt the whole situation draining me further. Something else I'd have to fix before I left.

"I'll patch it up for you so you don't have to worry about anything else, Pop," Snake offered from across the room.

"Fuck man, I'm standing right here," Walker spat out at him.

"Not blind, brother. Also know you're the one that caused the damage. I'm just trying to patch it up so it'll stop bleeding out all over the place. Been trying to do that all this time, but you wouldn't pull your head out of your ass and listen to any-fuckin'-body." Snake shook his head. "A year ago we had a talk, and I told you then that this outcome was your future if you didn't put that pride of yours aside and realize what you had in front of you instead of dwelling on the obstacles.

"You didn't listen then. Six months ago, I pointed out shit was sliding further, bleeding more, and that your woman never smiled anymore. You didn't fuckin' listen. Told you a month ago your woman lost weight, wasn't eating, and was barely hanging on, and instead of coming to her you got pissed that I was 'in your shit again' and took one of the club bitches to your bed." I winced at that, because hearing Snake say it made it so much worse, especially knowing he did that on the heels of hearing how poorly I was dealing with things.

"The guys – the ones without women – have been envious of you for years. You got the best of them right there." Snake pointed at me. "That woman is gold, and we didn't have as much history as we do I'd be all over picking up the ball you dropped, brother. She deserved a fuck of a lot more than you gave her. And make no mistake, because I won't allow you to think differently, I watched as she tried, repeatedly, to bring you back to yourself over the past couple years. After things went bad I watched, as you did nothing but make it worse. I can't watch that shit anymore. It's not right. It sure as fuck ain't fair to her. You are my brother, but I'm fuckin' human and I won't stand by and watch her bleeding out for nothing any longer. Enough is enough, man." Snake turned to me then. "Poppy, you need help with what you got going on here, you have my hands at the ready, including patching that shit for you so you don't have another thing to worry over."

"Thank you," I told him honestly, and sort of wished I hadn't heard him tell my husband that he'd go for me if there weren't so much history. There was a time I would have went for Snake too, but that time was about five minutes before I'd met Walker, and I wasn't one to look back and ruminate on what could have been. That way lays madness.

"This is your family's place," Walker finally said, looking around at all the boxes. "What are you doing?"

"Walker, I'm leaving. I can't stay here, because all the memories are ghosts that are haunting me instead of comforting me like they once did. We've had two bad storms since..." I didn't bother saying since the night we split. "We've had two bad storms and it almost killed me to go through them here alone in this house."

His face scrunched up with emotion as tears once again fell down his cheeks. He stared at me through them and then glanced around again. "I did this," he muttered on broken words. I didn't confirm or deny that sentiment. It was, for the most part, true. He had done this. "I broke the place you loved. I took that along with everything else, and all because I couldn't get over the fact that I was the broken one and not you." Well, that was a slap in the face. At my reaction Walker held out a hand to calm me. "No, you don't understand. If it had been you, I would have been okay with not having kids, or doing whatever we had to. When they told me it was me, I felt like I'd failed you. I failed us. My body is broken, and can't give you what you wanted. What we wanted. I couldn't handle being the one... not being man enough..."

"You're a fucking idiot then!" I yelled, finally, for the first time in months. "You're not broken. You're sperm count was lower than normal is all. If you had listened to the doctors and done one fucking thing they suggested we could have had a baby by now." I started ticking the things off on my fingers. "Wear loose fitting underwear," ticked off with my forefinger. "Stay out of hot tubs and the like," I ticked off with my middle finger. "No climaxing the week before I ovulated," I ticked off with my now empty ring finger, and that's when all hell broke loose.

"Where are your rings?" he shouted.

"This is not about my rings. This is about how your stupidity broke our marriage. You broke us because you couldn't handle being told you needed to work harder at something." I huffed out. "Unbelievable."

"Where the fuck are your rings?" he demanded on a shout again.

I ignored his shout and stomped into the kitchen and pointed to the note I had written that was stuffed into an envelope on the counter along with the boxes that held my engagement and wedding bands. "There," I yelled as I pointed. "I was going to have Snake drop them off to you since I didn't want to stop by the clubhouse and chance seeing you with one of the whores who were more important to be with than your own fucking wife!" I screamed at him.

"I think maybe you should be going, man, before this turns ugly." Snake stated calmly to my husband.

"Where are you going?" Walker asked me instead.

"That's not your business anymore. You lost the right to ask me that when you forgot your wife and your vows to her."

"Where the fuck are you going?" Walker shouted again.

"You didn't care where I was, how I was, or what I was doing for two fucking months while you screwed everything with a pair of tits, Walker. You don't get to waltz in here and pretend to care now."

"I'm not pretending," he stated on a defeated note.

"Well, it's too late to start caring again," I informed him.

"It's never too late," he answered back.

4. THE NEW

Saying goodbye to the people and to the place you had known your whole life should be hard. It should be wrought with emotional hugs, kisses, and a huge fanfare seeing you off on your next journey. It should be all of those things, but for me it meant my brother coming to town with a moving truck, and Snake helping him load it up. Snake was the only person there to hug goodbye. The realtor had come by while we were busy to put the for sale sign up in the yard. The tears came then, because it was a sight I never thought I'd see or be ready for. The fact that I was ready now spoke to how broken I was inside.

When I hadn't responded to Walker telling me it's never too late he had turned on his heel and walked out of our house for the last time. Two days later I watched from the window as he brought his own truck and loaded up the things that belonged to him that were in the shed. He never approached the house and I never bothered to leave it. I watched as the man I thought would be my everything climbed into that truck when he and Tank were done filling it and drove away. It was the last time I saw him. Now, I stood watching a woman hammer the for sale sign into my family home's yard and I wished for the briefest of moments that things had been different and Walker had come to me before he broke things so irrevocably.

"You ready, sis?" Keith asked me. I looked at my brother, who was wearing his MC kutte stating his name was Chief now, and I had a moment to think to myself that I needed to remember to call him that from here on out. I'd forgotten he earned the moniker because our Cherokee roots came out full blast in him when he was born. He had the high, pronounced cheekbones, darkly tanned skin, midnight hair, and deep brown eyes that our father had given him.

Our father had been nearly full-blooded Cherokee with a white woman thrown in the mix a few generations back to muddy up the line, as he used to joke. Our mother was of Irish and Scottish descent, and I took mostly after her. I got my dad's warm brown eyes, but that was all I'd inherited from him. The nearly red, curly hair I had been graced with my entire life was straight from my mother's gene pool, as were the freckles across my face, shoulders, and chest. I tanned, but in doing so the freckles ran amuck and reproduced all over my skin. I was not in any danger of being dubbed some crazy Native American name as my brother had been. Instead, I usually was forced to prove my heritage to anyone who hadn't been around since forever to know who my parents were.

"I'm ready," I finally responded, as thoughts of my

heritage drifted away. My hands were shaking as my brother took them in his and pulled me in close for a hug.

"I know this is tough, but I think getting away from this town, and all the memories is going to help you heal finally, lil' sis. I promise this isn't the end of your life, it's the damn beginning."

I had no choice, but to believe in the words my big brother spoke. It was all done now anyway. My house was up for sale, cleaned out, and everything I owned was stuffed in the back of a moving truck heading for a new town. Cedar Falls, West Virginia may have only been a bit more than a six-hour drive, but it was a world away. I'd only been there twice since my brother moved there after our family was killed. Both of those times I had gone with Walker, because there was a club thing to attend. This was definitely going to be a change. That being said, I knew I'd have to come back home to Sierra High at least one more time. I'd filed for divorce through an attorney just the day before. Walker should be served his paperwork today, according to Thom Lincoln, my attorney, and then we had no less than 30 days to wait for that to go through, unless Walker contested it for some reason. We had already split all of our marital assets. The house belonged to my brother and me in equal shares so Walker was not entitled to anything from its sale. He could try to fight for a portion of my part of the sale, but he'd be dumb to attempt it since the whole town knew he stepped out on me and Georgia didn't look kindly on cheaters in court.

Once I was settled in the passenger side of the moving truck my brother hopped in. He'd been making sure that my

Subaru was attached properly since we were towing it behind us. My brother, in all his infinite wisdom, thought driving myself out of town might be a bit too emotional for me and he didn't want me behind the wheel if and when I broke down – emotionally, because my car was in perfect working order. He most likely wasn't wrong, but I was not about to tell him that.

"It's going to be okay, Sis." His kind, soft words struck a chord in my heart, but I definitely disagreed with him. It was not okay now, and I didn't foresee any of it being okay in the near future. It probably wouldn't be okay in the distant future either.

"Sure," I muttered instead as I watched the town that held nearly every memory of my existence pass as we drove by like it was nothing more than forgotten scenery.

"I still think you should have let me go hunt that fucker down. Just the fact that he left you alone on the anniversary gets my goat, especially in a storm." My brother tried to swallow back his anger before he blew his top, and I wondered how he knew that, because I certainly hadn't been the one to spill the beans.

"How did you know that?"

"The question that needs to be asked is why didn't I know it sooner? Hell, I would have been down here two months ago to collect you had I known how bad shit had gotten."

"I didn't even know how bad shit had gotten until that night, Keith, and when it happened I wasn't really in a sharing kind of mood, you know?"

"I know," he said, softening his tone again. "Believe it or

not, you have friends in the club. They informed me. They did it fuckin' late, but they finally did it."

"Snake?" I asked already knowing the answer.

"He was the first one to let me know. Asked that I wait to hear from you before I made my way down, because he thought, wrongly, that Walker would get his head out of his ass in time to save shit." My brother hissed out. "I wish my sister would have told me, though."

"I know. I'm sorry. I thought..." I started, stopped, and then sighed out a breath that I couldn't keep contained anymore. "I thought things had to get better, you know? Then they didn't. Then they got worse, and I needed to figure out what I was going to do with my life without someone else telling me what to do. I went straight from mom and dad's house to being with Walker. I've never done anything on my own without guidance, so I wanted to just make that decision without having to wonder if someone else had made a bad choice for me. This way, it's all on me."

"It's not all on you, and don't you fuckin' take it all either. Walker fucked your marriage up, Pop, not you. He's the one that got you started on the kick to make a family. He should have sucked up his bullshit and finished what he started, any way that was possible once he got you excited about it. He didn't do that. Then he dropped his stress, wounded pride, and whatever other bullshit burdens he carried in your lap without a care for your feelings. Then he really fucked up, and continued to do so once you took your space. From what I hear, none of the burden of the loss of your marriage falls on your shoulders, so don't try to carry it."

"I know that," I told him. "I also know that what I chose

to do after was on my shoulders. Will be for some time. I'm having to start new, and scrape off the old, and the old still has a grip on my heart, Keith. Whether I want it to or not, it's there. We spent ten years together," I reminded him.

"Yeah, and from what I hear the last few of those haven't been roses. You made the right call, Lil' Sis. If his answer to you kicking him out to give you time to sort your thoughts was to bang through club whores, then I guarantee that shit would not have ended with a reconciliation. I liked Walker for you back in the day, but something happened to break that man along the way, and you can't heal what doesn't want to fix itself."

"I learned that," I told him as we crossed the state line into North Carolina. "Thanks for coming to help me, Keith." I finally said as I glanced over at my brother who would end up being my strength for a while.

"Should have forced that move on you when I made it. I've been worried with you so far away and our visits so few and far between. We lost everyone else, sucks that we haven't been closer. I know that's partly my fault since I left, but not a day goes by I don't regret not bringing you with me. Living with their ghosts wasn't a good idea. Living where I couldn't make sure Walk was doing right by you, less of a good idea."

"Okay, big brother, well you get to see me every day now and I'm sure it's going to get old, so be prepared." I tried to lighten the mood with that. Keith took it for what it was and just smiled and then turned the radio up, and thank goodness for satellite radio, because there certainly weren't any quality stations in these parts.

Thankfully, my family's house had been paid off when I inherited it so I simply put aside the money that I would have used as rent somewhere else so that I would have a rainy-day, house-fixing, whatever I needed it for savings to fall back on in hard times. That fund was what I'd planned to use for the IVF with Walker before everything fell completely apart. Instead, I was going to have to use it to help maintain my new place until I could get a steady job in Cedar Falls and get my feet under me again. I did some freelance work with graphics and building and maintaining websites for businesses, but the pay had just been the extra stuff I hid away in my savings account. It was more of a hobby, but I was hoping I could pick up a few more clients in addition to a steady paycheck somewhere once I got to Cedar Falls.

Keith had found a small two-bedroom house in his neighborhood that was within the budget constraints I asked for. He had taken care of getting everything set up for me beforehand, so now all I had to do was get there, unpack, and start looking for a job. Granted, he had not sent me any pictures of the house or anything, so it was kind of a crap-shoot as far as what I'd be walking into.

Ten hours later we had made it to Cedar Falls; and with the help of my brother's friends Wren, Bender, and Dragon everything had been unloaded from the truck; and I was already starting to sort through and unpack boxes. "You gonna be okay if I take off now?" My brother asked in the midst of a wide-mouthed yawn as I pulled the silverware from the box labeled kitchen. Everyone else had already gone once the truck had been unloaded.

"Sure, Keith." He gave me a look and tapped his kutte

that he had donned sometime after the last box had been brought in. I rolled my eyes, but smiled at him as I stated, "Chief. You know, that should probably be offensive somehow."

He just shrugged. "Dad would have thought it was funny as shit," he told me on a chuckle. He was right. Our dad didn't have a politically correct bone in his body. Funny was funny to him didn't matter if it was completely inappropriate or not.

"As long as it comes from a good place, we can find humor in it," I repeated what he'd always told us. This made my brother's smile widen. He came over and grabbed me up in a big bear hug, lifting my feet off the floor as he did so. "I'm a phone call away, Sis, but I'm wiped out and needin' sleep about now."

"Thanks for everything, Chief," I told him as I hugged him back and then released him.

"You do not have to thank me for that shit. Should have been here all along," he murmured the last.

"Hey doll face," Wren called out, having popped his head back in my front door. I had thought all the men had gone, but apparently Wren had just been outside on a phone call. "My old lady already put word out she's wanting to meet you. I think her and Leanne are chomping at the bit to take you out to lunch tomorrow if you're up to the company. They could also help unpack some." I smiled at Wren's offer. After the freeze out I got from the old ladies belonging to the club down in Georgia I wasn't sure I was ready to jump back in to socializing and making friends with the women of the club here. At my hesitation Wren's face screwed up in puzzlement. Obviously, he knew I'd been an old lady before, so I guess he assumed I'd jump at the chance.

My big brother came to the rescue before I had to stumble over my excuses. "During her split from her old man the women from Sierra High stopped checking on her and speaking to her. Her man was up to no good, they knew about it, and I guess they thought it was too awkward a situation so they stayed away. I think my lil' sis is gonna be a bit gun shy where the old ladies and club are concerned," my brother informed him as I marveled at the depth of his understanding.

"Well, shit," Wren hissed out. "I swear, there are times I think we need to forget the patch, and just kick some much deserved ass to help straighten a brother out instead of allowing him to dig a well-deep hole for the woman propping him up."

"You and me both," my brother stated.

Wren patted my shoulder then, and smiled at me. "When you're ready then. I'll explain why they need to bottle that shit up for now."

"Thanks," I managed to get out quietly.

My brother left, along with Wren, and as I closed and locked the door behind them it took approximately two point five seconds for it to sink in that I was alone. Completely alone. There was no promise of Snake dropping in here to alleviate some of that loneliness with his quick check-ins. The house wasn't familiar to me like my family's home had been. Most of the things that would have made this place seem more homey and familiar still sat packed up in boxes. I glanced around the open plan house where the space before me seemed to double, then triple as panic set in about the decision I'd made to come here and start fresh.

I was about two seconds from full blown, can't breathe, sweat dripping down my back, heart hammering anxiety attack when there was a knock on the door. Oh, thank God. This meant my brother probably forgot something, and maybe I could convince him my couch was the place to be tonight. I moved quickly, turning around and throwing the lock, then swinging the door open to a complete stranger. Granted, he was a beautiful stranger, but a stranger none-the-less. The only thing that kept my already accelerated heart rate from ramping up again was seeing the Aces High Kutte he wore.

"You okay, honey?" he asked, taking in what were probably my wide eyes and rapid breathing.

"Um," I started and failed.

"I came by to see if Chief was still around," he stated quickly thinking I must be freaking out because of him.

"He, um," I put my hand to my chest, as if that would help calm my overactive heart and make things better. Then I took a breath, and let it out slowly. All the while the man stood on my doorstep keeping a watchful eye on me as he took out his cell. I held my other hand out – the one not holding my heart in my chest – and shook my head no. He halted his movements. "Sorry, you caught me at the start of an anxiety attack, I think."

"This happen often?" he questioned with careful consideration.

I shook my head again. "Nope, just when I move from the only home I've ever known to a new town, to look for a new job, while I'm in the middle of divorcing my cheating husband," I over shared.

"Mind if I come in, check to make sure all is well while I'm here?" he asked as he tapped the patch on his chest. "Name's Smoke. I'm a good friend of your brother's, and he's told me a bit about your situation already, but if you need to share more with someone who isn't family, I'm all ears. Even if you don't, might help to have someone around for a bit while you adjust. Not sure what Chief was thinking leaving you alone in a strange place your first night here."

"I'm pretty sure he wasn't thinking. He was tired; so don't hold his poor manners against him. It's been a long couple days."

"I can imagine," Smoke nodded his head towards the house again. "You gonna let me in, or I gotta call your tired brother and get his ass back over here? Whatever makes you the most comfortable, honey."

Holy hell. I moved out of the way to allow the man into my home. As he brushed past, I could feel exactly how solid his muscles must be under that kutte. It was obvious by his arms since his biceps were larger around than my thighs, but still the man must have lived in a gym. Combine that with the chiseled features he was rocking, the well-trimmed full beard, and the nearly shoulder length chocolate brown hair, and he was any woman's dream come true. Then there were his eyes, the ones I'd had to take a moment to look away from, because I swear they were dazzling me with their imperfect perfection. They both appeared to be a jeweled mix of colors; only one was more in the blue green spectrum while the other was a mix of green, brown, and gold.

"Sorry, I don't think I have much in the way to offer you," I told him as I closed the door behind Smoke. "Just got here and all."

Smoke smiled, and his straight white teeth shining out of his full lips and that beard ramped up his beauty tenfold. "You should probably check your fridge and cabinets. Pretty sure the old ladies had you set up before you got here."

"What?" I asked the question as I moved to the kitchen and started opening the fridge, then the cabinets, and seeing that they indeed had stocked me up on all the basics, as well as some of my favorite things. "Chief must have told them," I stated out loud, using my brother's road name for the benefit of his brother.

"Imagine he did. That's how it works around here." His voice from right behind my shoulder surprised me and I spun to see he was so close I could feel his body heat rolling off of him in waves, or maybe I was just having hot guy hot flashes. Jesus, what was wrong with me? I hadn't so much as looked at another man in anything other than a friendly way since I started dating Walker way back when. Now, here I was practically panting after one of Chief's club brothers. He was one of Walker's club brothers too, even if he was in a different chapter. I was pretty sure there were rules about picking up another brother's ex-old lady. Then again, maybe there weren't since nothing stopped my old man from getting with every available woman around the club while we were together.

Smoke's fingers came up and caught a curled tendril of my hair between them. He studied that piece of hair as if it had the answers to all of life's questions. "Chief never mentioned you were beautiful, or a red head," he muttered. "This is real." I assumed that was a statement about my natural copper colored hair so in lieu of answering I just gave him a slight nod. The movement seemed to pull him out of whatever trance he'd been in and Smoke quickly took a step back from me, releasing the curled lock of hair, and smiling at me once again. "Did you see any beer in that fridge?" he asked, but proceeded to look inside for himself. He had a beer in hand, popping the top off as I finally got around to answering.

"Sure, help yourself," I muttered.

"You drink beer?" he asked.

"Sure, it's a hell of a lot better than wine, but not as good as rum." At that he laughed and then gave me a once over.

"You don't look the type to pound down the hard liquor."

I just shrugged my shoulders. "There's a time and a place for everything. I don't drink tequila, wine sucks – mostly, and beer is good for everyday things like watching a game or whatever, but when I go out for fun with the girls or something it's rum and coke all the way."

"Rum and coke," he repeated thoughtfully. Then he pulled his phone out and appeared to send someone a text before slipping the thing back into his pocket. "What kind of game?"

"Sorry?" I asked, not really sure what he wanted to know.

"You said beer is for when you're sitting around watching a game. What kind of games do Georgia girls watch when they drink their beer?"

At that, it was my turn to laugh. "Well, most Georgia girls are probably watching football, but I went to see the

Thrashers with my dad when I was sixteen, and it was so damn exciting. I fell in love over three periods, and have been a die-hard fan since. Of course, the Thrashers mostly sucked, and were sold to Canada, but I still go watch the Gladiators once in a while, and hope for those guys to get the call up to the Bruins, because some of them really deserve a shot at the big time." I crossed my fingers in the tradition of good luck.

"No shit?" he asked, looking completely blown away by my response.

"No shit," I responded. His grin grew wider still.

"My brother plays for the Penguins," he stated nonchalantly as he stood there sipping on his beer afterwards like he hadn't just dropped a major bomb.

"As in the Pittsburgh Penguins?"

"Is there another?"

"Well, I'm sure maybe somewhere, but..." I laughed then. "You're kidding, obviously. Making fun of the only hockey fan from the south," I proclaimed.

"Hardly the only one, and I'm serious as a heart attack, honey. Kent Lewis is my younger brother. He was..." I cut him off before he could finish.

"First round draft pick, right winger, three years ago," I finished for him. He stood a little straighter as I rattled off the information he had surely been about to tell me.

"You're from the south, doesn't that make you a Predators or Hurricanes fan?"

It was my turn to grin now. "Well, yeah, but the game I went to with my dad was the Thrashers against the Penguins, so when my Thrashers were sold I transferred my fandom to the Penguins and they definitely work harder to put me in my happy hockey place." I glanced around like someone might be listening in. "Do not make that common knowledge. I'm still not far enough north, and will possibly be lynched for my disloyalty."

That sent Smoke into a fit of laughter that only served to ramp up his insane handsomeness by another bajillion notches. Jesus.

"Fuck, am I glad you showed up just before the season kicked off. These fuckers are all about football and baseball around here, now I know where to go to find a hockey buddy to swill beer with while I yell at the screen."

That had my grin amped up too, and before our hockey bonding could commence there was another knock on my door. Smoke's grin did not die as he announced, "I got it," and proceeded to saunter over to answer my door like he was at home here. He spoke to someone outside, not letting them in, and then grabbed a brown paper bag from them while handing them money. "Thanks man," I heard him say as he shut the door on whoever had been there and brought the package to the kitchen.

He held it up victoriously when he got closer to me. "You have some glasses unpacked yet? Maybe a spoon or something too?" I gave him a funny look and just pointed to the box I'd been working on before my brother took off. He reached in, came back with two glasses and a spoon, and set it all down on the granite countertop with the mystery bag. Then he began unpacking the bag. Two, two liters of coke, one of them diet, and then a bottle of Captain Morgan Black was set beside them. Oh dear lord.

"First night in a new home seems like just the thing that

requires rum and coke instead of beer, honey. Figured we could kick this shit off right, especially since we'll be best hockey buds from here on out."

"You know what?" I asked quietly.

"What's that, honey?"

"I like you," I stated simply as I snatched the rum from his hand and poured a healthy double shot into the glass he'd just rinsed out, not realizing as I did so that I had forgotten all about my earlier panic, the mess my life had become, my failed marriage, the lack of babies in my belly, and pretty much everything else that had been on my mind and bogging me down lately.

"That's real good, honey, because the feeling's mutual." His beautiful, multi-colored eyes twinkled in the minimal light of my kitchen as I splashed Coke into my double shot of rum and stirred it. He laughed as he took the bottle from me and began pouring his own. "So much for southern hospitality, huh?"

I graced him with a large, toothy grin as I responded. "You seem capable enough," I told him before tipping my glass up for another healthy gulp. His top row of straight, white teeth bit into his plump bottom lip as he continued to mix his own drink while not taking his hypnotic eyes off of me. Once he was finished he glanced away long enough to take a swig of his own and then he turned those eyes back to mine.

"Honey, fair warning, I really like what I see before me, so you keep throwing challenges out there and I will end up showing you exactly what I'm capable of."

Oh. My. Wow. He did not just say that.

Our eyes still locked, his twinkling with both amusement and seriousness, I realized quickly that yes, he absolutely did just say that. The truly disturbing thing was how my body reacted to his words, because I know he took in the full body shiver that ran through me. Thankfully, he couldn't know the state of my panties, because that would have been super embarrassing. Good lord, what had I gotten myself into when I opened up that door?

He tipped his head in a gesture indicating my living room area. "Let's go settle in, and you can tell me how you think my baby brother's team is looking for the coming season."

Just like that, he'd tamped down the fire blazing in my belly, but not so much that he didn't leave me behind, smoldering a bit as he took off for the couch while I watched his fine – and I really do mean fine – ass walking away from me. 'Lord, Jesus, if this is not part of my moving on plan, you might want to send some help!' That prayer was sent up while attempting to look through my ceiling into heaven itself. I knew when I met Walker that he was the one for me, but even our immediate – or subsequent – chemistry had not been this combustible.

5. THE BED

SHOTS HAPPENED.

How in the heck we went from sipping on rum and coke to straight shots of Captain Morgan Black Label was beyond me, but it definitely happened. The other thing that took place was the laughter. Smoke was a funny guy, and he kept me in stitches with stories about the guys at the club, my brother, and the men he worked with at Cedar Falls Fire and Rescue, which was apparently what he did for a living outside of the club because it was 'his calling' as he put it. I had to admire that in a big way, because any man who found his calling tended to be passionate in a way those who hadn't found it weren't.

"So, did you ever play hockey like your brother?" I asked after his last story about Kent Lewis, the famed right-winger.

"Sure. I was damn good at it, too. I had to quit so that Kent could look better," he stated solemnly and with such a straight face, I damn near believed him. Instead, I threw the hand towel I'd been using to mop up a spill at Smoke. He caught it and tossed it on the floor with a wet-sounding plop.

"You did not!"

"Well, I did quit, but long before my baby brother got good."

"Why'd you quit?"

"I was at my high school girlfriend's house, and her grams lived two doors down. When I headed out that night, I smelled smoke pretty strong and turned to notice Gram's house was ablaze. I yelled for Stacey to call 911 and I took off like a rocket. Grams was no spring chicken, and I knew she'd need help if she was even awake. I tore into that house, fought through smoke that immediately blinded me since there also weren't any lights on, and made my way back to the bedrooms. Her house was a smaller version of the one Stacey lived in, so it made finding my way easier."

"Anyway," he continued after another shot was consumed. "I found Grams. She was out like a light. I wasn't sure if she just slept heavy or if the smoke had gotten to her, but I closed her bedroom door, got her window opened, kicked the screen out, and then I snatched Grams up. Almost dropped the poor old lady twice. I was a freaking weak ass motherfucker back in those days. Sixteen, still growing, and hadn't figured out what hitting the gym could do for me, you know?" I did not, but I figured it was a rhetorical question.

"Got her out safe just as the CFFRD and an ambulance were rolling up to the scene. A firefighter took her out of my struggling arms, and ran her straight to the ambulance where they put oxygen on her. The fire chief was on scene, and he clapped me on the back, told me 'good job, son,' and started barking orders to his men to get shit done and put the fire out before it had a chance to spread to the other houses in the neighborhood."

I was smiling while listening to his story. "So, that's where you discovered your passion?"

"Yeah, took off the next day to hit up the fire station that responded to the incident. I went in, requested a meet with the chief, sat my ass down, and laid it out for him."

"Wow!"

"Yeah, wow," he chuckled. "So much 'wow' that good old' Chief Murdock fuckin' laughed his ass off for a solid five minutes before he sobered up and told me how it was really gonna go. He said, 'son, I appreciate ya, and you did good yesterday, but you're gonna finish up high school, move on to college, and start hitting the gym, then you come to me if you're still ready for this. I need men with brains and brawn to fight fires and save lives. You ain't ready yet, but you will be one day if you stay smart about it.'" His eyes glimmered as he recounted the speech he'd been given by the fire chief. Then he grinned at me as he took a swig of the beer he had to chase his shot with.

"So, you followed his instructions and here we are?" I asked.

He laughed again. "Well, I almost wasn't. See, when I started hitting the gym, I met Wren and Heavy. They saw to my training, and I got a gleam in my eye for the bikes they always rode away from the gym on."

"Wren was here earlier, helping out with the unloading," I told him. "I liked him."

"Yeah, he's a great guy, and even better now that he's settled down with his woman and little girl."

"So, the call of riding free nearly derailed your plans?" I asked, still curious.

"Yeah, you could say that. Once I graduated high school, I enrolled in the community college like I was supposed to, but I also started prospecting for Aces High. They understood I was a student, and Ghost liked the idea of having a guy who actually wanted to get an education too, so they worked with my school schedule. I just had to prospect a little longer than the norm." I nodded my head understanding this since I had both a brother and a soon-to-be ex-husband in the club. "I got caught up for a little while in the life. Even prospects get their pick of women and fun when they're off duty, so long as they aren't stepping on the brothers' toes."

"Yeah, so you're saying you discovered easy pussy and partying," I laughed out the words, knowing full well I'd never say pussy in mixed company if it weren't for all the alcohol loosening my tongue, or the residual anger. Still, I felt the heat of a blush staining my cheeks when I did it, and Smoke's eyes went liquid at the sight of it.

"Exactly that." His voice held a lower, huskier quality as he spoke those two words, and the sound did something to my insides I wasn't sure I was ready to acknowledge. So, I prodded some more.

"So, what then? Obviously you still went on to be a fire-fighter."

"I did. Around the same time I was earning my patch, and in danger of actually flunking out of a couple classes, my mom had her first stroke. She was young for that shit, and the doctors told her they thought her birth control, and the fact she smoked cigarettes like a fuckin' chimney were probably to blame. While she was getting healthy, I figured I needed to pull my head out of my ass and make sure my ma stayed that way. I'm eight years older than my little brother, six up from my sister. They were 12 and 14 at the time. I was 20. My mom couldn't work for a while, and I needed to get my ass in gear and make some money for my family. I was pulling in some cash working for the club, but definitely not enough to keep a family of four afloat while paying for college, and then the medical bills started piling up."

"That's a lot to put on your shoulders. Where was your dad?"

"Gone. That bastard ran out when Kent was three. Never saw him again. My mom worked her ass off to keep us fed, clothed, and a roof over our heads. Lucky for her, the house was paid off. They'd inherited it from my dad's family when I was a baby. Only decent thing my dad did was put that house in mom's name before he took off. I guess it was her parting gift since he was leaving her to raise three kids on her own with no help and no other financial support."

"That sucks," I managed to get out even while my tongue felt heavy and thick from the alcohol. Actually, it sounded more like 'that thuckth" so I started giggling. Then my hand flew up to try to hold the giggles in so I wouldn't offend Smoke. I definitely wasn't trying to make light of his family's situation. He didn't seem offended, though. Instead, he got up, went to the kitchen, and brought back a couple bottles of water.

"I think it's time for these," he stated as he handed me one.

"Oh Jeezzzzus, I'm a meth," I tried to say and ended up in the midst of another giggle fit.

"She develops a speech impediment when she's drinking heavy," Smoke said to absolutely no one. "Good to know," he added as he watched me, the fine lines near the corners of his eyes crinkling with the humor that caused the unusual, mismatched gems themselves to twinkle even brighter.

"Mesmerizing," I managed to mutter as I took in the sight of him. That when his eyes changed again, becoming darker, and something more. His gaze began to appear almost lazy as his lids slid down to half-mast and got closer, much, much closer to my own. I didn't even register the fact that his eyes getting closer to my own meant he, himself, was moving in. At least, I didn't register it until his lips were on mine, and then sweet lord in heaven, nothing but bliss followed.

Smoke's arms wrapped around my body, one moved around my shoulder where his hand cradled the back of my neck, while the other wrapped around my waist and pulled me closer to him. Our lips scored each other with their heat, and when mine parted for him, he wasted no time dipping his tongue into my mouth to taste more of me. I felt that kiss from the roots of my hair to the tips of my curled toes. For some odd reason, Stone Sour's version of Wicked Game started playing in my head. Maybe it was a warning of things to come, maybe it was just the perfect mood music I was conjuring, because God rest my wicked soul, but this man's kiss was about to burn me to the ground where I stood.

Somewhere in the background, I vaguely registered thunder cracking, but it was at the same moment that I was divested of my shirt, and I couldn't bring myself to be concerned with a late summer storm. Instead, my body caught fire as Smoke blazed trails of heat up and down my ribs from his deft fingertips before he latched onto my full breasts, only separated from skin on skin contact by the sadly utilitarian, and slightly worn out, cotton bra I had donned for comfort on the long ride from Georgia to my new home. Thankfully, I was inebriated, and didn't give a hoot what my bra looked like in that moment. Tomorrow, I'd be embarrassed a plenty. For that matter, it only took a moment, maybe Smoke's mind powers, to melt the bra from my body anyway. It would seem there really wasn't much to be concerned with. If there was, I felt I sufficiently distracted him by tugging his t-shirt up his beautifully crafted body, helping him to pull it over his head, and toss it aside wherever the rest of our clothes had settled thus far.

"Please, tell me you have a bed set up." Smoke mumbled the words into my kiss-swollen lips as I nodded and then pointed down the lonely little hall off the side of the living room that lead to one bedroom on either side and bathroom separating the two in the middle.

"Left or right, babe?"

"Left," I explained as he lifted me in his arms forcing me to wrap my legs around his hips for balance while he maneuvered us to the bedroom. Luckily, Chief had put the bed together first thing, and I'd made it up once the guys were busy unloading the boxes into the other rooms. I made the bed thinking I'd be ready to crash at the end of a long day.

Never in my wildest dreams did I think I'd be tossed on top of it as the most gorgeous man in the history of manly men stripped me of my yoga pants and my equally sad cotton panties that matched the worn cotton bra of a woman who had been married and underappreciated for far too long.

I refused to dwell on those memories as Smoke leaned in to cover me with his own body, and I realized the only thing he had on was a pair of boxer briefs, color dark, but otherwise unknown in the dim light of my bedroom. Lips moved a warm trail of kisses up my thighs, teeth nipping here and there as he went, hands trailing on my outer thighs until he moved up far enough that he needed me to spread for him. Then he didn't ask, he didn't demand, he just slid those fingers around from the outside of my thighs to the inside and gave a gentle push that had me obeying the unspoken command. I dropped the tension holding them in place and allowed them to fall to the side as broad shoulders slid in place between them and hot breath trailed over my sensitive, wet flesh. I just knew I was at the gates of heaven waiting to be admitted, and then his tongue flicked over my hard bud before sliding thickly through my folds from bottom to top, ending with a seductive suck and nip of my clit that nearly sent me over the edge all on its own.

"Shit," I whimpered out as my back arched and my head flung to the side, eyes closed, and hands trailed to that gorgeous, thick head of hair Smoke had. I weaved my fingers into those locks and tugged him back down when he chuckled at my quick response to his mouth. It had been far too long since a man had taken his time with me, made me feel good, and enjoyed giving the pleasure instead of looking at the act as a chore to get me prepared. So. Damn. Long.

Smoke's fingers glided up my sides, tickling my ribs lightly as they moved to reach above him and grab hold of my breast as he continued to dip his tongue into my folds, suck relentlessly on my clit, and giving an encouraging nip now and again when I tugged at his hair. That beautiful beard of his scraped ruthlessly at the insides of my leg and the space where leg met groin. The extra sensations were both relentless and delicious all at once. One final pull on my clit as he pinched both of my nipples simultaneously sent me flying over that precipice into a momentary beautiful oblivion. "Shit, holy..." I panted out. "Jesus, God." My fingers clamped down as my body grew tight just before the ripples of pleasure blew through me, squeezing and releasing in equal measure. I released Smoke's hair and felt him roll his body right up mine, maintaining maximum contact as he maneuvered his muscular chest, with its light sprinkling of dark hair up and over my body. The friction – so sweet on my nipples – held me in the throes of my orgasm just a little bit longer while he got into position, wrapped his arms around me as if he was cradling my shoulders while slipping inside me and filling me up in a way I'd never experienced before.

"Ungh, Smoke!" His name pulled from my lips on a breathy moan just as he captured my mouth with his and matched each stroke of his tongue with the movement of him pushing into and pulling out of me. My eyes were forced open with the perfection of the moment, and I found myself lost in those fascinating multi-hued eyes of his.

"Honey," he drew that one word out on a sexy growl

before dipping his head and planting a slew of open mouthed kisses along my jaw, my neck, and down to my collarbone. "Never before," he huffed out as he started picking up his pace. I wasn't sure what he meant by that, but it didn't matter, because I was lost once again, dangling on the edge as his thick cock started hammering into a place deep inside me that was sending sparks shooting through my insides, tingling in my limbs, communicating the promise of imminent rippling waves of ecstasy.

"Smoke, I'm..." I couldn't get the words out quick enough.

"I know, honey. Feel it. Let go, because it's not going to be the last one tonight. Not done with you yet." Well, hell. That did it. Heat suffused my entire body, barreling through me on waves that carried with it the pleasure that I had been promised just moments before.

He didn't lie. It was not the last one. The last one came in a fevered moment with me on all fours and Smoke behind me, pounding into me with an abandon I'd never known from either of the two lovers I'd had in my life prior to this man. Somewhere in the recesses of my mind I knew I'd feel every minute of tonight, probably for the next week, but I wouldn't stop it to save my life. My nerve endings were all on a crash course with my next orgasm, chasing it like the pot of gold at the end of the rainbow and fearing I wouldn't get there, but hoping like hell I did in time.

"Honey," Smoke breathed into my ear as he draped his body, slick with sweat, against my back. His hand came around my waist, arm resting over my belly as his hand dipped between my legs and fingers went to work on my clit while he continued to pump into me at a desperate pace. "Let go, sweetheart. Can't. Hold. Onnnn," that last came out as a tortured growl as my release hit and swamped me just as Smoke let go, too. His hips jerked into me, hand holding me as close as he could get while he rooted there, coming deep and hard while my muscles clamped and released in rapid succession around him.

"Fuck, honey, never in my life..." he husked out as I took on some of his weight before we both collapsed down to the bed with me hitting face first and him following, riding my back down, still fully lodged inside of me as we went. He immediately rolled off to the side so he wouldn't hurt me and we both started chuckling. "Sorry," he grumbled out amidst his own laughter.

"Not a damn thing to be sorry for. I'm amazed you held it together as long as you did."

"Shh," he huffed out and tugged me to him so that my body rolled, putting my back to his front, then he swiped the blanket at the end of the bed up and over our rapidly cooling bodies. His other hand swiped the hair off my face in a gentle gesture that felt a little too intimate, but beautiful neverthe-less. His lips touched down on the top of my head before leaning in closer to my ear and whispering, "Get some sleep, honey."

"Mmm," was the only response I had, because the beating of his heart at my back, the warmth of his body against mine, and the exertion of the day and night mixed in with the drinks we'd consumed had me tipping over into sleepy la-la land before words could form.

6. THE WAKE UP

THERE WAS A DULL, THROBBING ACHE IN MY HEAD AS MY BRAIN peeled slowly back from sleep and into the waking world. The dull throbbing in my head was quickly dismissed as the ache in other places of my body made themselves known. There was also the warm, weighty body plastered to mine that took precedence over all of those aches. For one brief, heart-wrenching nanosecond, the fantasy that the husband I knew from our early years had come to me to tell me what a huge mistake I was making was in my thoughts. Then I remembered he'd stopped holding me like this long before we ever even tried to have babies. He liked his space, and never once thought about what I liked in that regard. If he had, he'd have known there was no better moment than waking up in the arms of the man you love. I supposed in my reality this morning, in the arms of the man who gave me the best sex I'd ever had.

No, it was not my husband wrapped around my body as if he were protecting me in our sleep. This was the man I'd met last night. The man I formed an instant friendship with, and the one who may or may not make things awkward this morning when he woke and realized we were spooned up together. Last night might have been a hit it and quit it fun little tryst for him. Hell, it may have been more. If I weren't in the situation I was currently in, attempting to divorce the husband who had let me down in every way possible, then I might consider the explosive and undeniable chemistry I'd encountered with the man who was still offering me peace and safety even in his sleep. I sighed thinking about how things were going to go when I attempted to remove myself from his arms. The other thing I'd realized in my quick assessment of my situation was that I had to pee, so escape wasn't only eminent it was necessary.

The arm wrapped around my waist slid up my body to position itself between my breasts while the hand attached to it cradled my shoulder. "Honey, go back to sleep," a raspy voice called from just behind me causing my body to tighten with both want and fear of the unknown. Let me be clear, I was not afraid of him, just where this situation would take us this morning.

The arm around me tightened momentarily before he spoke again. "Listen honey, I realize things carried further than either of us intended last night, thanks to our amazing chemistry and I don't regret a single second, but I know you're going through shit right now. We need to put this part on hold; I'll step back for now. We'll be friends, and go from there. No awkward moments, no wondering or worries. We're going to be straight with one another because I don't regret last night, I don't want you to, and what we started out there with the bonding we did is too important to kick away with morning after awkwardness. Never in my life been so instantly comfortable around a woman. Don't want to lose that for anything."

I turned my head into my pillow since I couldn't control the huge grin that was threatening to split my face. This man. He had just cleared up all my worries in one go. Once I got myself back under control I turned in his arm and planted a quick kiss on the tip of his nose. "That's all really good to know, Smoke, but right now you're still gonna have to ease up on the grip you have because nature calls." I raised my eyebrows as he tightened his grip and then proceeded to start tickling me. Tickling me... when I had to pee... Oh dear lord. I dissolved into a fit of giggles just as a loud banging pounded on my front door startling me and pulling Smoke from his teasing playful manner into a serious growly one.

"Who the fuck is banging on your door at the ass-crack of dawn when you just got to town last night?"

I shrugged, eyes wide with worry as I bolted out of the bed and then promptly realized I was still buck ass naked and most of our clothes had been discarded in my living room. Well, shit. I wrenched open the closest box, and praise Jesus, it was the one with my hoodies and sweats in it. I snagged a pair of jogging pants and a hoodie, tossing them on quickly as the banging on my door ramped up and the doorknob jiggled.

Smoke pulled his pants up his thick thighs and over that delectable ass of his, effectively snagging all of my attention from the person now attempting to gain access to my house without waiting for me to come open the door. I attempted to rush out of the room when I realized this, but Smoke threw an arm out blocking my path. "Let me go first, because whoever that is, they're fuckin' determined, honey." He sauntered out, no shirt, bare feet, zipping his pants up, and I followed closely behind. We rounded the corner of the hall with me on his heels as the door burst open, and my brother stood there looking supremely pissed while he took a moment's pause to assess the situation.

"What the fuck?"

"Hey man," Smoke called out lazily, no longer on edge.

"Jesus, Chief, you scared the shit out of me," I huffed out.

"Scared the shit out of you?" he asked seeming awestruck. "I came to check on you as soon as I woke and realized we had a hell of storm blow through last night. I can't believe I left you alone instead of staying here," he managed to get out as he dragged his hand through his hair. Then he glanced between Smoke and myself a moment, took in the rest of the room, and a grin spread across his chiseled features.

"What storm?" I asked. I don't know what was so funny, but my brother threw his head back and laughed heartily at my question instead of answering it.

He walked over and picked up the nearly empty bottle of rum from the coffee table and his laughter only died down to a mild chuckling as he tipped it in my direction. "I see why you weren't aware of the storm, Lil' Sis." Then his attention turned to Smoke as he cocked his head a bit to the side in question. "Any particular reason you're barely dressed at my sister's place this morning, Brother?"

I saw the shrug of Smoke's shoulders as he sauntered

forward and reached down for his shirt, tugging it back over his head. I watched as it slid down across his shoulders, muscular back, and the achy place between my thighs I'd almost forgotten about twitched with the memory of last night. Lord help me. I didn't know how I was going to deal with this while figuring out everything else I needed to do.

"Came by yesterday hoping to catch you still here. Didn't think you'd leave your sister alone her first night," there was a bit of a bite to his tone as he said the last. My brother just raised a brow at him. "You weren't here, and Poppy was in the middle of a freak out when she opened the door." This revelation received more attention from my brother.

"Pop, what the hell?"

It was my turn to shrug as I walked over to the chair in the corner and plopped my ass down, wishing I'd done it a little more gingerly as a spike of pain shot through my body. "Everything kind of hit me all at once, and I..."

"She was mid-panic attack man, so I wasn't gonna leave her like that. She didn't want me to bother you, because she said you were exhausted. So, we started talking, she mentioned hockey, and..."

"Fuck me," my brother muttered, cutting Smoke's recap off. "Should have seen this shit coming. Didn't even think," he continued to mutter. I don't even think he was talking to either of us, but more to himself.

"Anyway, had a prospect drop a bottle and some coke by, and the rest isn't really anything you want to hear."

Chief's eyes snapped up to his club brother then, because he'd obviously already surmised where the rest of the night took us, but to my surprise my brother did not look the slightest bit pissed off. Instead, he was grinning again. "Yeah, I'm guessing that's the reason my sister, who hates storms, didn't even realize we had a major one blow through last night."

"Shit man, I didn't realize either," Smoke mentioned.

"Bike's fine, man," my brother told him. It occurred to me then that my brother had to see the motorcycle sitting outside of my house when he rolled up so he knew someone was here. "Though, it's not your normal ride," my brother stated, which I was guessing was the reason he'd been banging on the door the way he was.

"Nah, had to snag a loaner while mine's getting the paint job," he told Chief.

"Forgot about that," Chief nodded then turned in my direction. "The old ladies sort you for food, or you wanna get dressed and go find some breakfast?"

"I could eat, and I don't feel like cooking, so breakfast out sounds about right."

"Okay, well go get ready," he told me. I glanced between Smoke and my brother wondering if he was just trying to get rid of me so he could have the big brother chat without my prying ears sitting here listening. He smirked my way when he realized what I must have been wondering. "Not gonna give him a lecture, Sis. You're both grown ass adults and fuck if I'm gonna complain about someone taking your mind off the shit you've got on it." With that, I stood and removed myself from the room, especially since I remembered I also had a very desperate need to pee.

As I was leaving the bathroom and heading back to my bedroom, I overheard my brother. "Heard her laughing when

I was rolling up to the door. Haven't heard her laugh like that in a long damn time, man."

There was a silence that followed his statement, and I waited while holding onto the last breath I'd taken as if it were all I'd ever get. "Hearing it can't possibly compare to seeing it in action," Smoke informed my brother.

"Fuck me," my brother muttered again. "My lil sis has always been able to enchant people. She has no clue she's capable, because Walk snatched her up and sure as fuck wasn't letting go when he first saw her. I knew back then it wouldn't last, but she wouldn't hear it. He was good to her in the beginning so I had no cause to step in, until recently, and if Pop had been honest with me sooner about what was going on I would have stepped in a few years back."

"He's a fuckin' fool. I think he'll realize that sooner or later and come callin'. I'm telling you now though that I am not stepping aside. Informed her this morning, I'll step back and be a friend while she adjusts and goes through her shit, but the minute I think she's ready for more, she's mine."

"You sure you want to make that promise after less than 24 hours with her?"

"Not my style to do so, you know that considering how long I was with Julie before. Two hours in with your sister and I wondered how I was capable of wasting all that time with a woman who could never compare."

I wondered then who Julie was and if she was still in the picture. I got my answer before I had to worry if I had unwittingly been the other woman. "Good you got shy of her when you did then," my brother murmured and I moved to find the shoes I had stuffed in boxes. "Take shit slow with her, man.

That fuckwad ex of hers did a number on her in more than one way. If I'd known she was spending the anniversary of our family's death that way I would have been there kickin' that fucker's ass and getting her the fuck out of that town a whole hell of a lot sooner than I did."

"You'll tell me about that later," Smoke demanded. I didn't hear a response from my brother, and I figured it was time to get my booty out there before they could continue this conversation. I wasn't sure I wanted anyone else privy to my humiliation. It had been bad enough that Snake had been there to witness most of it.

"Ready, sorry, I'm moving a little slow this morning," I apologized before locating my purse, digging through it, and coming out with a triumphant fist in the air, filled with my bottle of Ibuprofen. "Thank you, sweet baby Jesus," I called out. This made the guys chuckle. I turned, pointing a finger to my brother. "You hush." Then I turned to Smoke. "You too since your devil's juice brought this on."

"Sis, I do not need to know about Smoke's juice – devilish or otherwise," my brother called out on a sigh. For a moment I was actually caught off guard enough to be puzzled, then it hit me.

"Eww, nasty! I was talking about the rum, you idiot!" This had both men laughing as they moved closer to the front door.

We were seated in the local pancake house that the guys assured me was far and away better than the popular chain restaurant just down the street. I took their word for it, figuring it was never too soon for me to get to know some of the local gems since I'd torn up my Georgia roots and moved to Cedar Falls. My hometown of Sierra High didn't have any chain restaurants outside of usual fast food joints. Everything else had been locally owned and operated and the people from Sierra High preferred it that way. I did as well, if I was being honest.

Our waitress finally made her way over to us with a giant smile on her face as she took the guys in. "Hey there, fellas, how are y'all doing this morning?" I wasn't going to find offense in her 'fellas' only comment, because I figured she knew them since they'd bragged about this place at the house. "I didn't see the bikes outside," she mentioned, pointing towards the window as if they didn't know whether or not they'd ridden here.

"My sister drove since we were all headed to the same place," my brother told her as he scanned her with narrowed eyes.

"Oh," she perked up, even brighter, if that were possible. "Sorry, didn't see you sitting there," she amended, her words obviously a lie. There was no way she missed me as she scanned the occupants of the table when she walked up. I'd dealt with this shit whenever I traveled away from home with Walker and the guys, too. This type of thing did not happen at home though, because it was a small town atmosphere and everyone knew exactly who I was and whom I belonged to. That being said, her slight didn't go unnoticed nor would it go unaddressed. I'd been in and around the MC life for the past ten years. You either demanded respect or people would walk over you without thought.

"Yes, you did," I hesitated as I took in her nametag, "Sally." She attempted to sputter out a denial, but I held my hand up to stop her. "Listen, I watched you clock our table, me included before you even sashayed your hips over here – which by the way, I was going to check in on you and make sure you hadn't thrown one out of place, because sweetheart that was some serious hip swishing going on – and you locked eyes with me before purposely not including me in your greeting. Bit of advice to you, don't disrespect any of the women the MC brings around, because you never know who they are, how they're attached, or how your rude ass bullshit will play out for you. Now, find us another waitress, because I won't be ordering from you."

"This is my station, you can't..."

I moved to stand up then. "Then we'll move, no sweat off my back," I stated plainly as the guys just took in the scene as if it was highly entertaining.

"Please, look, calm down or something. My boss will not be happy if..."

"The way you treat your customers, your boss shouldn't be happy, sweetheart. Now, do I have to go get him or what?"

"That won't be necessary," a woman with big hair, also a redhead, stated as she came sauntering up with a natural sway to her hips and a grin on her overly made up face. "What seems to be the problem today?" she asked as she eyed the boys who were still just watching with amusement evident in their demeanor.

"Your waitress is rude, I requested someone else wait on us. Preferably, someone who doesn't ignore the patrons who don't have a dick swinging between their legs." At this, my brother couldn't hold his composure anymore and burst out laughing. Not that I could blame him since it was rare that I used questionable language outside of my home, and even rarer that I got my panties in a twist over pretty much anything. I was sweet and southern as you please, normally. That hadn't gotten me anywhere before except walked all over, so I was turning over a new leaf.

"Damn it, Poppy, I missed the shit out of you," he admitted through his laughter. "Daisy, can you send one of the other girls, let them know we'll tip well for covering a table that's not in their section?"

"Sure thing sugar," the overly done woman told my brother, smile still in place on her face. Then she turned back to me and pointed. "Not sure who you are, sugar, but I like you already." She stated this in a no nonsense way that brokered no arguments.

"Daisy, this is my little sister, Poppy. Poppy, Daisy here owns this fine establishment."

I held my hand out to her. "Nice to meet you, Daisy. My brother and Smoke have been bragging your place up, and since this is my first day here since I moved yesterday, and this is where we ended up for breakfast, I'm guessing that means good things."

Daisy grinned big, swatted my brother in the shoulder and hooted out a laugh. "Lord, Chief, you bring your sister 'round more often. I am thinking good things about this one." My brother beamed at me. I smiled back at Daisy. Daisy turned to see the waitress, Sally, still standing there gaping at all of us. "Don't you have tables with people you haven't offended to go see to?" The woman asked.

"I," the girl's lip trembled as she glanced back at my brother and then flipped her nervous, and very longing gaze, across the table – not to me – to beg with pleading eyes to Smoke. He just sat there, and stretched his arm out behind me, tucking his hand behind my shoulder. He spoke not one word, but his message was sent loud and clear, because the girl stumbled backwards as if someone had physically pushed her back. Then she took off for the back of the restaurant.

"Damn, there goes another one," Daisy complained. "Can't keep the young, decent looking ones long with the way you guys run through them." I scrunched my nose up at that making Daisy laugh. "Yeah, it's like that, sugar, but I'm guessing the way you lit Sally Mae up that you already know that. Even when they don't get their claws in the guys, the minute they see their crush wrapping those arms around another woman they can't handle it."

"That's why they never get what they're after to begin with," Smoke finally spoke. "It's easy to see the ones who will be a problem, and won't be able to handle their shit."

"You got that right, Smoke. I need to have you all sit in on interviews from here on out so maybe my employee turnover won't be so high." She smiled at him genuinely then as if it was no sweat off her back that she'd apparently lost another waitress. "Now, since I'll be taking over her tables anyway, what can I get you all?"

We ordered our food. It was fantastic, and I immediately understood why the guys loved this place. Everything was spectacular from the food to the company, since Daisy joined us for a bit and talked to the guys about how things were going, and to me about how my move was going. Daisy was apparently the old lady of Mick, the security officer for the club. Daisy turned back to me before walking away.

"I don't suppose you're looking for work?"

"I still have a few jobs that carried over from my old place, but if you need a website maintained, graphics made, or any advertisements done, you let me know, and I'll be all over that."

Daisy cocked her head towards me, thoughtful for a moment. "I'm all good with things for now, but I have a friend interested in rebranding a store she just purchased. I'll give her your information." I nodded to Daisy, and she walked away.

Smoke looked at me then. "What is it you do again?"

"Just what I said. I'm part graphic designer, part website guru, part marketing and advertising genius. I used to handle more than a few of the accounts for businesses in our town, but when everything went down and my dumbass ex-husband started running around, I lost a few accounts, because some of the businesses there are only loyal to the club, and they thought they were doing right by dropping me since it looked as if Walker had already done the same. They learned they weren't correct when Snake dealt with them, but I wouldn't take them back on as clients after that, so I don't really have enough work to keep paying the bills long term at the moment, but I'm hoping to branch out now that I'll have more time on my hands to do it."

"You ever handle social media for people or companies?" he asked.

"I did for the two bars in our town for a while until the one changed owners who didn't like social media and the other was one of those businesses that sided with Walker when we split."

"Might have something for you, let me check on a couple things first," he suggested. Then he glanced down at his watch. "Shit, I need to get going. Promised Soph I'd watch the kid today." I stiffened a bit as he stated this, wondering if it meant he had a kid, if Soph was his woman, baby momma, or what? Shoot. I felt a kick to my shin under the table and my brother shook his head slightly at me as I sat watching Smoke get himself up from our table.

"You guys stay and enjoy, Granger's on his way to take me to my bike."

"All right man, give little man a hug for me," my brother told him. Smoke gave him a chin lift before turning to me, putting a hand on my shoulder and giving it a squeeze. "I'll give you a call later, Poppy. Enjoy your day. You need anything, just let me know." With that, he turned and left. I watched him go then glanced out the window to see him get into a black Ford Expedition before it shot off into the light traffic of the morning.

"The kid isn't his," my brother told me, snapping my attention back to him instead of where it currently resided in la-la land outside the window. I didn't say anything, just raised my brow in question. My brother grinned at me like the idiot he was. "Sophie is his sister," Chief clarified, and I felt my shoulders go slack as the tension I didn't realize I'd been carrying was swept away. My brother noticed then pounced. "So, you guys bonded over hockey, huh?"

That did it. I bounced excitely in my seat. "Did you know his younger brother is Kent Lewis of the Pittsburgh Penguins?"

Chief laughed then, shoulders shaking, eyes twinkling, and head shaking back and forth at my excitement. "Yeah, Pop, met him last year when he came in for a visit."

"What?" I shrieked.

"Pop," my brother attempted to calm me with his tone.

"What? You mean to tell me you met Kent Lewis last year and you did not share that information? You didn't invite me up to meet him? What kind of brother are you?" I didn't give him a chance to answer. "Never mind, I know. You're a horrible brother. Holy shit, Keith! Kent Lewis was here! You met him! You... you... you should have told me!"

My brother was full out laughing at this point. Daisy had emerged at some point and was standing at the end of our table looking just as amused. "I take it your Poppy here is a hockey fan?"

"The biggest," my brother informed her.

"Oh lord!" She sighed out. "Does Smoke know that?" There was a glimmer of worry before she buried it and went back to focusing her attention on my brother's answer.

"Oh yeah. Seems when Smoke went looking for me last night he found Poppy here, and the two of them bonded," Chief explained with a waggle of his brows.

"Is that..." she was clearly struggling with whatever she wanted to say, and didn't know if she could say in front of me.

My brother waved off whatever concern she was attempting to show. "Nothing to be concerned about, Daisy. Should have seen the two of them this morning. Like they'd known each other forever." Daisy visibly relaxed then, and I wondered about why she was so affected by the fact that I was a hockey fan. Weird.

Once we left the restaurant and were headed home, I asked, because I never was one to leave questions unasked or unanswered if I could help it. "What was that about?"

"What do you mean?"

"You know with Daisy getting weird about me being a hockey fan?"

"Oh. Not really my story to tell, but I don't think he'd mind, so..." my brother started. "Smoke had a girl for four or five years. It ended about six months back. He broke it off with her after Kent spilled the beans during an argument with Smoke that Julie had come on to him after he'd been drafted to the Penguins. She apparently thought she'd be able to trade up to the more successful, and famous, brother. Kent never told Smoke."

"Why the hell not?" I asked pissed off for Smoke.

"Didn't want to hurt his brother, I guess." Chief shrugged his shoulders. "Maybe thought his brother was in so deep he wouldn't believe him. Not real sure what motivates people to do the things they do, Pop. Anyway, every time Smoke wanted to go see him Kent would get sketchy and ask if he was bringing his girl. If he said no, his brother was all over the visit. If he said yeah, Kent would make excuses. Didn't take a fuckin' genius to put two and two together that little brother didn't like the girlfriend. They fought about it the last time, because Julie was adamant that she go on the trip with Smoke to see his brother, because she didn't want to be left behind. Kent finally lost his shit when they got there and he hadn't realized she'd be tagging along."

"Oh wow, that sucks."

"Yeah, probably for the best that it happened when she was there. She broke down and admitted Kent was telling the truth, but swore that she had caught feelings – true feelings – for Smoke by then, and that she didn't want anyone else. Not even his famous, rich, much younger brother."

I scoffed at that.

"Nah," my brother cut off my noise. "She fuckin' meant that shit. Watched that girl go from only somewhat interested in those early days to being completely gone for him. She caught feelings all right, but the uncomfortable, disloyal history she'd cultivated sealed her fate." My brother shrugged. "Smoke cut her loose then and there, sent her packing back home with a plane ticket instead of on the back of his bike the way she'd arrived."

"Oh, wow," I muttered.

"Yeah, I imagine he felt a little of what you did when Walk fucked up so big. They weren't together as long, or as legally committed, but they'd been living together for a few years, and working towards getting there. Don't know if it was his brother's sketchy behavior about her holding him back or what, but doesn't matter. It's been over for a good while and he hasn't even thought about moving on with anyone since."

I raised my brows in question then.

"He's had his share of post break-up ass, Sis. He just isn't dating anyone seriously."

As disturbing as that was to hear, considering how much I enjoyed the previous night with him, I could totally understand wanting some no strings fun after going through that. I'd thought about it myself, and until last night, I'd decided against it. Then again, last night seemed like anything but no strings fun, especially considering Smoke's little speech when we woke up.

7. THE DOGHOUSE

As it turned out, I had a few days to think over what my brother had said about Smoke. Those days of thinking were thanks to not hearing from Smoke or my brother during that time. As in, not hearing from them at all for three solid days now. I knew the life that came with the club sometimes meant being shut out and not knowing things, but this sucked far worse than anything I had endured over the last 10 years in the life, because I didn't know anyone else in my new town, and didn't have anyone's phone numbers who were involved with the club. Sure, I'd met Daisy at breakfast my first full day here, but I didn't know her well enough to go hunting her down to find out what was going on with my brother, or anyone else. I'd know when I knew. So, I threw myself into unpacking, getting some work done, and beefing up the advertising for my website.

I also took a trip to the local SPCA, because they had requested some work from me for an up and coming fundraiser they were having. When I got everything together for their invitations and signage I decided to take samples to them in person so that I could get a feel for how they really liked or disliked the ideas I had. Sandra Keeton, the woman who was my point of contact, was thrilled to death with what I brought her.

"Oh thank God you moved to town. These are gorgeous! Perfect! I can't even tell you how darn excited I am about these!" Her praise left me blushing a bit since her exuberance wasn't something I was used to. "You'll have to come to the event," she finally told me. Unfortunately, I had stopped paying attention, because something else caught my eye. A gorgeous midnight black dog with bright blue eyes and pointed ears that had been docked to make him look even more ferocious than he already did sat staring at me. His head was cocked just so as if he were attempting to determine if I should be his new person or not. I cocked my head too, taking him all in. His shoulders had to be at least thigh high on me standing on all fours. That meant he would definitely be nearly waist high with that big head of his. His muscular frame led me to believe he had to tip the scales well over 100 pounds, probably closer to 120. Sandra's eyes followed mine, and she sighed.

"That's Bubba," she told me. "He had one owner from birth, but the poor man died last week. I've had quite a few people interested in him, but either he didn't like them and let them know or I didn't think they had the best of intentions for our boy."

I nodded, and hadn't even realized I'd been on the move until I got near him. "He's gorgeous," I stated as I knelt down on the opposite side of the cage from the dog. "Hey there,

Bubba," I cooed to him. He nuzzled his nose through the crack in the fencing and I reached through to rub my finger over his nose. He huffed out a doggy sigh and leaned the full weight of his body against the cage in an attempt to get closer.

"Seems like you two have decided on one another. Were you thinking about adopting?" Sandra asked.

"I had thought about getting a dog since I'm living on my own in a new place, you know a little added security, plus the company would be nice. I mostly work from home, so I'll be around a lot." I informed Sandra of my sad, lonely-girl life. She clapped. Kid you not, she started clapping and then moaned out a happy sound that forced my eyes away from Bubba and onto her. "This makes me extremely happy, because Bubba needed someone who would give him plenty of love. He's fully trained, walks on a leash well. Heck, I'm sure he'd walk off leash well, but maybe you shouldn't attempt that until after you get to know one another better. He'll definitely scare away any unwanted individuals around your house too," she attempted to sell me on the dog, but I was already gone for him. "He's a Cane Corso, which means he's one of the bully breeds, but not many people realize that until they see him. How do you think your landlord would feel about him?"

I had my phone out in my hand already calling Todd Anderson, the man I was renting the house from. Todd was giving me the option to buy once my lease was up since Chief had informed him that I would probably be purchasing a home once our family's house sold back home. It was the reason he was able to talk Todd into a six-month lease instead of a 12-month. "Hey Todd, it's Poppy." I listened as he asked if everything was okay with the house. "No, everything is just fine. I love the house, but I was wondering how you would feel about me getting a dog? He is fully trained, and I would just feel a whole lot better having him as a bit of security since..."

"Not a problem," Todd cut me off to tell me.

"I can bring you a pet deposit..."

"Not necessary," he again cut me off to say. "If it makes you more comfortable, get a dog. If there's a mess later, we'll deal with it then. I trust you. More importantly, I trust Chief. Do what you need to do. Hopefully, you end up buying the place anyway so just treat it like it's yours in the interim."

"Thanks, Todd."

"Sure thing." There was a pause and then he asked, "just out of curiosity, what kind of dog is?"

"A Cane Corso," I told him.

"Damn girl, you do not fuck around when you say you want a dog for security, huh?"

I laughed at that. "No, I suppose I don't." After that, we said our goodbyes, and I set about filling out the paperwork to adopt Bubba and bring him home with me. As we were about to leave Sandra quickly came running over to me waving a piece of paper. "I almost forgot these," she stated as she passed me the paper she'd been waving about to catch my attention. I glanced down and started reading out loud.

"Sitzen," I started reading and Bubba, who had been standing next to me, parked his butt on the floor. I glanced at him them back to the paper. "Platz," I said, and Bubba laid down on the floor at my feet. I cocked my head sideways then glanced back up at Sandra. "Is this German?" I asked.

"Yeah, apparently the dog was trained with German commands and possibly already trained as security, so I'm going to stop you from reading the rest out loud. Familiarize yourself with them all though, because from what we've seen if he respects you, Bubba will follow those commands to the letter."

"Wow," I stated as I glanced back down at Bubba. "How has no one adopted him yet?"

Sandra grinned and shrugged her shoulders. "That's mostly my fault. I was waiting for the right person to come along for Bubba," she told me.

"Well, I'm so freaking happy I was the right person. I promise, he will only get the best treatment from me."

"Oh, I know he will. Besides, Bubba chose you." As if he wanted to let me know Sandra was right he bumped my leg with his nose. I glanced down at the paper in my hand and looked for the correct word to use.

"Foos!" I stated and Bubba jumped into action coming up from his position lying on the floor to stand directly beside my leg. Cool. Bubba and I were going to be best friends. "Come on Bubba, we have to stop by the pet store and nab you some new stuff, then get you to our new home.

Bubba and I had been home getting to know one another for two days, making me realize how extremely lucky I had been to adopt this beautiful boy. He stayed near me wherever I went. He did not attempt to get up on the furniture, which made me wonder if that was one of his previous owner's rules. I figured I would stick with that, and didn't encourage him to do it since he was so large he'd probably take up the entire bed, couch, or whatever he attempted to get on anyway.

During those two days that Bubba and I were getting to know one another, I still hadn't heard from my brother or Smoke. I wasn't ready to forgive my brother for keeping me worried; he was going to get an earful from me whenever he deemed me important enough to show his face again. I stood hand washing the dishes while eschewing my dishwasher in order to keep my hands and mind busy with the menial task, and started talking to Bubba so that I wouldn't continue thinking of Smoke and the fact that we'd shared a pretty spectacular night only to have him never contact me again. Sadly, I was a little more upset by that fact than I was by the fact that my ex-husband hadn't bothered to check to see if I made it to my new home okay.

Sure, I told him I was going and there was no changing my mind, but I thought for sure if he still had any hope he would have at least pretended to care. Snake had texted a few times to check on me. He seemed to be the only person from my old life who remembered I existed, because outside of him and the few clients I kept, no one from Sierra High contacted me at all. "Once I'm finished here we'll go take a walk, Bubba. I know you must be tired of being cooped up." Bubba's ears perked up, and for a brief moment I thought maybe he'd speak back. Instead, he shifted so he was by my side, but looking back toward the front door. He moved from siting there to standing and alert, something I hadn't noticed him do in the past two days.

"What's up, boy?" I heard a low rumble coming from

Bubba just before a knock on my front door startled the crap out of me. Bubba huffed out a low woof, but otherwise refused to give up his space by my side as I moved to the door. I did not have a peephole. That was something that needed to be remedied. In my old house I had plenty of windows near the door that negated the necessity for one, but this door had no windows on either side of it.

"Who is it?" I asked as I got close enough that someone could hear me through the door.

"Poppy?" A male voice asked.

"Who is out there?" I asked again since I didn't recognize the person.

"Poppy I'm with the Aces High MC, your brother sent me to check on you since he's been out of communication for a bit."

"I don't know you," I stated plainly. The handle of my locked door twisted a bit, and Bubba was done being patient. He let loose a series of loud, vicious sounding barks that would have scared the pee right out of me if I'd been the person on the wrong side of that door.

"Jesus Christ!" The man shouted, sounding as though he stumbled back as well. "Fucking hell," I heard shouted. Then I heard laughter. The laughter was very familiar.

"Pop, open up. It's me," Chief called out. I glanced at Bubba then.

"Bubba, foos!" Immediately Bubba was by my side as I moved out of the way of the door so that I could open it. "Sitzen," I told Bubba, but I also took hold of his collar just in case.

As soon as the door swung open, my brother went to step

in and stopped upon seeing my new best friend. "Holy fuck, Sis. What the hell is that beast, and where did he come from?"

I smirked at my brother considering the joke he tried to play on me was now on him. "This is Bubba. He's my new buddy," I explained as I reached down and rubbed across Bubba's midnight fur. Normally when I did this Bubba would nose into my leg, but this time he stood stoic and on guard. "Good boy," I told him.

"Seriously, Poppy, I left for a week, and come back to you having a hell hound in your house. What gives? You have trouble?" he asked,

"Nope. I did some work for a charity thing at the SPCA, and when I was dropping off the mock-ups, Bubba was there watching me. It was fate, and I brought him home to hang out with me since I'm in a new town where I know about five people, have numbers for two of them, and none of them have gotten in touch in five days," I chastised.

"Shit," Chief called out. "We had some club business to deal with out of town."

"Uh-huh and your phone doesn't work when you leave town?" I asked as I planted a hand on my hip. Bubba actually broke his pose then to glance at me, trying to ascertain what this new gesture meant, no doubt.

"Shit," my brother hissed out again.

"Hey man, is it safe to come up there?" The disembodied voice that I'd heard through the door called out again.

"Yeah man, just maybe approach slowly."

I still had hold of Bubba's collar and the minute he felt me twitch on it a bit he went back on guard, bowing up his shoulders and cocking his head at the man who slowly moved through the door. He was a cutie.

"Poppy, this is Hold 'Em. Brought him by to introduce you in case I'm ever gone like that again. It doesn't happen often, but just in case."

"Hi," I offered to the man who was staring at my dog like he was going to attack at any moment.

"Good job, by the way, not opening the door." My brother was saying to me as I checked out the man he'd called Hold 'Em.

"I'm not a moron, Chief. Of course I'm going to check before opening a door. Besides, I had my Bubba with me."

"How long you had him here?"

"Two days," I responded.

"Gotta tell ya, I'm feeling a fuck of a lot better about the time I had to leave you alone now," my brother admitted.

"Yeah, I was feeling better about it once I had Bubba, too. He's great. Plus, I always wanted a dog, and Walk wouldn't let me..." I started to say, making my brother angry. The dog responded to his body language and his guard went up once more, an audible grumble growling from him.

"Bubba, foos!" I commanded as I moved to go sit on the couch. Bubba followed right beside me, but that darn dog stayed aware of the two men in my house the entire time. When we got to the couch and I took my seat, I commanded Bubba with "Platz," and down he went right at my feet while watching the boys.

"Wow, that's awesome." My brother commented. "What were you saying?"

"She told him to heel and then to lie down." Hold 'Em

explained. When I glanced in his direction he smirked at me. "I have a buddy who was a handler with a K9 unit in the Army." I just nodded.

"Do I even want to know how you got stuck with that road name?" I asked in order to break the ice of getting to know a new person.

"Name's Holden. I um, had a few girlfriends while prospecting, and the guys said I had a hard time holdin' on to them. Jokes ensued, and the sentiment got shortened down to a play on my name." If I wasn't mistaken, Holden was blushing as he told the story. It made him even cuter. He had fine, sandy brown hair that flopped over his forehead and into his eyes a bit in the front, but was short as hell, almost buzzed in the back. His eyes were either a light blue or gray, and he had one dimple that popped up on his right cheek when he smiled.

"Poor you!" I laughed. "At least you have an interesting story to tell with your name, though. My friend Snake literally got his because he snatched up a snake that was sitting beside his bike when he came out to hop on it."

"That's a cool story too, though," Hold 'Em told me.

"Nah, it was a garter snake." We all laughed at that.

"Chief tells me you been in and around the club life a while. You didn't get your own club name?"

I shook my head. "No, never did. Down there, all the women are darlin', sweetheart, or sugar. I don't think any of the guys have it in them to learn any more names than they have to," I offered on a chuckle. Hold 'Em just glanced at my brother, giving him an odd look. "I know it's the norm up here with your club so that seems weird, but truly they are all a little bit different."

"True, the chapter up in South Dakota calls their club whores BRATs." My brother offered up to take the heat off of me. I had been finding out little by little over the years that I'd been kept out of a lot of the club life that other old ladies experienced. I didn't really pay much attention before, because I was so ensconced in trying to procreate that I didn't see the writing on the wall. Belatedly, I wondered if the club whores had always been a problem in our relationship, and if my husband had just done a better job at keeping it a secret when he thought he had to. It didn't matter now, because I wasn't about to go backwards and wander down that road of questioning everything. It was what it was. And what it was at this point was over.

"Yeah, I heard that last year when we went to Sturgis," Hold 'Em admitted bringing me back to the conversation. "Forgot what that shit stood for, though."

"Bitches Relinquishing Ass and Tits," my brother chuckled out. "Those guys are not right up there."

"Probably because they have to give up riding for too much of the year when snow's falling," Hold 'Em offered.

"Shit man, you're probably right."

"I think it's really cool that you guys came here to banter about club life, but was there a point to this visit other than to tell me your phone is broken or something?" I asked while glaring daggers at my brother. "Bubba and I were about to go for a walk." My brother sat back, shook his head, and I'm pretty sure he hissed out 'damn,' but he did it low enough that I knew he did not want to get into any more trouble with me.

"I just thought you might like to meet more people, especially the ones who will be around when I can't be most of the time."

"Nice to meet you, Hold 'Em." I stated without much enthusiasm.

"Damn," my brother muttered for sure that time. "Don't hold her attitude against her, man. She's pissed at me."

"I don't blame her. I'd be pissed too if my brother moved me to a new town and ditched me days later with no warning and no communication for five days." Hold 'Em explained to my brother before turning his attention to me. "I didn't know where you lived or how to get a hold of you without asking someone from Sierra High. I didn't want to call any of them, because I didn't want to bring any unnecessary drama down on you, but I did want to stop by and exchange numbers in case you ever need anything, could use someone to talk to, or whatever."

I offered him a genuine smile then. "Maybe you could teach my brother some manners?" I asked.

He laughed.

Chief scowled.

I just sat there watching them both watching me. Then we managed to exchange numbers before I told the boys they were welcome to hang out, but that I had a dog to walk. Chief protested saying he'd come with me, but I refused. "You've been gone a week. I've managed on my own in that time. I don't need you holding my hand through my new situation now."

"Poppy," he lamented quietly.

"Nope." I stated firmly. "It's a good thing this happened, because it forced me to realize I'm going to be just fine. Seriously, I'm not even mad aside from being angry about you being an inconsiderate bastard and not even letting me know you weren't dead in a ditch somewhere. I appreciate you stopping by now and introducing me to someone else, but I really need to take Bubba for a walk, and I honestly want to do that by myself. I'll talk to you later, Chief."

"Okay, fine, Poppy. I get it, and I'm sorry. You're right I could have called, at the very least when we were heading out. I just didn't think about it, because I'm not used to having to think about it." Well, now that he put it like that I guess I kind of understood. He was right. He'd been living here for six years without checking in with me about his every movement. When I'd lived in Georgia and he was here we talked a couple times a month on the phone, tops. He never told me about his travels or what he did for the club unless it was just to pass on a funny anecdote to make me laugh. So, I nodded to my brother and finished tying my tennis shoes. I was looking supremely unattractive in my sweats, but hell, who did I have to impress? I had absolutely no one to impress, that's who. Bubba certainly didn't care what I wore so long as he got his walk in, and was able to strut his terrible, horrible, fiercely beautiful self all over the neighborhood, letting everyone know I was not a person to be trifled with or else he'd be taking a bite out of them. Bubba was my hero!

I SAW the bike sitting in my driveway as Bubba and I approached my house, and I knew immediately it was not my brother's since his had a bluish tint to the black and chrome look the guys at the club favored. "I wonder who that is?" I asked Bubba. I also wondered, briefly, why there was a bike outside of my house when there didn't seem to be anyone attached to it. Then I watched as a man came from around the side of the house with a cell phone to his ear. "What do you mean she's walking the dog? She doesn't have a fuckin' dog." I recognized the voice before he came fully into view and I recognized the man, too. Smoke was at my house, and he was clearly speaking to someone on the phone about me. I could only assume it was my brother. I sighed loudly and glanced down at Bubba.

"Here we go again, boy," I huffed out as I moved closer to the house ignoring the man who was hanging up the phone and approaching me cautiously while eyeing my dog.

"Poppy?" Smoke questioned.

"Yeah?" I asked as I took to the task of unlocking my door without so much as a glance in Smoke's direction.

"Poppy?" he asked again in a more demanding tone. This put Bubba on edge and he bowed up beside me, going on alert, which halted Smoke's approach.

"What do you want Smoke?" I asked, still not bothering to look his way.

"I came to see you," he stated plainly, as if that said everything. I turned slowly towards him then.

"Why?" I asked as flatly as I could get the word out.

He appeared taken aback by my question. "What do you mean 'why?' I thought I made it clear that we were going to be friends and then something more when you were ready."

I laughed at that. He stared stone-faced at my response. "Oh, I'm sorry," I started in on him then. "I know I've forgotten a lot about what it was like to have friends as I'm just now realizing most of mine back home were of the fair-weather variety, but I'm pretty sure that when you agree to be friends with someone you don't walk out on breakfast with them promising to call, and not speak to them for five days expecting to show up to their house afterwards to a warm reception."

He glared in my general direction then. "Chief knew what was going down, hell he had to come assist," Smoke barked out.

I laughed again. "Yeah, and I just got done chewing my brother's ass for not getting a hold of me to let me know whether he was dead, alive, or otherwise engaged for the past five days, too."

It was then I watched as Smoke's shoulders slumped, his hand raked down his thicker than it had been five days ago beard, and he shook his head. "You have got to be shitting me," he hissed out. Then I continued to watch as he pulled his phone back out, waited a second, and started talking. "You mean to tell me, knowing that my phone was toast and I couldn't do it, you didn't bother to tell your sister what was going down?"

He stopped and listened for a minute. Then he blew up. "She hadn't even been here 48 hours and you forgot? Are you fucking shittin' me? Now she's pissed at me too, and I wasn't the asshole who had a way of getting a hold of her." He listened again. "You did what, now?" Anger seemed to be rolling off him in waves at whatever my brother was telling him. "You tell that fucker he needs to stay the hell away." I could actually hear my brother's laughter through the phone before he apparently hung up. Smoke glared at his phone, pocketed it, and started moving toward me before he was halted in his tracks by the growling dog at my side.

"You might want to calm yourself before you approach me," I warned him.

"Shit," he hissed out. "Sorry," he huffed then. "Can I come in and explain some things to you?" he glanced at me then tacked on, "Please." I just nodded my head as I swung the door open.

"Foos," I gave the command and Bubba turned to follow me inside. I moved directly to the chair on the opposite side of the living room from the door, sat down, and started untying my shoes as I murmured, "Platz" to Bubba. He immediately laid down at my feet, but his eyes stayed trained to Smoke.

Smoke smiled at my dog as he came in, shut the door, and took a seat on the couch across from me. He clapped his hands together and then pulled them apart and whipped his phone back out of his pocket. "I need your number again," he stated quickly.

"Lost it so soon?" I asked with a raised brow.

"Some asshole nearly ran me off the road shortly after I left you guys at breakfast. Granger, my brother-n-law, picked me up, but then he informed me my babysitting services were no longer necessary. Something he should have confirmed before he picked me up, or I would have stayed with you that morning. That's where it all started going downhill, because as he was taking me back to your place to grab my bike, I got a call from my buddy, Shep. He needed me to come do him a favor, so I snagged my bike, and headed over to his place, but on the way, he called again. I went to pull my phone out of my pocket since I was rolling up to a red light, and the damn thing fell and took irreparable damage when a car almost clipped me.

I just got a replacement this morning, because we've been handling Shep's situation this whole time. His mom and sister were attacked. They live four hours away now, moved there with her new husband only to find out he has some gambling debts, and a few goons were sent to collect. They thought to do it using Shep's mom and sister."

"Oh my God! Are they all right?" I asked, quickly forgetting any earlier anger and disappointment I had felt towards Smoke over not receiving a phone call all week. I'd actually been more disappointed in not having heard from him than my own brother.

"They're fine, a little banged up, but otherwise good. They're both staying with Shep for the time being. Took us a little longer to handle things than expected since we helped pack them up and get their shit in storage until Tammy can figure her shit out. She left a good job here to follow that asshole, and I'm not so certain she'll be able to get it back."

"That sucks," I told him.

"Yeah, but as much as it sucks, it's not my problem any longer. That's for them to figure out as a family. What is my problem is the fact that you were angry with me. I'm truly sorry, Poppy. I thought your brother was in communication with you while we were out there handling things. If I'd known..." he started, then hesitated. "Doesn't matter. I should have taken a moment to get my shit together, grab a new phone, and get your number from Chief."

I waved him off. "It's whatever. Sounds like you had your hands full, especially with two women who were most likely at least a little bit traumatized." A warm look slid into Smoke's eyes as I said that, and he stood to come to me, but stopped when he saw Bubba's head perk up. "It's okay, Bubba," I told the dog, and just as quickly – as if he understood – his head went back down to rest on his paws by my feet. Smoke moved in closer and came to me. He took my face in between his hands and ran his thumbs over my jawline.

"I missed you. Crazy to think that I knew you less than a day, but I missed you more this week than I knew what to do with." Butterflies ran amuck through my belly at his words. "When did you get the dog? More importantly where did you find a beast that behaves that well?"

"I did some work for Sandra at the SPCA, and he was there watching me when I took the samples to her. She said his previous owner had him for protection, and that he died. Apparently more than a few people inquired about him, but she had put them all off. Anyway, she says Bubba chose me, whatever that means, so I brought him home, and he's been keeping me company the past couple days."

"Gotta say, I'm real fuckin' happy to know that he's been here with you. I was worried with you just moving to town and all the boys you knew being gone on that run," he informed me. "Of course, I thought your brother was in touch that whole time," he sighed. It was then he reached into his pocket and pulled out a pair of tickets. I watched as his face lit up. "We'll have to see if your brother can watch Bubba though, because I have tickets for us to go see the Penguins kick some Predator ass in two days."

I stared at the tickets.

I hadn't been to a major NHL hockey game since the one my dad had taken me to as a kid. That made the tickets in Smoke's hand the holy grail of oh my god moments for me.

"What?" I finally asked, stupefied.

"We're going to see my brother play, honey."

"Oh my God," I whisper-hissed. "Are you serious?"

"Yeah, honey, I am. You'll have to see how your pup responds to Chief. If they can get along well enough you can leave him since we'll be gone overnight. If not, I'll grab us a hotel with a pet friendly room, and we'll just have to make it clear that no one is allowed to enter the room. Think of it as my apology for being gone a week right after we started something."

"You didn't owe me an apology or anything, but um, I'm not turning it down either, because it's the Penguins!" I almost shouted at him by the end of my statement.

"Good to know honey." His smile nearly blew me away, and I think even Bubba could tell because he made a snuffling noise at my feet as if to say, "Women!"

8. THE GAME

TWO DAYS LATER, I FOUND MYSELF SITTING JUST BEHIND THE GLASS as Kent Lewis was smacked right into it. Before he peeled himself off, he grinned big at his brother, and then tore off after the asshole that had slammed him there. The gloves came off and a fight ensued ending with both players in the sin bin for a bad boy hockey player time out.

"I can't believe that just happened," I yelled enthusiastically to Smoke as we retook our seats after standing to yell at the refs. Clearly, any retaliation should have been overlooked. Jeez.

"I think Kent just wanted to get a better look at who I had sitting over here," Smoke mumbled. I glanced at him, saw that he was serious and did a double take.

"You're not serious," I stated. He just looked at me. "Oh my God, you are serious!" I glanced over to see Kent waving to us from his place in hockey jail and I huffed out a laugh.

"Honey, my brother would not let someone stuff his face into the glass that easily for any other reason than he was curious who was on the other side of it," Smoke explained.

"Unbelievable!" I shouted as I tossed my hands in the air and then started gesturing wildly to the ice where his brother should be playing. "Now they're a man down!" I moaned. "What was he thinking? He could have waited to appease his curiosity after the game. Holy, holy hellfire."

Smoke was full on laughing at my tirade, but he didn't realize I was serious. Kent Lewis just earned an ass chewing from me, and I was going to seriously see to it. Who cares that he'd probably earned one from his coach as well. Mine would be far better. "Maybe I should have a talk with the coach about his behavior," I mumbled. This too earned more laughter from Smoke. Suddenly, I forgot all about his brother's ice troubles, because Smoke throwing his head back in unbridled laughter was the most glorious thing I'd ever seen. His throat worked as his head tipped back, and his eyes were glittering with mirth. The wide smile that graced his bearded face damn near stopped my heart, and before I knew it I had reached my hand up to touch his cheek as he brought his head back down and his features shifted from lighthearted fun to a look so heated I felt it all the way down to my soul, and other places south of my waistline.

Smoke's hand came up to capture mine and hold it against his face as he spoke. "You keep looking at me like that, honey, and we won't be sticking around for you to see the end of the game let alone have the opportunity to chew my brother's ass for his stint in the bin."

"Um, okay," I murmured dazedly. He leaned in then and captured my lips with his. I did not even think to stop him and so when cheers went up close to us, it caught us both by surprise. It would seem that we had been featured on the kiss cam since we were both decked out in Penguins gear – my idea – to support Kent. "Oh my Gosh!" My face started turning red with a blush so bright the camera was bound to notice, because that kiss had been hot, and probably not meant for PG audiences. Smoke chuckled beside me as he tossed an arm around my shoulders and pulled me close to him. I hid my face in his neck and almost wished I could stay there, because he smelled so good. The leather smell from his jacket clung to him along with a fresh, almost minty scent that drove me wild.

I glanced up from his neck after a minute to find him smiling down at me with such a soft look on his face that I was struck stupid for a moment. "Thank you," I whispered, so close my breath probably tickled his chin as I did.

"Honey," he said and stopped there. His hand came up to cup my jaw then he kissed me lightly before sitting back and refocusing on the game. I turned my focus too, just in time to see his brother was watching us from his place on the bench. I hadn't even realized his shift was up until then. I smiled, not certain Kent could see it, but it didn't matter. I wasn't sure what any of this meant for me right now, so I certainly didn't need him trying to figure us out either.

Once the game was over – the Penguins won over the Predators 3-2 - Smoke took me to the tunnel where the guys would come out to see family, fans, and whoever else had access. There were plenty of women scantily dressed in not much more than a fitted hockey jersey adorned with which-ever player's name they were fishing for. I didn't think many of them would be too picky if they nabbed someone else, though. A few had asked Smoke if he played. After the first two, he used me as a human shield while he stood against the wall and pulled me in front of him. He wrapped his arms around my waist to keep me there, and I wasn't really about to complain, because it felt nice to relax back into his solid frame while we waited.

"Yo, Jared!" I heard called out at the same time I felt the arms around me lock down a little tighter. I glanced over to see a freshly showered Kent come bounding toward us in a bit of a rush.

"Kent," Smoke stated sharply as tension filled his body. "Everything good?"

"Nah man. I know you came all this way to hang out, but I have a situation I need to handle. Can we do this another time?" he asked his brother as he swirled a finger to indicate the three of us.

"You need me for anything?" Smoke asked him. Kent shook his head and looked a little grim.

"Got my own woman troubles at the moment. I need to see to her before she sees her way out of my life for good," he explained quietly so the vultures standing nearby wouldn't hear him. Good call on his part too, because they were definitely leaning in attempting to glean some juicy tidbits.

Kent glanced at me then. "I promise, we'll get together soon so we can meet in a more official way," he offered his hand though and I took it quickly giving him a quick smile.

"I hope everything goes okay for you tonight," I told him. He grinned then.

"Me too, sweetheart!" With that, he clapped his brother

on the shoulder and then took off for the locker room once more.

"I guess that means we are on our own now?" I asked.

"Yeah, honey, seems so." He reached out to take my hand, but his arm was pulled back by one of the vultures.

"How do you know Kent?" The woman asked.

Smoke glared down at the hold the woman had on his bicep and then back up at her. She put on something that was supposed to be a sexy grin, I'm sure, and then she batted her fake eyelashes his way. She definitely didn't have enough going on upstairs, because she did not clue in to the fact that Smoke was not happy about being touched by her. I stood there, cocked my head in her direction, and waited.

"You're his brother aren't you?" she cooed, finally. "I'm Mandy, a good friend of his. I'd be happy to show you around the town and take care of you while you're visiting since Kent's busy with things. Just so you know," she leaned in conspiratorially. "It's not anything more than friendship with Kent and me. I've never taken him for a ride, but I'd definitely be up for it with you." I just stood there watching this go down, and waiting for Smoke to blow his top.

He grabbed her hand that was still stupidly attached to his bicep – honestly I couldn't blame her for wanting to hold on to it as long as possible – and he removed it quickly, efficiently, and with zero care as to how it felt to her to be snatched away from heaven. I had to stifle a giggle at her fish out of water reaction with her mouth gaping and closing in repetition.

"I don't know you. I don't care to know you. I know you watched me standing here with my woman before he ever came out, so you knew damn well I was already here with someone. No man worth his salt would take a second glance at trash that behaves the way you do especially when he already has heaven on his arm.

"Knowing my brother, that means you aren't even close to being in a league where you could be his associate, let alone a friend, let alone anything else." Some of the other people waiting in the hallway with us – the ones who appeared to be family and real friends – started laughing heartily at what Smoke told Mandy. I was guessing this was normal behavior for her and they were enjoying seeing her being put in her place. One woman had her cell out, and I would bet money she was shooting video.

Smoke turned to me and took my hand then. "Sorry, honey," he apologized.

"No need for you to apologize for the behavior of skanks who don't know their place," I informed him.

The woman stood there, red-faced and fuming. I turned with Smoke – who was apparently my man tonight – and we left her there. I found myself hoping that the woman who had been holding her cell up was going to send that video around to everyone who needed to see it.

"I think you just made the night of all the normal people that were standing there waiting," I informed Smoke.

"Normal people?" he asked.

"Yeah, you know the ones who weren't puck bunnies."

"Jesus," he laughed out loud. "You even know what their whores are called."

"Doesn't everyone?"

"No, honey. Everyone does not know what they're called."

"Oh, I guess they don't read then," I suggested. He just shook his head and laughed at me again.

We ended up going straight back to our hotel, The Omni William Penn, to check out the speakeasy lounge. We each enjoyed a couple drinks, the atmosphere, and then headed up to our room. The anticipation of getting there had us both suffering some seriously pent up frustrations. It was a little strange for me, because I kept waiting for my old life to step in and tell me that I wasn't ready. It never happened, though. I didn't feel like I wasn't ready to move on. I didn't feel as though I was doing anything wrong, or moving too fast. Everything just felt right. Because it all felt right I refused to second-guess my growing feelings for Smoke. I refused to put a stop to his mouth when it found mine, traced down my jawline, and suckled at my neck before he lifted the jersey I'd worn to the game over my head and trailed more kisses down my body while divesting me of my pink satin bra.

All the while, my hands were not idle. I helped remove Smoke's jersey too and ran my fingers up his abs, through the trail of hair that started below the waistband of his jeans and moved up to his naval, then further in a thin, light line until it spread out over his chest in a sexy sprinkling of hair that made it apparent he was all man while not completely overtaking the beauty that was his sculpted body underneath. 'Sheer perfection,' I thought as I trailed my nails lightly over his nipples that had perked up in the cool air of the hotel room.

As my bra fell away, my attention on Smoke's body was

challenged when he dipped and bent in order for his mouth to seek out my nipple and give it a quick tug with his teeth before licking the sting away. He then sucked it to pert attention again before releasing it with an audible popping noise as he shifted to the other nipple, laving it with the same attention from tongue, teeth, and mouth.

The rest of our clothes quickly followed those removed before. His, mine, ours. All of it tossed to the hotel room floor and before I knew it Smoke had me lifted up with my legs wrapped around his waist, and he was carrying me to the bed. Along the way he managed to slip himself inside me. Never in my life had I been carried while connected to a man. Never. Holy, holy Jesus! There was nothing quite like it in this world. The insanely intense feeling in combination with the strength Smoke exuded while holding me aloft and managing to pump me up and down his shaft as we moved was so arousing I had already reached my first climax by the time he got us to the bed, and it hadn't been that far away.

"So fuckin' wet, honey," he told me as if I didn't know I was dripping wet thanks to his feats of greatness whenever he got me naked. Granted, this was only the second night we'd gotten naked together in the eight days since I first met him, but damn if he wasn't going for the gold in the sexual Olympics every single time.

The hold he had on my ass as we walked changed, and suddenly his hands were moving up the length of my back as I started tipping backwards. It was an unsettling feeling, but I went with it as I was secured as both of his arms slid around to secure my backside while his body curled around mine in the front. Magically, seamlessly, before I knew what had happened in my foggy-brain sexed-up state I had been placed so gently onto the bed that the transition couldn't have been real. What was real was the fact that the man hovering over me was slowly pumping in and out of my clenching sex. My eyes lifted slightly from their hazed, barely seeing anything state, and finally took notice of the pair of mismatched hazel orbs that were watching me so intently as he moved.

The glide of our bodies coming together sent zinging little electric shocks through all my sensitive places especially as Smoke got closer and his chest hair started tormenting my nipples with each plunge he took into me. The man was giving me a full body seeing-to as he moved and I managed to reach around and grab hold of his taut ass to hang on for the ride. Such a firm, fine ass it was, too. The minute my nails dug in he started moving faster, thrusting harder, and suckling at my neck again. "Honey," he called into my neck, the whispered word sending a puff of air to tickle the skin there. "You feel so fuckin' good, Poppy."

I ran my fingers up his back, trailing my nails along the way as I did while I whispered back. "So do you, Smoke." He pulled out, flipped me over, tilted my hips up at just the right angle and slammed back into me. "Oh God!" I breathed out as the new position added a different sensation to the mix. Smoke was not a small man in any way, and he was hitting a place so deep inside me it sent thrills of electrical pulses that both stung and elated me at once.

"So fuckin' sweet and sexy," he rasped out each word between thrusts inside me before he wrapped an arm around me and his fingers found that sweet little bundle of nerves that he began to manipulate. That was probably overkill as I was already about to tip over the edge into beautiful, oblivion, but I also wasn't about to argue with anything this man made me feel. Everything he did to me was heavenly.

"Smoke," I huffed out between labored breaths as he used his other hand to pull me back into his body harder with each thrust. "Oh God, Smoke, don't stop, please... don't... stop..." I murmured before my head tipped down toward the pillow. I couldn't quite reach it after the hand at my left hip moved to grasp a tight hold of my hair and tug.

"Stay with me honey, I want to see the minute I take you there." The slapping of his thighs against my own, the smell of sex on the air, and the tug at my nape from him controlling my position with the grasp he had on my hair combined with the throbbing, heavy pounding his body was giving mine as he swirled those strong fingers around my clit one more time sent me sliding right over the edge.

"Smoke," I called out, loudly as my toes curled, my muscles clenched, and sweet, sweet nirvana enveloped me. "Sm-oooo-ke," I managed to pant out with each thrust he was still thrusting into me as my insides clenched and released around his cock.

"That's it baby, milk that cock," he grunted as he slammed into me hard and deep one more time before his chest came down on my backside as he released inside me. "Fuck, Poppy," he hissed out again before rolling us, still connected, to our sides on the bed where I curled right into his body as if it were something I'd been doing my entire life. It felt right. So damn right I didn't ever want to lose the feeling that startled me a little bit and caused me to stiffen in his arms.

Smoke kissed the top of my head, squeezed tighter with the arm he had wrapped around me and whispered in my ear. "I'm not going anywhere, honey. Right here with you," he finished with another kiss, this time just beneath my ear. Holy, holy Jesus. The man could read my mind!

WE WERE STOPPED at a rest area on our way home the next day when Smoke got a call from his brother. Kent went about thanking Smoke, which only caused a puzzled look to appear on Smoke's face until he burst out laughing as his brother clarified why he was being thanked. "You're welcome, Brother. Shit, you should have just told me about it then. I would have taken care of the problem, and we could have met your girl while I introduced you to Poppy properly." There was a momentary pause and then Smoke was speaking again. "Nah, it's not like that. Yeah, she is. Yeah, next time. No excuses. Later."

I didn't know if I had the right to ask questions about the conversation he'd had with his brother, but as it turned out I didn't need to. Smoke grinned at me and then laughed before recounting what his brother had just told him.

"The bitch from last night was trying to cause problems for my brother and his girl." He shook his head then. "Didn't even know the little fucker was seeing someone. He's managed to keep it quiet, which is a fuckin' miracle in itself considering who he is. Anyway, the bitch who got up in my shit last night had strongly insinuated she'd been fucking Kent. She did this in earshot of his girl. Kent's never touched the bitch. He's steered clear of puck bunnies since he got his first taste of their brand of trouble in college. Had one claim he knocked her up back then."

"She wasn't really pregnant?" I asked.

"Oh, she was, just turned out to be Kent's teammate's kid. Kent dodged that bullet, because the poor guy whose number was up ended up flunking out of school the next semester. He wasn't good enough yet to go up for the draft so the bunny screwed them both out of their hockey dreams. Thank fuck that wasn't the road Kent ended up on."

"So what happened with the woman from last night?" I asked.

He grinned. "One of the player's wives shot video of what went down last night. It made the rounds through the wives and girlfriends by this morning. Dumb cunt told me she hadn't had my brother yet, but wouldn't mind taking me for a ride. Every word came out clear on video. I guess that clinched things for Kent's girl that he was the one telling the truth." Smoke's features distorted a moment in an almost angry look. "Sucks that she didn't have enough faith in him to believe him outright, but apparently they're still somewhat new, so he doesn't blame her for that."

"Well, I'm glad it worked out for him then. I'm also happy to hear that the video made it happen. Kind of made someone propositioning you right in front of me worth it."

"Honey," Smoke spoke softly into my ear as he pulled me into an embrace. "I really am sorry that happened. I promise you, if any bitch tries to disrespect you, me, or what we have together; I will take care of it immediately. That is not something I will ever tolerate."

I nodded my head against his chest and couldn't help thinking back to memories I'd apparently blocked out for some time. Memories of attending club functions where whores draped themselves over my man and it took him far too long to get them off, or he played it off as a joke later. Not once, that I could remember, had he nipped the problem in the bud for my benefit. I squeezed my arms around Smoke's waist a little tighter, because even though he couldn't possibly know what that proclamation meant to me, he deserved extra appreciation for initiating that response without me having to ask for it.

9. THE SISTER

Smoke had to go back to work the day after we got back from the hockey game. He was on for twenty-four hours and then he'd be off for the next forty-eight. I found I liked the sounds of that since it meant we could possibly have a full day, at least, to spend together if he didn't have obligations with the club during that time. In the meantime, I had Bubba to keep me company, and he seemed a bit clingier after having to deal with my brother during my absence.

"Poppy, I'm telling you the dog doesn't like me," My brother tried to convince me.

"Did he tell you that?" I asked on a laugh.

"He didn't have to, smartass. It's in his eyes. He kept watching me, like he was waiting for me to fuck up so he could eat me."

I glanced down at Bubba, and I swear I could see a grin on his doggy face. Yup, Bubba was my new favorite person. Yeah, I know... dogs aren't people. Whatever. Some of them are better than most of the people I know so I think it counts.

"You have a screw loose. Maybe he was just waiting on you to give him belly rubs," I suggested, and as I did my dog laid down and rolled over immediately. He obviously knew exactly what belly rubs were.

"That's just nuts. I swear he's not a fuckin' dog. He's a shape shifter, hellhound, demon, or something. No dog knows that much." I laughed again as I leaned in and rubbed Bubba's tummy. "You got plans tomorrow?" My brother asked with a knowing grin.

"Nope," I informed him to which his eyebrows shot up damn near to his hairline.

"Seriously?"

"Seriously, why?"

"Um, the club's is having a barbecue. I figured you'd be coming with Smoke so I didn't say anything."

I just shrugged my shoulders. "I don't know what we're doing yet, if anything. It's not like he pinned me and we're going steady or something, Keith."

"You just went on a trip, out of town, on the back of his bike yesterday. Same fuckin' thing for bikers and you know it."

I just huffed. "It's not the same for all bikers, and you know that, too."

"I know Smoke, so I'm telling you it's the same. That man has you on the back of his bike at all, it's because he expects to keep you there."

That caused me to smile. It also caused my brother to shake his head. "Jesus. You're already gone for him too," he muttered. Then he moved to me and pulled me into a hug. "I'd pick him a thousand times over for you, Pop. Seriously, never liked you with Walker all that much past the first few months. I do like Smoke for you though, for what it's worth."

"It's worth a lot," I told my brother as I hugged him back. "But just so you know, we're taking things slow and seeing where they go. Walk is not being very cooperative with the divorce. My lawyer called, said he's refusing to sign the papers and grasping at every straw he can to stall."

"What the fuck straw does he have to grasp for? The bastard cheated and the whole fuckin' town knows it."

I shrugged. "He's saying I inherited the house while we were married so a portion of the sale will belong to him if we divorce."

"You have got to be shitting me!" The gruff rumble to my brother's voice spoke of the violence he wanted to commit against my ex. "Seems like maybe I need to take another trip down to Georgia to straighten some shit out. Does he even realize I'm half owner of that house?"

"He knows, Keith. He's just doing this to stall the proceedings. According to Snake, he's supposedly coming up with a plan to come get me back."

"You still talk to Snake?" My brother asked cautiously.

"He checks in every couple days. Snake felt bad for what went down before. He thought my leaving was because he didn't tell me what Walker had planned. I've told him that it still would have happened because I can't stand by a man who won't stand by me."

"You tell Snake you're seeing someone else?"

"Nope," I answered with a slight pop to the p. "Not his business or anyone else's that he might pass that information along to."

My brother grinned then. "Probably for the best. You let me know if this continues to be a problem with the house and the divorce. You know I already told you I kept my half of the stake in that house to protect you from this shit, so even if by some demonic miracle he gets half of your half, you'll still get my portion, too." He glanced at me then grumbled under his breath, "I'll take care of shit before it comes to that."

I knew that. When my brother and I had split my family's estate after their death, he took a lump sum from the insurance money, and left me with enough to cover the taxes and whatnot for a couple years. I got the house and land. They equaled about the same amount, but Keith had kept his name on the house and land in case Walker ever tried to screw me over. I had told him that it wouldn't be a problem at the time, but I'm glad that my brother refused to listen to me. Apparently, he'd seen the writing on the wall long before I clued in to it.

As we stood there, each lost in our own thoughts about the situation, my cell started ringing. I glanced down and smiled when I saw Smoke's name there. "Hello?"

"Hey honey, just calling because I forgot about the barbecue at the club this weekend. You think you can be ready to hit that up with me tomorrow?"

"I'm sure I can. Do you need me to bring anything?" I asked as I glanced up at my brother's grinning face.

"You know the drill. If you want to bring a dish, you can, but make sure it can travel with the bike." I laughed. Of course he'd be picking me up on the bike. "It's a family thing, so you'll get to meet my sister while we're there. She's the reason I remembered about the damn thing to begin with."

"Oh, okay." I didn't know how I felt about meeting Smoke's sister. His brother, I'd been excited to meet because being one of my favorite hockey players took my mind off of the fact that I was meeting someone who was Smoke's family. Odd as that sounded, it was true. His sister was an entirely different scenario. I worried she would hate me and tell him then that would be the end of whatever we were starting, and I really liked what we were starting.

"Honey?" he asked, sounding hesitant.

"Sorry, lost in thought. Sounds good. I'll make some cookies up to take with so that they travel easily. I'm assuming by family barbecue that means kids will be there, too?"

"Yeah, honey. My nephew will be there as well."

"Okay, cool," I exclaimed before glancing nervously up at my brother who looked ready to laugh at me. "I better get to the store for cookie stuff then."

"Okay," he hesitated a moment. "Poppy, no need to be nervous. Soph will love you, and I'm sure that Brantley will."

"Brantley?" I questioned.

"My nephew," he explained.

"Oh okay. How old is he?"

"Three."

"Awesome, I will make a special cookie just for him," I announced, because I knew exactly what I was going to do. I had seen these cool cartoon and animal shaped cookies on Pinterest, and I had been dying to try them out on someone. I also had a motorcycle cookie cutter that would probably make a fitting cookie for a biker kid.

Smoke laughed. "Well shit, he'll definitely love you if you're bringing him his own special cookies." I heard an alarm sounding in the background. "Gotta go, honey." The phone disconnected before I could tell him to be safe. Damn, it sucked knowing he was possibly rushing into a dangerous situation while I was rushing to the store for baking supplies.

"His sister is going to be there," I informed my brother as I pocketed my cell.

"I figured. Her old man is Bender," my brother informed me.

"Bender?" I asked. "Wasn't he here helping move my stuff in?"

"That would be him."

"Oh, okay. I liked him."

Chief grinned at me then. "He liked you too, so you shouldn't really have a whole hell of a lot to worry about. I'm sure he already told Soph about you."

I couldn't help ringing my hands in worry anyway. "I never had to worry about meeting the family with Walk," I admitted. I'd already known his mom and dad. Walker didn't have any siblings so that wasn't an issue, and I'd already known the guys from the club thanks to my brother being a patched member.

"You'll be fine, Lil' Sis. Everyone loves you when they meet you."

"Not enough, apparently," I mumbled thinking about all the people who had turned their backs on me in favor of my philandering husband.

"No accounting for stupid," my brother informed me before we both got ready to head out for wherever our days were going to take us. For me, it was the grocery store. For my brother, I assumed the day would take him back to the clubhouse. For Bubba, he'd be waiting for me to get home and show him how much fun baking cookies could be, because I was going to make some special peanut butter biscuits just for him, too. Not that he really knew that was going to happen, but the dog was so good at anticipating my next move, I couldn't help but believe he did really know.

I GRABBED THE SMALL, beat up leather backpack I'd had for years and tossed it over my shoulders. It had the special cookie packed gingerly inside so as not to mess it up before the little boy it belonged to could tear into it. All the rest of the cookies had been packed neatly into Tupperware containers that now resided in Smoke's saddlebags. It had been a couple years since I was last at a function in Cedar Falls, and even then it was a multi-chapter function so I had never been too certain just how many members they had. Chief never really talked about it aside from little stories of specific events and people before. I knew a good eight or so guys he always talked about, but I was sure there were more. The problem was, I didn't know how many had old ladies, girlfriends, or how many kids there would be. I'd made enough cookies to feed an army, so I hoped they were plenti-ful. If not, I was positive big, bad, burly bikers enjoyed cookies just as much as the next person. It just so happened that they washed them down with beer or whiskey instead of milk like everyone else.

I laughed at my own thought as I threw a leg over Smoke's bike to straddle up close behind him. He felt warm and solid there in front of me as I wrapped my arms around his middle and held on. I had always hated wearing my helmet since it made me feel like a bobble head figure, but now I had a new reason for hating it, because I wanted more than anything to rest my head on Smoke's shoulder and cozy into him even more. The intermingling scents of mint, leather, and masculine perfection were lulling me into a space where I'd rather say forget taking the cookies to a barbecue, and let's stay home cuddled up in bed.

Thanks to his schedule at the fire station, Smoke and I hadn't been able to spend another night together yet since the hotel in Pittsburgh. His hand came down and squeezed my thigh before he took off out of my driveway and brought me back into the moment. It was almost a surreal moment, because the last bike I'd been on the back of regularly had been Walker's, and now that I'd thought of that, it had been almost four months since I last rode with my soon to be ex-husband. I hadn't even been on the back of my old man's bike for two months prior to our end. That was unheard of. The more little thoughts like that crept into my mind, the more I wondered what kind of rock I'd been living under during the time I'd spent with Walk. We were no longer the couple we'd once been. Instead, we had grown to be more like roommates who didn't exactly enjoy being around one another. I wished I had woken up to that fact sooner. I didn't want to be thankful for the storm. I didn't want to be thankful for the day I dreaded every year, but if it weren't for those circumstances I wonder how long I would have continued living in the shadows, unseeing?

I shook off that depressing thought and focused on the wind blowing the tendrils of my hair that managed to slip free of the quick bun I'd wrapped it into at the base of my neck in order to keep the wind from wreaking havoc on my long locks. I'd worn my comfortable skinny jeans, noting that there was a chill in the air already, despite it only being early October. I had definitely moved to a slightly different climate than what I was used to in northern Georgia. I was also wearing a simple dove gray t-shirt with a navy-blue Harley logo on it alongside the words "live free". Over that t-shirt I wore my black leather riding jacket that Chief had purchased for me years ago when he found out I'd taken a trip to Cedar Falls with Walk while wearing no riding leathers. Chief had been pissed that Walk hadn't been taking care of me. Walk had been pissed that Chief made him look like an ass in front of their club brothers for not taking care of his woman properly. Even though it didn't take Chief pointing it out to the other men, hearing someone say it out loud clued Walker in that he looked like a jackass, whether he realized it on his own or not. It was the last time we had gone to Cedar Falls.

There was yet another memory of something I hadn't wanted to see or admit to while I'd been with Walk. My brother had been right. Walker hadn't been taking care of me like some of the other brothers did with their old ladies. Steel, Quickshot, and Sweet would never allow their women on the backs of their bikes without their leathers. Not that they had to worry about it since all of their women rode their own bikes too and equipped themselves, but even Stone had equipped his woman, Mercy, with leathers that were patched to claim her as his old lady. Walk had never done that for me and we'd been together for ten years. The closest he had come to that had been to demand that I get a property patch tattoo with his name on it. I never did. My skin was as yet unmarred by ink, and not because I was against inking my skin, I just wasn't going to make a property patch the first thing I put there, especially since Walk was dead set against getting me inked into his own skin.

When we'd discussed it – read had a heated battle over it – he had told me 'my dad told me you never put a bitches name permanent on your body, not about to start now'. Needless to say, I used his own words against him in my refusal and neither of us ever wore each other's names. Looking back, that should have been a huge red flag for me. That was only six months after we married, and only after a man visiting from the Charleston Chapter tried to pick me up at an event.

We slowed as we turned into the Cedar Falls Complex and, once again, I was pulled from the morbid thoughts of all the things that should have been warnings of what was to come when I was with Walker. I squeezed Smoke extra tight before releasing him and dismounting the bike. There were only a couple of guys hanging around outside in the lot, and they all glanced over curiously as we started pulling tubs of cookies from the saddlebags on Smoke's bike.

"Thought you didn't let bitches ride on your bike, man?"

One of them called. I glanced up to see he had reddish hair, and appeared to be in his 30s with a well-trimmed beard that was just a couple shades darker than the long locks flowing down his muscular form. He was grinning at Smoke, but that grin slipped at whatever he was seeing from Smoke's expression. I didn't bother to turn and look. Instead, I stood there studying the man as his features shifted from grinning idiot to questioning and thoughtful.

"Call her a bitch again and we'll be talkin' out back in the shed," Smoke called out. The red-haired man took a harder look at me then before moving his attention back to Smoke, and nodding to the man while awaiting an explanation.

Smoke didn't give one until we had everything unpacked, and then he walked us over to the three men, of which Red had been one, and started introductions. "This is Poppy," he started when he was cut off by another man whose kutte told me was called Crutch.

"Poppy?" he questioned then smiled. "You're Chief's sister, right?"

"That I am," I offered on a smile.

"Oh, Chief asked you to bring her by?" Red asked, and then added, "I'm assuming that means he's bringing one of his bitches then?" This made me cringe, because I knew my brother played the field since the woman he followed to Cedar Falls all those years ago broke his heart, but the way this man, Red – who was apparently known as Heavy – had spoken my brother had several 'bitches' that could have been in contention for a place on the back of his bike.

Smoke growled at the man, tossed an arm around my shoulder, and shook his head. "Poppy's with me, because she's mine," he informed them. "Don't know what Chief's up to or if he's bringing anyone." As he spoke I noticed the third man, finally, who was grinning at me.

"Oh, hey!" I exclaimed.

"Hey, Poppy," he called. "How's that monster of yours?"

I laughed. "He's good, although he didn't seem too happy to be left behind today," I informed him. The him being the man my brother had brought by to introduce me to the other day, Hold 'Em.

Smoke's arm tightened on me. "You know Hold 'Em?" he asked quietly.

"Yeah, Chief brought him by when he got back from the run the other day and realized he'd left me without a way to communicate with anyone." Smoke studied the man who was still a prospect for the club, but from what Chief had told me was soon to be a fully patched brother.

"Take it you met Bubba?" he asked the man.

"Damn near pissed my pants meeting Bubba, thought he was gonna fuckin' tear my leg off," Hold 'Em admitted. Smoke cocked a brow up.

"There was a strange man standing on my porch, and it made me nervous. I'm sure Bubba felt that, and was feeding off my energy."

"Like that Bubba was doing his job, honey," Smoke told me, ignoring the confused glances the other men were throwing his way.

"You two know each other before Poppy moved here?" Heavy asked.

"Nope," Smoke answered and turned me with his body so that we could move to go inside. "I'll catch up with you guys later. We need to go deliver these cookies Poppy made." He motioned down to the containers of cookies he and I were both holding on to as we went.

"I'll grab the door for you," Crutch called out as he moved to lead the way.

"Thanks, man," Smoke told him and Crutch just nodded, smiled at me, and then opened the door to the clubhouse. It took a moment for my eyes to adjust to the dimness of the interior as opposed to the bright fall sunlight we'd stepped in from.

Just about the time my eyes adjusted, and I was able to take in the once shadowy figures on my periphery, a tiny little body slammed itself into Smoke. "Unc Moke," he yelled. I grinned down at the cuteness that was the toddler boy hanging on to Smoke's leg as he took his arm from around my shoulder and patted the boy's head. The boy latched on to Smoke's leg, wrapping arms and legs tightly around them in what was apparently a familiar game for them to play, because Smoke pretended it wasn't happening as he moved forward through the room until we got to the bar, where he placed the two bins of cookies he was carrying down on the counter as I followed suit. Once my hands were free, I reached up to the straps on my shoulders and moved to pull the bag off, but Smoke beat me to it. He helped me off with my bag and placed it gently in front of me on the bar.

I offered up a beaming smile to him as he reached down to snatch his nephew off his legs and tossed him into the air. "No free rides," Smoke called out to the giggling boy. As he landed firmly in Smoke's arms again he turned the boy so he was looking at me and then he whispered something in the boy's ear. "Can you say hi to my girl?"

The little boy shook his head, no as he blushed.

"Why not?" Smoke asked.

"She pwetty," he answered as he ducked his chubby little face into his uncle's neck making me smile even bigger at the little guy.

"I'm just Poppy," I told the boy. "Can you say that?"

"Popwee," he told me while shaking his head in the affirmative. I held my hand out for him to shake, and as he did I asked, "What's your name?"

"Bwantwee," he informed me. I glanced up at Smoke for a translation. I was pretty sure he meant Brantley, but with little kids you never knew.

"Brantley," Smoke confirmed. "Where's your mom?" The boy pointed across the room to a couple that was standing watching our interaction with heightened interest.

"Why don't you go ask your mom if you can have a cookie. I think Poppy made a special one just for you, bud."

"You did?" The angelic little face gazed up at me in wonder.

"I did, but you can only have it once your mommy says it's okay."

"Momma!" He screamed across the room while struggling for Smoke to put him down. Smoke did and his little legs took off full steam ahead towards his parents. "Popwee made me spetial cookies!" He exclaimed. "Can I eats them?"

I took the special cookies from my pack and started heading in their direction with Smoke hot on my heels. When we got closer it became very noticeable that Smoke's sister was a beautiful, feminine version of himself. The woman was tall with legs most other ladies would kill to have, long and slender, yet well-toned. She was wearing shorts and a tank top, something I thought was not quite up to par with the weather we were currently having. Her tank was a black support tank for the club, and she also had a female version of the kutte the men wore. No doubt, hers held a property patch on the back. Her long, dark brown hair was pulled into a fancy fishtail braid that wound down the right side of her neck and hung loosely over her shoulder. Her eyes were a hazel mix of greens and golds that were stunning in their own right, although not as in your face amazing as her brother's multi-hued eyes.

The woman was not smiling as we approached. She wrapped her arms around her wiggly son and glanced down at him as he tugged on her tank top. "Momma, can I haz a spetial cookie pweeeez?" he begged. The man standing next to her laughed at his son. He was a tall man with dirty blond hair and a slightly darker goatee. The laugh caused tiny little crinkles to form at the corners of his eyes that made me suspect that he was prone to laughter and smiles. If I hadn't been in such a daze when he helped unpack my moving truck, I might have remembered that about him.

I responded in kind as I leaned forward to hand him the special cookie his son was talking about. "Whenever you're ready for him to have that," I suggested and the man took it while smiling at me then he held out his other hand. "We already met when you moved in, but I'm Bender. This is my old lady, and Smoke's sister, Sophie. This little guy," he added as he took his hand back from shaking mine in order to ruffle his son's hair is our boy, Brantley." The pride in his voice and his eyes could not be missed. That man was all about his family.

"Thanks again for helping move me in," I managed to flounder out before putting my hand out to shake Sophie's. She took it a bit reluctantly. I didn't know what to make of her reluctance, so I decided to not let it bother me just yet. "I'm Poppy," I offered. When she just stared blankly at me and didn't engage in conversation, I let go of her hand while I mumbled, "I'm Chief's sister." Bender was staring at his woman with confusion written all over his face and when I chanced a glance up at Smoke he did not seem very happy with his sister. She noticed where my eyes traveled and hers moved in the same direction. Whatever she saw in Smoke's fierce look shook her out of her stupor.

"Sorry," she rushed out quickly. "I was just confused by you showing up with my brother since you're married and all," she stated nonchalantly causing a couple gasps to go up from people who had been standing close by and watching this all play out. I was so damn embarrassed I could feel the flames of a deep blush rushing to my skin, which was going to suck, because when I got embarrassed it left a mark on my pale, freckled complexion, making those freckles stand out even more.

"Are you fuckin' kidding me, Soph?" Smoke called out. I just put my hand on his elbow to get his attention and shook my head, not wanting any more attention drawn to our little corner of the room.

"I am still married," I spoke, addressing Sophie. "I'm in the middle of a divorce at the moment, and while I would love that it was all over already, my ex is being a pain in the butt and trying to stall in order to get money for the sale of my family's home and lands." I put it out there as honestly and succinctly as possible. Sophie seemed to pale a little bit.

"He's a brother in the club," she whispered as though this meant something.

"Yes, he's with the Sierra High Chapter," I informed her.

"Why would he need your family's money?" she asked.

I just shrugged. "I don't begin to understand anything Walker does, so I couldn't tell you. If you'll excuse me, I'm going to see if my brother's around yet," I told her, because I certainly didn't intend to stand there airing my dirty laundry for anyone else in the club, least of all Smoke's sister, and especially because Smoke and I hadn't even discussed the latest news in my divorce drama.

"Poppy," Smoke called to me before I was more than a couple steps away. I hesitated long enough to hear him say, "I'll be right behind you in a minute. Chief's at the pool tables."

I nodded and walked off, headed in the direction Smoke had pointed me to, but I still heard him speaking in a scathing tone to his sister. "What the fuck is your problem?"

"I – I don't know," she admitted. I was on the move so I didn't get to hear the rest of what was said. Instead, I searched out my brother, found him, gave him a big hug, and informed him the cookies were on the bar. He glanced over in the direction of Smoke and his family and frowned.

"What was that about?"

I shrugged once again, something the day seemed to be

bringing out of me. "I'm guessing Sophie isn't a fan of her brother hooking up with a woman who is still married."

"What?" My brother hissed out angrily.

"Leave it," I told my brother. "It is what it is. I'd probably feel the same if it were you until I got to know the woman and her circumstances."

"Still, Poppy, she disrespected you by bringing it up in the clubhouse with people around to hear that shit?" he asked, knowing she must have since I knew why she didn't like me.

"It is what it is, Chief. Let it go. I'm used to being the outcast in the clubhouse, remember?"

This did not appease my brother in the way I thought it would. "Yeah, and I wanted better for you here, because that shit should have never happened back home. Walk was any kind of man he would have nipped that shit in the bud for you instead of perpetuating it by not bringing you around and staking his claim the way he should have." Chief shook his head at me while thinking before he spoke. "I always thought it was you just being shy or something, but I'm seeing that wasn't the case. He was hiding shit from you, or keeping you away from his other shit all this time. I know it."

I cringed. "Can we not talk about this right now. It's bad enough to know what went down in the last couple months of our marriage. I don't want to speculate that I was dumb enough to allow that to happen throughout our marriage. That will kill me, Keith," I whispered the last to him, but he heard me, and managed to pull me in close to him while giving me a big brother hug I hadn't realized I'd been missing out on all these years since he'd moved to Cedar Falls.

"Should have went with you when you left," I told him which earned me a kiss on my head before the warm presence of another body was at my back. I knew that body just by the scent of him, and I turned to smile at him as his arm came around my waist and gently pulled me from my brother's embrace.

Chief just grinned and went right back to his game of pool that had been put on pause while I was talking. Again, something my ex-husband wouldn't have done. He would have made me wait until the game was over before interacting with me. Why was I just now seeing all this? Why couldn't I see it before, as I was wasting ten years of my life with a man I thought I loved and whom I thought had loved me?

"Food's up out back. You want to go grab something?" Smoke asked me, and I nodded while following him as he took my hand in his own and led me to the back yard area of the clubhouse. They had an amazing array of multi-level decking leading to a sunken large deck in the middle that had a fire pit, coolers along the sides, and plenty of benches wrapping around the whole thing, except where narrow steps came in down the middle of all four sides. Those steps lead up to a deck on the right where all the grilling was apparently done, a deck on the left that held a hot tub that was already seeing some action, although from clothed individuals since there were children present. There was a slim deck beyond that funneled out even lower into the grassy lawn area that seemed surprisingly well maintained. Then there was the deck I was currently standing on that opened up from the clubhouse to the others. Scattered lawn furniture and deck chairs were everywhere. Personal coolers were sitting beside some of the chairs and there were men all over the place decked out in denim and leather, t-shirts and a few flannels. The women seemed to be congregating around the food to serve the men or take care of the smaller children.

I wasn't certain of my place in all of this since I wasn't an old lady to Walker anymore and Smoke and I were something new. At best, I was now simply family to Chief. So, I stayed glued to Smoke's side as he moved us over to where the women had set up an elongated table with tons of sides, chips, and cupcakes all over it. Smoke walked us over to the table and smiled at the women who were eyeing us curiously.

"This your new woman?" A younger girl with bleach blond hair and bright blue eyes asked. She was wearing what I'd normally associate as club skank wear consisting of shorts so short parts of her were hanging out that shouldn't be on show and a top that was cut off to a point that her under-boobs were going to be visible to any of the children who dared get too close to her. Her tone was not exactly mean or anything, but she did not acknowledge me at all, aside from asking Smoke the question.

"Poppy is my woman. She's also Chief's sister." He scored her with a heated look before issuing a warning. "Be nice, or we'll have problems. Don't care who your dad or your man is now."

Well, obviously there was a story behind those words, and it made me wonder what, if anything, had gone down with Smoke and this woman previously. She sucked her lips into a pucker as if she'd tasted something sour. Then she turned and walked away from the table.

"Don't mind her," an older, blond haired woman told me with a smile. "That one has always had a bad attitude. She didn't grow up in the club thanks to her no-good momma. Didn't have much of a good influence for the same reason, so make no mind." She held out her hands. "I believe we actually met a few years ago when you came up for an event. I'm Cindy, Hopper's old lady."

I smiled at her. "Hi Cindy, I do believe we were introduced once before." I looked around at all that was on offer at the table and then laughed. "We left the cookies I brought on the bar inside," I lamented.

"Oh lord, those boys probably done ate them all up then," she laughed. Then she mock-glared at Smoke. "You should have known better than to do that."

He gave her a sheepish grin before picking up a plate and starting to pile sides on it. "We got sneak attacked by Brant, and then I had to introduce Poppy to Soph."

"How'd that go over?" Cindy asked cautiously.

"Not as well as I'd have liked," Smoke told her honestly which made Cindy sigh.

"I was worried about that since everyone was gossiping about what went down in Georgia to bring Chief's sister up here." I turned all my attention back to Cindy then.

"Gossiping about me?" I asked.

"Sure, sugar. Nothing bad was mentioned, just that you were leaving your old man, and from what everyone says, he deserved to be left."

I nodded, and was happy to hear that I wasn't being

made out to be the beast in all of this, but it still sent my stomach to turning on itself, and suddenly the food I'd been placing on my plate didn't seem quite as appetizing. Cindy reached over and patted my hand in a kind gesture. "You ever need to talk, a shoulder to cry on, or just someone to vent to, you call me up, sugar. I might listen in on the gossip, but I don't run my mouth. You have something to say or get off your chest it'll stay with me if you need it to."

"Thank you, Cindy," I told her as Smoke took my hand again and began walking us toward the deck with the grill so we could go grab some of the ribs the boys were cooking.

"Cindy's a good woman. You can believe her. That woman locks secrets up tighter than a vault.

"Good to know."

When we got to the grill I noticed Ghost, the president of the local club, as well as the national president of Aces High, was standing there manning the ribs. He tipped his chin up to Smoke before his piercing turquoise colored eyes landed on me. The smile he gave me then was genuine. "Hey there, Poppy."

"Hi, Ghost. See you're the one to complain to if the ribs suck," I teased. He grabbed at his chest as if I'd just broken his heart and he was holding the organ in.

"You wound me!" He exclaimed loudly.

I just giggled. Ghost and I had a cook off once when he was down visiting with his daughter who was married to the president of the Sierra High Chapter as well as being President of her own female motorcycle crew. We pitted our ribs against each other and came out with a draw in the end. No one could decide whose were better because they liked them equally and for different reasons.

Ghost pointed to the two different containers holding the ribs that were already done. "I made two batches, darlin'. There's my brand of spicy and your brand of sweet." He pointed in kind to each dish.

"You made my ribs today?" I inquired on a surprised breath.

"Been making both since we had our cook off all those years ago. Thought it'd be prudent since most of the women preferred your sweet to my spicy." He offered with a wink.

"Well, damn, now I have to try them and make sure you're doing my recipe justice." He laughed then.

"Shit! Do not shoot the cook! I make no promises that I got them right. They're always missing a little of your magic when I attempt them." Smoke had remained quiet during this exchange, but when I glanced over at him he was grinning from ear to ear.

"What?" I asked.

"Didn't know you were the one responsible for the sweet, southern ribs Ghost started making, honey." I didn't know what to say to that so I didn't say anything at all. "They're my favorite."

Ghost laughed at that. "He isn't joking. The women always complain when he gets to them first, because there are never enough."

"Maybe you should take a hint and make more of the superior ribs then?" I asked on a laugh.

"Blasphemy!" Ghost bellowed out while both Smoke and

I laughed. "Okay, darlin' what's it gonna be?" he finally asked.

"I'm having some of each. Have to make sure you're doing my recipe justice, but I also love your spicy ribs. It's a good change of pace from mine." I offered up on a wink as I grabbed a couple of each.

"Well, next time, you can prep your own recipe so that you know it gets done right."

"Absolutely," I agreed with a smile.

"And maybe some of that triple chocolate cake you made before because Leanne loved that shit, and I was supposed to get the recipe for that too, but I didn't and she's been harping on my ass about it for years. Woman's tried to find something similar since then and to no avail."

"Aww, you could have called. I would have given it to her."

He looked at me funny then, almost hesitantly, before he spoke. "I did call. Walk told me he didn't know what I was talking about that he thought you bought it at the store."

I know I must have paled considerably. "Are you serious?" I gasped out. Ghost nodded as I shook my head. "It's my grandma's recipe that I tweaked a little over time. I can't believe he told you it was store bought."

"Sorry to bring up bad shit, darlin'."

"No worries. Just another reminder why my recent life change was for the best."

Ghost nodded then tipped his head to Smoke. "I need you both to know something before you run off today." He had both of our undivided attention with that statement. "If I were to pick a person for each of you, this would be it.

I approve. No matter that her divorce hasn't gone through," he told Smoke. "No matter that you were once with another brother," he informed me. "I like the two of you for each other. So, if it works out, you have my blessing all the way. It doesn't work out, make sure you don't disappear on us, darlin', because you'll always be family. That's something Sweet should have conveyed to you, and I'm damn disappointed he didn't." Sweet was Ghost's son-n-law and the president of the Sierra High Chapter of Aces High.

I felt tears brewing at the backs of my eyes then. "Thanks," I whispered as Smoke let go of my hand in order to put an arm around my shoulder and pull me into his side instead.

"Appreciate all that, Ghost," Smoke let him know before we moved off to find ourselves a table to sit down and enjoy our feast.

"That was sweet," I told him, speaking about what Ghost had just said to us.

"Yeah, honey, it was. He likes you. Never seen him joke around like that so easily with any of the other women outside of Leanne and Angel Girl when she's around."

"We bonded over our ribs years ago," I explained.

"I see that. Damn proud to know those ribs I've been eating up all this time came from you in a roundabout way." My smile lit up my face with his praise.

"Thanks. I'm just glad someone other than the club-women actually likes them. "Ghost won't tell you this, because it might mean he loses the cook-off you had, but the sweet ribs are always gone long before the spicy ones and that isn't on account of just the women eating them." At that I laughed.

"Good to know," I told him.

"Make sure no one gets eager enough to touch my food, honey. I'm gonna go snag us some drinks. You want beer, water, coke, or something else?"

"Coke's good to wash the ribs down. Little too early for beer for me." He gave me an odd look, but went about going to procure our drinks anyway. I never drank early at the few club events I went to. Mostly, I knew that I'd have to pace myself, and stop drinking after one or two anyway, because Walker almost always got out of hand and forgot I was there. I'd have to find a ride home or be the one to drive us home on the days I'd driven my car to the clubhouse because Walker had taken off without me. Most times he'd told me it was because he knew I'd have a bunch of shit to take with me that wouldn't fit on the bike. It still sucked to show up alone and have to drag my stupidly drunk husband out after he allowed other women to paw on him in front of me without putting them in check. It was definitely making me wonder how long Walker had been messing around behind my back and just being more cautious about who was seeing it.

Once again, I attempted to remind myself that it didn't matter what Walker had done, what I had been ignorant of, found out about too late, or anything else. The only thing that mattered was that moving forward I didn't have to deal with any of it. It was my past. The speculation could stay buried in the past with all the other not so pleasant memories our separation had allowed to surface. Instead, I decided to tuck into the ribs on my plate, and the minute I did, the flavor exploded on my tongue. Ghost had done my recipe proud.

"Poppy?" A female voice called to me from just behind my shoulder. When I looked I realized it was Sophie.

"Oh, hi," I managed to get out as I wiped the sauce off my mouth with my napkin. "Have a seat," I offered, gesturing to the empty side of the table across from where I was sitting.

"Where did Smoke get off to?" she asked while eyeing his plate of unattended food.

"He went to snag us both a drink."

"Listen," she started as she sat down across from me. "I wanted to apologize for being rude earlier. That's not normally like me. It's just that I watched my brother with that undeserving skank ex of his for far too long. She dragged him and our brother, Kent, through some shit."

"I know," I interrupted to tell her, because there was no need to hear the story retold again.

"You know?" she asked while sounding surprised. I nodded so she continued, "The thing was, I watched my brother just getting by with her. He never really seemed happy. The light he usually had in his eyes wasn't there. It's almost like he was always on edge when they were together, and you could almost physically see him waiting for the bottom to drop out, you know?" I nodded again, because I was discovering that was what my own life had been like with Walker for more than a few years now.

"The other guys used to refer to her as his old lady, and while he never corrected them, he never said the words himself. Five years they were together and there were no proposals, and never even a thought about buying a ring to make one either. That said a lot about how my brother was feeling, even if he didn't realize it himself."

I was really beginning to wonder where this was going, but I didn't bother interrupting again. I just sat there and listened as Sophie went on.

"I see him with you today, and he's lit up like the damn Fourth of July." She shook her head then, as if doing so would lead to understanding. "Saw you guys on TV at the game the other day, too. That's when he first talked to me about you. I had to call him and ask who the woman was. He told me your story about your husband, or at least what he knows of it."

"Ex-husband," I corrected her.

"Thought you weren't divorced yet?"

I shrugged my shoulders. "Semantics. I don't have the paperwork, but when I left there was no looking back for any reason, other than to sign papers making it official."

"That's what worries me," she stated solemnly.

"What do you mean?"

"You're not divorced yet. You were with the man a decade or so right? From what I hear, you were trying pretty desperately to have kids with him, too." That stung a bit, but I just bit off my bitchy response I wanted to lob her way and shrugged my shoulders as if to say... 'And, your point is?' She nodded her head. "I worry it's too soon. That either you're not really over your ex and just mad that he made some dumb decisions or that my brother is your rebound and he'll be the one to get hurt either way."

"I understand your concerns and if it were Chief and some woman in my shoes I'd be feeling the same way, so I don't blame you for it either. The thing is, you don't know the whole situation, because no one outside of me does. Yes, we were trying to have kids, but the trying part died out a long while back. He gave up, because our failure to have them was his problem physically and he couldn't cope with that. What I've come to realize since our big blow out and the mess that followed was my eyes had been shut for a long time during our marriage. I hadn't been happy. He wasn't happy. We were roommates living a lie of a life, and I allowed that to happen, because for a long time I was too consumed by the grief of losing my family to acknowledge the fact that I was lost right alongside them.

"My husband never tried to find me. He never bothered to help me heal, to put me in the arms of others who could help, or anything. He just concerned himself with the club, came home, and had me there to care for him. It took a huge epiphany for me to see that my life was a joke, and that my husband didn't care beyond my convenience any longer. It took that same epiphany for me to realize I hadn't been in love with the man in a long time. He was just all I had left since my only other living relative had moved away to be here, and for whatever reason I didn't think I could leave behind the memories of the rest of our family. I allowed myself to remain stuck for far longer than I should have, but rest assured my eyes are wide open, my heart accepting, and my brain has caught up to everything I was ignoring.

"My divorce will go through. My ex is just that, an ex. And as far as your brother is concerned, I have no clue where the future will take us. I'm making no promises to him, to myself, and definitely not to you that our futures will be entwined. How could I know that? We're new. What I do know is that from the moment I met Smoke, he has captivated me. He has shown me some of the things that I'd been missing from my marriage. We have fun together, we have like interests, and we have amazing chemistry.

"Will that lead us to an amazing future together? All I can say is I hope so. I'm not on the rebound, because I wasn't looking to begin with. There are just people in this life that you meet and there's no denying they belong to you in a way. They are meant to be your people. Smoke is one of those people for me. He just clicked into place immediately."

Sophie smiled at me and, for the first time that day, it was a genuine smile. She looked beyond me, over my shoulder, and a moment later I felt him there. His warmth embraced me seconds before he did as he took the seat beside me, deposited our drinks on the table in front of us, and then had one arm wrapped around my shoulders again. "Soph," he grumbled out.

Sophie continued to smile at her brother. "Brant loved the cookie you made him," she claimed as her smile moved from her brother back to me. "You'll have to share your recipe with me, because I tried a bite, and it was heaven in my mouth."

"Lord, woman, everyone wants your recipes," Smoke declared. When Sophie sent a questioning glance to her brother, he held up one of his ribs. "The sweet ribs Ghost makes are Poppy's."

Sophie sucked in a breath and then grabbed my hand. "You're kidding?" I shook my head.

"They're mine." I affirmed after I swallowed the drink of coke I'd been taking when she asked.

"Oh my God, those things are to die for. When Ghost started making that second batch, I thought he'd found his true calling. I can see we'll have to spend a bit more time in the kitchen together. You're the one that made that chocolate cake Leanne has been going on about for so long then?" I nodded once more. "She's had us all try so many chocolate cakes it's ridiculous. I feel like a chocolate cake connoisseur by now, but Leanne says nothing compared."

"If I'd known I would have brought that instead of the cookies."

"Next time," Sophie insisted. "You have to make a few of them though, because I promise you that they will be devoured quickly. Everyone has been in on Leanne's chocolate cake quest." She laughed and so did Smoke.

"She is not wrong about that." Then he grinned at his sister. "Where's the demon spawn?"

Sophie sighed. "He had a bit of an accident since he was so excited about the cookie. Bender took him to get cleaned up before anyone noticed." She whispered conspiratorially.

Smoke grinned wider. "Poor kid. Though, nothing these morons don't do themselves during a good party when they tie one on too hard." He offered with a laugh.

"Truth!" Sophie stated with an exasperated huff. "Still haven't forgiven Bender for the time he came to the bedroom and pissed in our laundry basket thinking he'd made it to the bathroom." She shook her head as my jaw dropped. Then she looked right at me. "It was full of clean clothes too, and my old leather jacket was right on top."

"No way!" I cried out in disbelief.

"Oh yeah, he ended up buying me a new one the next day, because I refused to wear the jacket he pissed on ever again. Taught him a lesson, because the replacement was not cheap!" She offered as she snickered.

"Tell me you are not extolling the virtues of me watering the laundry again," Bender said as he found his way to the seat beside his wife and tucked in along with his son and a plate of food.

"Oh yeah, I did."

"Jesus, woman. You ever gonna let me live that down?"

"You still tell people about the first time I farted around you when we were dating?" Bender started chuckling immediately, and looked guilty as hell while doing it.

"That's what I thought," Sophie scoffed.

"Babe, it wasn't just a fart. When you go all in, you go ALL in." He glanced my way, eyes crinkled with mirth as he explained. "It was a full-on shart. Didn't stop laughing about that shit for a solid week." Sophie's face was buried in her hands as her shoulders shook.

"You're an asshole," she grumbled from her hands.

"Babe, it was epic. One minute you're talking to me as we step off the curb to cross the street to the movie theater, next thing I know a liquid rumbling is coming from your ass, and you got this look on your face." He had to stop because of his laughter at that point. Smoke was belly laughing with him. Obviously hearing this story retold was still just as funny as when it first happened. Probably not for Sophie, but she seemed to at least be able to laugh about it now.

"Her hands clamped down on her ass like something had

just been shoved up there, then she started hopping around like a lunatic, before she dodged back into the restaurant we'd just come out of and then she refused to come out of the bathroom." Bender was still laughing as he finished telling this story, but then he pointed at Smoke. "This one shows up fifteen minutes later with a backpack on his back. Looks at me, breaks out laughing for a solid five minutes, and then heads into the restaurant. Sophie called him to bring her a change of clothes and barricaded herself in that bathroom until it happened." He was shaking with laughter at this point. "Damn woman refused to talk to me for two weeks after that. She left with her brother that night. They snuck out the back and left me high and dry standing on the curb."

"I texted you," Smoke put in.

"Yeah, but I didn't realize that until after I heard your bike start up and watched you pull away from the curb with my woman on the back of your bike."

"Oh my God!" I hissed out amidst my laughter. "I'm sorry, Sophie, I don't mean to..." I couldn't get the rest out through my laughter.

She waved me off. "Don't worry about it. Everyone here knows the damn story, and every single one of these fuckers laughed their asses off about it, too."

"Dees fuffers," Brantley put in, causing us all to laugh even harder.

"That's a bad word, Brant," his father corrected.

"Whats is bad? Fuffers is bad?"

"Yeah, bud," he told him while trying to hold back his laughter.

Brantley shrugged his itty-bitty boy shoulders and glanced around the table. "Mommy says fuffers."

"Mommy's gonna get a spankin'." Bender told him while winking at his wife.

Brantley's eyes grew wider. "Oh, mommy youz in tubble."

"Christ!" Sophie muttered. I just giggled while hoping that someday I had a kid as cute and unassumingly hilarious as her son. For the first time, in a long time, that didn't seem like an unattainable goal either. Maybe it would happen with Smoke, maybe not. I just knew that I was in a position to make it happen finally, since I got clear of my ex who did everything in his power to make sure I didn't have options once he realized it wouldn't be an easy thing to accomplish.

"Popwee?" Brantley called out from across the table.

"Yeah, buddy?"

"Youz cookie was good. You not gon' get spankins like Momma."

"Good to know!" I told him. He then looked at his uncle.

"It was a voom bike, Unc Moke."

"I know bud, I saw it."

"You did?"

"Sure did. Poppy showed it to me."

"Popwee is good," his nephew told him, making both Smoke and me smile.

"Yeah, she is bud." At least I knew I'd earned the approval of the toddler in the bunch. "Momma, you like Popwee too?"

"Sure do, Brant," Sophie told him softly as she glanced back to me with a smile.

"She not get her spankin'. You gets a spankin'." He reminded her.

"Okay, one-track," his dad called out to him. "Let's go grab you a cupcake before they're all gone." The little squirt did a fist pump with a solid, "YES!" hissed out as he squirmed from his mom back to his dad and then slipped through his grasp and took off like a rocket across the deck to get to the food. Yup, one day, I hoped like hell I had a little boy just like him.

"It's moments like those that keep me from trying for another one right now," Sophie stated to no one in particular. I didn't bother telling her that her moment of cautionary tale was the opposite for me. I just smiled and went back to tucking into my food while being thankful that Sophie and I were able to have our little chat. It left me feeling far better about things than our initial meeting had.

10. THE FIRE

SMOKE AND I LEFT THE PARTY FOR A BIT TO GO SEE TO BUBBA, AND our insatiable need to get one another naked. We actually ended up staying locked away at my house long enough that we had to see to Bubba one more time before we left again to head back to the party.

By the time we returned, the barbecue was over and family time had come and gone with the old ladies and the children retiring to their homes for the rest of the night. The women who were able to find babysitters, or didn't have younger children to tend to, found their way back to the clubhouse for the late night festivities. I was surprised to see that there didn't appear to be many club whores hanging about so I asked Smoke why that was.

"Jewel, the girl who asked if you were my new woman when we got here earlier?" he asked to see if I remembered who he was talking about. When I nodded my head he continued. "She was a club whore for a short time before it came out who she really was. Hopper had a thing with one of the club whores back in the day after his woman left him and took his son to South Dakota to be with another man in the club. The whore he had a fling with got herself knocked up, but she never told him. Jewel comes of age and heads to the club to be a whore, at her mom's behest, in order to help pay the bills since the girls who lived on site got a financial stipend."

My eyes had to be bugging out because I had never known that was a thing. "Each club runs that shit differently. The club up in the Dakotas actually pays college tuition for some of their girls. The one in Charleston doesn't fuck around with whores in their clubhouse anymore at all after some shit went down there that got a club member killed. The guys in Georgia don't allow them to stay overnight, and that's mostly because their top dogs have women in the S.H.E. MC and from what I've heard, those girls don't tolerate the whores' attitudes too well. They just show for parties and whatnot. Here, we had a few that lived at the clubhouse and earned a stipend for being on call all the time." I didn't have anything to say when he paused so he continued on with his story.

"Well, we were on the verge of kicking Jewel out because she refused to be with any of the older guys, and wouldn't give a reason why. Finally, she mentioned her mother told her not to ever have anything to do with any of the guys over 40. We asked who her mom was and all hell broke loose, because everyone knew she used to be one of the club's whores, and considering Jewel's age, any of those older guys could have been her daddy."

"Jesus, are you kidding me? That woman sent her

daughter in to be a whore where her own father could have... where he could see things... what the hell was she thinking?" I gasped all that out, completely astonished that a mother could put her own daughter in that position or that she would put the father in that position.

"Yeah, it was fucked, because Hop had seen his little girl getting banged on more than one occasion. Lucky as fuck he never got a hankerin' to participate. Then again, Hop has a good woman, and isn't one to run around on her." He shook his head back and forth with whatever memories were running through his head then. "Jewel ended up catching the eye of Phoenix, one of the club's nomads. They're still together, but after everything came out and it was made clear that Hop was Jewel's dad, he lost his shit a bit. When I say he saw her in the middle of doing some things, I mean he got the full view, and he was not happy to find out that was his daughter afterwards. He pushed to have the whole practice of keeping whores at the clubhouse abolished. He also pushed to keep the guys from having sex in public spaces. We have wild throw downs and sometimes you'll see some heavy make out sessions. Tonight, you might even witness a blowjob in the corner or something, but it's rare here now. Hop was obviously torn up about his daughter's situation, but the other guys were just as disturbed, especially the ones who were with Jewel when Hopper saw. It caused a lot of friction in the club, so when the vote went up it was damn near unanimously passed. Didn't hurt that most of the guys are settling down with women of their own now anyway."

"I can't imagine how humiliating that was for everyone involved. I hope Jewel wrote her mom off after that."

"That woman dug her own grave and stepped in it knowingly. She's not in this world anymore, and no, it wasn't the club who took her out, though I'm sure Hopper and a few others would have loved the honor after the shit storm that bitch caused and the life she brought that girl up in. It was the bullshit she had going on with drugs and owing money to the wrong people that got her dead in the end."

"That's nuts," I hissed out through my teeth.

"It is, but I'm going to warn you now, that girl is still getting her shit together. She's not here often, because her old man, Phoenix, is a nomad in the club. When she is here, you'd do best to steer clear of her. She's working through her demons from what Phoenix has passed on to Hopper, but she's still prone to causing drama, and she used to be friendly with my ex, so rest assured if she's wanting to cause drama you make a pretty target."

"Fantastic," I muttered. Smoke rubbed his fingers along my back as we moved deeper into the clubhouse where people were dancing, playing pool, drinking, and generally carrying on as only adult aged children can. Despite the fact that I'd been to the clubhouse a few times before when I was with Walker, I didn't really know anyone here. He had kept me mostly sheltered from club life, I was learning. I was also finding it strange that he had done so since most of these guys seemed to enjoy having their women close.

Once again, I had to take a moment to shut down the thoughts about my past. It wasn't that I wanted to dwell there, or go back, I couldn't help making the comparisons, because once your eyes are opened and you begin to see what is truly in front of you a person can't help chastising themselves for having been so blind to it all. I hoped this was all part of the healing process I was going through, and at least I wasn't in denial about the things I was experiencing now. I was learning from the past in order to make my future better.

Smoke and I were standing near the bar talking with Ghost, Leanne, and the prospect currently working behind the bar taking orders. His name was confusing, because I'd heard Ghost call him Gray and Smoke called him Surfer-Dude a lot. The Surfer moniker seemed fitting since he had that slow, southern California surfer speech going on and he had an affinity for the word 'dude' as well. Smoke had mentioned working with him before with CFFRD. It was just as we were all joking about the fact that Surfer-Guy Gray didn't know how to make silly frou-frou drinks when Hopper and a man named Tuck walked toward us with a purpose. A man named Mick joined them quickly.

"Ghost, we have a pretty big fuckin' issue we need to discuss in the office, possibly church," Hopper explained. Ghost immediately hopped off his stool and started heading in that direction. Hopper and Mick followed behind, but Tuck hesitated and he did so while staring at Smoke.

"I'm thinking you should come too, Smoke."

Smoke didn't say anything other than to nod his head. Then he turned to me with regret in his eyes. "Don't worry, you have to go, go. Handle your club business, and I'll see you when it's done," I assuaged his guilt with my words and I could see the relief as weight seemed to visibly lift off his shoulders. He glanced around before speaking though, then he sighed.

"Not sure how long this is going to end up taking, and Chief doesn't look fit to drive you home, honey."

"I've got her, Smoke. Go ahead to the office, and I'll see her home." Leanne lifted her glass to prove her point. "I'm just drinking Ginger ale tonight."

Smoke nodded his head and took off with Tuck in the same direction the other men had gone moments before. I turned and glanced in Gray's direction, smiling at him. "You better prepare your woman for the realities of that happening," I explained with a grin. He smiled back, but his smile didn't reach his eyes as they scanned the room looking for the woman he pointed out earlier. I looked too, and didn't like what I saw when I did. If I didn't know she had a man of her own I would think she was on the prowl in the clubhouse. Kayla, the girl Gray said he lived with, appeared to be flirting with a couple of guys over by the pool tables. That couldn't be good.

"Did you want to hang around a bit and see if the guys get done with their club business quickly, or..." Leanne started to ask when Smoke, Hopper, and Tuck tore off out of the building with Smoke yelling, "Gray, get your ass out here with us, gonna need you on this one."

"Shit!" Gray hissed, snatched up a set of keys from behind the bar, and tore off after the other men.

"Well, I'm going to take a wild guess and say they won't be back any time soon," Leanne amended.

I grinned at her. "I'm thinking you would be correct." At that point, Ghost had reemerged from his office and was stalking over to Leanne. "Babe, we're going to be tied up with club biz for a bit."

Leanne smiled sweetly at her man. "I figured. I'm going to get Poppy home since her ride just took off like a bat outta hell with the rest of the men. I'll be back soon as I drop her off."

Ghost didn't say a word, just leaned in and kissed Leanne long and deep. Then he swatted her ass as she moved off her bar stool and he took off at a quick pace back down the hall that led to his office. It was on the ride home that Leanne informed me that she would keep me in the loop if she could.

"Soon as I know anything, I'll message you. Lord knows, the lifestyle these boys lead, we women are left to worry too often. If I can help take some of that worry for you, I will."

I smiled at Leanne. "You make a good old lady for the Prez doing that."

She cocked her head to me then. "I imagine where you come from you know all about good old ladies for the Prez of the club." I saw the pride in her eyes as she spoke of Angel Girl, yet she still noted my hesitant response.

"She may be my step-daughter, but I will always take truth over lies."

"It's not that she's a bad person," I started out. "I like Angel Girl, but she has her own club to deal with. She leads those women, and half the time, club business for her club is the same as it is for the guys in Aces down there. She's too busy being a good president for her club to be a good old lady supporting the women of her man's club."

Leanne nodded her head. "I suppose I never thought about that. Some days, I wish she'd give it up, because I think her calling was supposed to be in that support role. Then again, I remember all those girls when they first came to me, and then started Sierra High Evermore MC. They were all so lost and not a one of them were found until they made their own purpose. So, while she's not supporting the women from her man's club the way I think she was always destined to, she's supporting all the women of hers in a way that they get a new lease on life when it's kicked them to the ground one too many times."

"I get that too," I agreed.

"She didn't step in and do anything in your situation?"

"Nope. I never heard from her or Keys throughout. JoJo came to visit me a couple times before I finally decided I needed to get out of that town, but there wasn't much she could do outside of giving me a shoulder to cry on."

"I suppose that's true. I'm a bit disappointed in those girls though, that being the case. I can't believe after everything Angel Girl went through with Sweet that she would stand back and watch all that go down without doing anything on your behalf."

"I think they've had their hands full with some things going on down there. I know JoJo hinted at something big with one of their security clients landing in a mess that was blowing back on the club."

"Still," Leanne muttered.

"Honestly, Leanne, she has her own family to worry about without having to deal with my soon-to-be ex-husband's problems with fidelity and not putting his pride above all else."

Leanne sighed. "You know, sometimes men can be really damn stupid."

"Amen to that," I agreed on a laugh.

"I have to tell you though, I like what I see going on between you and Smoke."

"I like it, too. His sister didn't seem incredibly happy at first since I'm still married, and everything started happening so fast."

Leanne pulled into my driveway, put the car in park, and then moved so that she was facing me. "Let me give you a little advice on that note. When I lost my first husband I thought I lost my world. One minute he was there, and we had been having some of the same fertility issues you had in your marriage, only we had to try getting pregnant around his deployment schedule. Around the time I finally decided it was never going to happen for me, and had given in to thinking about just adopting kids, I got word that he was gone. I swore I would be alone forever then. I just knew there was no getting over him. He was my first and only love up to that point."

I offered Leanne a small smile as we took each other's hands. "Then I met Angel Girl, of course I knew her as Jamie at the time. The thing was, I heard her story, and I saw her trying to put the pieces together. Watching someone else putting their broken heart back together one little tiny piece at a time does something to you. By the time her dad found her a few years later, I suppose I had been healing my own heart too, and just hadn't realized it. So, when he first approached me I was interested, but seriously conflicted. Had I listened to my family, I never would have given into him. Instead, I tuned them all out and went for where my heart was pulling me. Now, Ghost and I are happy, we have two beautiful children together, and then there's Jamie and our grand babies, too. When you're on the outside looking in, maybe it seems shitty or like I forgot my first husband, but he's still in my heart, and I have to think he'd be happy that I got the family I'd always wanted even if it couldn't be with him."

"I've always been a bit envious of what you have with Ghost. I guess being that way, looking back on it, I knew in my heart things were missing from my marriage."

Leanne nodded sagely. "My girl, I'm thinking you've had years to come to terms slowly with the death of your marriage. Doesn't matter that you think you were wearing blinders and suddenly woke up. It wasn't as sudden as you think, and you realizing what you just told me about feeling envious of Ghost and me, that says I'm telling the truth. You knew. It just took a bit longer for you to act on what you already knew. So, when people see that you are freshly divorced, and those same people haven't been living your life with you to know what was going on in it, they are going to have their own assessments about how you're moving on too soon. But they don't know that you've been working at moving on for a long while now in your heart. You've just gotten around to finally making it official." She leaned over then and hugged me, her warm cinnamon scent enveloped me and I melted into her arms for a moment before pulling away.

"Thanks, Leanne. I can't tell you how much it means to know someone understands where I am with everything."

She waved my words away in typical southern woman fashion. "We Georgia girls have to stick together, sweetheart. I have your back, and I will continue to do so whether things work out with you and Smoke or not. You are family, but more importantly, you're someone I consider a friend. I don't abandon my friends over petty lovers squabbles. So keep that in mind."

"I will," I said, and then, to lighten the mood before I got out of her car, I added one parting shot. "Besides, you have to keep being my friend if you want me to make my awesome triple layer chocolate cake for you again."

"Girl! I expect cake next time now that you said it!" I got out of the car and Leanne promised once more to message me as soon as she heard anything about the men who went out on an emergency run.

Since it was so late when I got back, and there was barely a sliver of a moon in the sky to lighten up my relatively dark neighborhood, I decided the walk I was taking Bubba on was going to be around the fenced back yard, off leash, while I watched him do his business from the door and then promptly took him back inside. He didn't seem to mind as he bumped my thigh with his head on the way into the house. I like to think it was his way of telling me he missed me.

"I missed you too, Bubba."

Bubba and I did our usual night time routine of me washing my face, brushing my teeth, and putting on the tightest, most comfortable sleep clothes I owned. Everything had to be tight when I slept, or I would go without clothes altogether, because I was not a calm sleeper normally. I tossed and turned a lot and in baggy clothing that became problematic, because then parts of my shirt or pants would get discombobulated and stuck under me and it felt like I was being suffocated by my murder-plotting clothing. Yes, I am aware that thinking those things makes me weird, but it's okay if I keep it to myself. I'm pretty sure I'm not the only one in the world who thinks their clothes might be trying to choke them to death at night. Why else would people opt to sleep naked in the wintertime?

Bubba was lounging just outside the open bathroom door as I did my thing, and he dutifully got up and followed me into my room where he proceeded to flop down on a doggy sigh at the foot of my bed once I climbed up and hopped under the covers. I wore a second skin tank top and panties when I crawled in. I was not getting trapped by my clothing tonight. No, sir.

It felt as though I had just laid my head down on my pillow when a banging on the front door set off Bubba who jumped to his feet and started emitting a low level growl as his eyes focused on my open bedroom door. "Shit!" I huffed out while clutching a hand to my chest. Then I glanced over at my alarm clock to see it was 3:52 in the damn morning. "Who in the hell is disturbing our peace this early in the morning, Bubs?"

I got up out of bed and started into the short hall that led from the bedroom into the living room with Bubba at my side. When I was close enough so that I thought I could be heard, I called out. "Who is there?"

"Sorry, honey, it's me."

"Smoke?" I asked to verify since I was still trying to shake off the cobwebs of sleep.

"Yeah, honey, you know someone else showing up at your door in the middle of the night?"

I moved over to said door, settled Bubba, and then

opened it to let Smoke in, and the first thing that hit me was the clinging scent of, well, smoke. As in smoke from a fire that was clinging to my man's skin, clothing, and it wasn't the good kind of campfire or cookout smell. It was an acrid, battling raging fires scent that caused my nostrils to burn slightly when he got close enough to push through the narrow opening I'd made with the door.

"What happened?" I asked as I shut the door behind him and locked it once more.

"Fire at one of our warehouses tonight. Looked to be deliberate since what Ghost and I were called away for was that our security cameras had picked up a couple people roaming around said warehouses. It wasn't until we were looking at the footage that I noticed what they were doing."

"Oh my God!" I moved to get a towel for him to sit on so that the blackened soot all over his clothing wouldn't mess up my furniture. "Here, sit on this."

Smoke smiled at me and then glanced down at himself. "Mind if I hop in your shower, honey? I didn't realize how bad I was."

"Only if you want to come out smelling like roses, and I mean that literally."

Smoke cocked his head in question, which made me laugh. "I don't exactly have manly fragrances in there. My shampoo and body wash are both rose scented. Apologies, because I used to keep gender neutral stuff in my old house for whoever stopped by, the club brothers, my brother, what-ever, and I just didn't think about the necessity here."

Smoke came over and brushed a tender kiss across my temple. "No worries honey. I just need something to clean me up. I can take a man-scented shower at home later to wash away the roses." He was chuckling as he turned and sauntered off to my bathroom. It was only after he was in the shower that I wondered what exactly he would be wearing out of it since he hadn't brought anything extra in with him.

I didn't have to wonder long. He came out with nothing but a towel and a smile on. Needless to say, sleep didn't find me for quite some time, and once it did, Smoke and I were both beyond exhausted and not worried in the slightest that he didn't have any clean clothing at my house.

11. THE BROTHER

It took right around three hours to drive from Cedar Falls to Pittsburgh, PA. We were back in Pittsburgh to watch the Penguins once again, and to finally meet Kent for more than a couple minutes. Smoke had planned on taking me, because he felt as if he had to make it up to me after leaving me stranded at the barbecue after party. His brother also had something to make up to him since he ditched us to work out problems with his woman the last time we had gone to see him play. None of that explained why my brother and Smoke's friend, Shep were tagging along. That involved the fact that they both had been sitting there when the negotiation of how Kent was going to make it up to Smoke went down; therefore they managed to yell loudly enough that they should also be included in the next game day visit.

That was how I found myself on the back of Smoke's Harley Dyna Wide Glide heading to Pittsburgh with my brother riding next to us and Shep trailing behind on his crotch rocket. The guys had given Shep plenty of flack over his choice in rides, but the man just shrugged it off and told them 'I like what I like, get over it.' So, they got over it. Eventually. The ride to Pittsburgh was a peaceful one. The traffic had been relatively light, the sun had been shining, and even though it meant three hours on a rumbling motorcycle that was going to make me walk funny when I finally got to get off and use my legs again, being wrapped around Smoke for those three hours made the trip worth it. I still had moments where I doubted myself, doubted what I had with Smoke, and if I were even able to have anything with anyone again after Walker. My judgment hadn't been the best with Walk, and I had so obviously been wearing blinders for the majority of our relationship. Now, it made me question if I was seeing everything clearly with Smoke.

The thing was, when I was touching him and in his orbit, I felt like my eyes were wide open and I was seeing everything for the first time. If only I could kick that niggling doubt out for good, because being wrapped around him on that ride had only reiterated to me how right everything felt when we were together. He had brought me to Pittsburgh, once again, to meet his brother. That had to mean something. Granted, the guys had conned their way in on the trip too, but even that meant a little more. This was my first time hanging out with Shep, who worked on the same engine as Smoke at the fire department.

"How'd you do on that ride, sweetheart?" Shep asked as we all got off the bikes outside of the PPG Paints Arena.

I glanced around and stretched a bit as I did. "I'm fine. I've done longer rides, just not recently," I admitted.

Shep seemed to blanch at my words, and then glanced at

Smoke guiltily. "Sorry, I forgot," he offered up in unnecessary apology.

Smoke just chuckled. "It's not like any of us were in the dark about each other's pasts, Shep. I know she was with a biker before" With that Smoke came over and tossed his arm around my shoulders and pulled me close. "You all good, babe?" he asked as his lips glanced over the hair on the side of my head.

"Yeah, just the tiniest bit stiff, but it's nothing." We started moving toward the building with my brother and Shep following along behind us.

"So, are you ready to see your brother destroyed on his home turf?" Shep asked Smoke.

"Shiiit, Kent is not going down easy, especially at home."

"They're playing the Bruins, dude. I hate to tell you, but they're no match this season."

"Bullshit," I coughed out.

Smoke grinned at his friend while Chief laughed at him. "Dude, she's a major Penguins fan. They'll win just through her force of will alone." My brother was not wrong. Well, in my own personal theory, I figured he couldn't be wrong, but what the hell did I know.

"We'll see," he sighed. "I can see I'll be outnumbered here tonight, though." Shep took his jacket off revealing a Bruins jersey making the rest of us groan in unison. It was just like his crotch rocket. He was going to be the odd man out, and I could already tell he didn't care what level of embarrassment he heaped on us as a result.

"No! It can't be," I lamented. "Your friend has to get new seats. This is unacceptable." Smoke pulled me closer; chuckling the whole time as if he was in on a joke and his best friend from work wasn't about to root for the team his brother wasn't playing for.

"It's okay, babe. Kent knows about this idiot's penchant for the Bruins. He also knows he'll be heckled to death before he even gets to his seat wearing that shit."

"Rightfully so," I explained unnecessarily. I did notice that Shep was grinning, Chief was shaking his head and trying to hold in a laugh, and I could feel Smoke's chest beneath me rising and falling in what could only be contained laughter. "Oh, whatever! Go ahead, laugh at me, but I'm telling you he's not wrong about the crowd heckling you to death." I warned.

"I'm a big boy, and this ain't my first rodeo, sweetheart, but thanks for the warning." With that Shep actually waltzed into the arena with his head held high and a grin on his face. Stupid man.

THE PENGUINS WON. Shep was grumbling about it as we waiting on Kent to come out and meet us. The rest of the friends, family, and puck bunnies waiting around were eyeing him suspiciously as if he were standing around waiting to attack their players simply for winning. When Kent came out, his face lit up and he, surprisingly, moved straight to Shep, picking him up off the floor in a surprise pounce-hug. "You should have known I'd give it my all when you showed up wearing that bullshit again. Thanks, for the extra motivation, bro."

"Damn it," Shep muttered. "Put my ass down, numb-nuts!"

Kent slung Shep back and forth another good couple times before dropping him on the floor. "I'll have you know, my nuts aren't numb, ya whiny little bitch." He then moved on to hug his brother, my brother, and then he stopped in front of me and opened his arms. I hesitantly moved into them and gave him a quick pat on the back before attempting to step back. "Oh no, that's not a hug. Come on, I owe you since I sent you away so quickly last time." Before I knew what was happening, I was smashed face-first into Kent's very muscular chest while he nearly squeezed the life out of me. I was tapping out before Smoke realized and rescued me from his overbearing, killer bear-hugging brother.

"Kent, if you could let my girl breathe, I'd appreciate it." Kent let go immediately.

"Sorry," he mumbled as he ruffled my hair. "Did you enjoy the game?"

"Of course I did. I even enjoyed the way all the people around us came together to give Shep shit about that monstrosity he's wearing."

"I like her," Kent informed his brother.

"Yeah, so do I," Smoke explained as he came up behind me and wrapped his arms around my middle. "So, where are we headed now?" Kent glanced around nervously before answering his brother.

"Let's get out of here, and head back to my place before we make any decisions," he told his brother.

It was then that I realized a whole lot of people had been watching our interactions. More importantly, the women I'd tagged as puck bunnies seemed to be salivating over Kent, and the three men I had come here with. Chief didn't seem to mind the attention which made me question his judgment just a bit, but as my mom used to say when she was alive, 'boys will be boys'.

It didn't take long to get from the arena to Kent's posh penthouse apartment. It was nothing like what I would have expected and my face must have shown my surprise, because Kent laughed and clapped one of his big hands down on my shoulder. "I know, it looks pretentious as hell, but it came already decorated like this. I haven't had the time to do anything with it since the season started right as I closed on it."

"Ah, okay. I didn't think this looked like something a major athlete would have going on, but then again, what do I know?" I shrugged my shoulders.

"Well, I bought this from a major athlete who was traded, but I think this was his wife's doing. She fancied herself an interior designer, but oddly enough her career never took off for some reason," he explained with a playful wink.

"Can't imagine why," Chief offered up with a certain level of disgust in his voice. His cell rang at that moment and he excused himself to walk down the hall away from everyone while he answered.

"You guys thirsty? I have water, orange juice, cranberry

juice, and milk right now. I don't keep sodas in the house, because I don't drink them, but I can order some or we can go out."

"I'll take some water, please." I moved toward the kitchen where Kent was headed, because I hated the idea of other people waiting on me, even in their own home. Smoke started following me, and then dropped off as his cell started ringing.

"I'll be right there, babe," he told me as he too moved to a quiet corner of the apartment to take the call. Shep shrugged at me and offered up, "looks like club business," before we both continued on to the kitchen with Kent.

"So, Smoke tells me you've been a fan of the Penguins a really long time," Kent started in as he pulled three bottled waters from his immaculate fridge that, when closed, looked like part of the cabinetry.

"Yeah, the first game I ever went to was with my dad when the Penguins were playing in Atlanta, back when we had a team."

Kent nearly choked on his water. "Jesus that had to have been a while ago."

"Yeah, it was, and since that team moved to Canada, I started rooting for the Penguins instead," I told him with a grin.

"Good call," he offered before chugging the entire bottle of water. He noticed me watching him as he chucked the bottle into the trashcan. "It takes forever to rehydrate after a game."

"Smoke said you have a new woman in your life. Are you still hiding her away from family and friends or what?"

Kent's grin lit up his entire face at the mention of his girlfriend, and it made me smile. It seemed the brothers weren't that different when it came to their love lives. They appeared to be either all in or not at all. "She had a family thing to attend out of town this weekend or she would have been here. I'm hoping to bring her down to meet everyone as soon as we catch a little break in our schedule."

"Smoke will be happy to hear that. He was concerned that you were hiding her for a reason." Shep chuckled at an apparent remembered conversation. I hadn't realized he'd followed us into the kitchen until then. "We discussed all the reasons you could be keeping her under wraps." He held up a finger, "she's butt ugly, but has a great personality," he ticked off before tossing another finger up. "She's a famous model, and you didn't want competition from the guys." Another finger went up. "She's a butter face, which kind of goes with number one, but personality be damned if she's all spectacular tits and ass."

I was laughing right along with Kent as Shep continued with all the reasons they had come up with for why Kent would hide the existence of his woman. They all added up to the fact that either she was ugly, and he was embarrassed; or she was exceptionally beautiful, and he was afraid of losing her to someone else.

Kent finally cut off Shep's ten-minute tirade. "Maybe, we're just both really busy, and I haven't had the chance to do it yet." I smiled at Kent as Shep waved him off.

"Likely excuse."

"Says the man wearing a loser's jersey," Kent tossed out.

I laughed at them, because they got along as if they were

brothers, too. Obviously, this wasn't their first time hanging out together. "How long have you known each other?"

Kent scrutinized Shep for a few minutes before answering. "I think about six years, right?"

Shep appeared thoughtful for a moment before nodding his head in agreement. "Yeah, that sounds about right. That's when I transferred into the station with Smoke and we started working together.

"Wow, that's a long time. I didn't realize," I added. They both smiled at me then with Kent about to say something when my brother and Smoke joined us, both looking grim.

"Club business?" Kent questioned. I couldn't tell if there was disapproval in his tone or if he was just frustrated by the prospect, but either way it was clear he wasn't happy about the interruption.

"Yeah," Smoke agreed while heading straight for me. "Chief and I have to go for a bit. You gonna be all right hanging here with Shep and Kent?" He glanced up as he asked me the question, seemingly asking his brother at the same time if he was okay with me sticking around.

"Sure, do what you have to do," I agreed. On the inside I wasn't too sure about it. I had just met Kent, and while he was someone I loved watching play hockey on television, he was still no more than a stranger to me. Shep, likewise, was someone I had just met. This was the life sometimes though, and I knew that going in.

Smoke nodded to whatever non-verbal answer he received from his brother then he pulled me close. "I promise I'll be back to get you as soon as possible, and if it's not soon enough, I'll have transportation arranged to get you back home. I'm so sorry about this," he apologized.

I swallowed down the little bit of hurt feelings I had over being left behind and just nodded into his chest as he kissed the top of my head, squeezed me a little tighter, and then let go for my brother to take his place.

"I would have gone on my own, but Smoke is needed," he tried to explain.

"I know how the life works, Chief. It's okay." It was okay, even when a little part of me thought it was unfair. I knew what I was getting into by saddling myself to another biker. The difference being, my ex would have just taken off and let someone else explain why he was gone again. Smoke was already making plans for getting me home safely, just in case. That was something new for me.

Once the guys were gone, I glanced between Shep and Kent who were standing quietly on the other side of the kitchen from me. "Well, since you two are stuck with me for a bit, what are we going to do with our time? You have any decent movies or what?"

Kent smiled at me then, and tipped his head toward the other room. "That is the one thing I've made time to set up. I have all the channels plus Netflix. You can binge to your heart's content."

"You are a saint!" I took off for the other room in a flash and plopped down on the surprisingly comfy couch, even if it was a butt ugly, putrid green color. "What was she thinking with this color scheme?"

"Who knows?" Kent looked around for a moment.

"Davey said she was going for spring time fresh since she was sick of winter, but I see more baby vomit than anything."

I laughed. "Yeah, she definitely missed the mark on spring time fresh, but at least this is comfy."

"The only reason I haven't had a real interior designer in here to fix this place yet. It's comfy until I can pick shit out myself. I've seen what those designer ladies did with my buddy's place, and let's just say it isn't much better than this. It's all stark black and white with no personality. I hate it."

"I thought they were supposed to design based off their client's personality and ideas?"

"I don't know, he hates it too so apparently she just went with what she thought a rich and famous bachelor pad should be." Kent looked away and then back at me before speaking again. "Does this kind of thing happen often?"

"What do you mean?"

"Where my brother just up and leaves you places. I mean, I'm his brother, but you don't know me from Adam, and I don't think you and Shep have known each other long."

I shrugged my shoulders again. "This is part of the life-style. I understand it because I've lived it for the past ten years, but believe me when I say your brother is at least more considerate than most, and no it doesn't happen like this often. This is the second time he's had to dip out on me since we've been hanging out, but from what I hear it's abnormal for the Cedar Falls Club."

"That's what you're doing? You're just hanging out?"

"Well, I don't know what else to call it at this point."

"So, you guys haven't had the talk about being exclusive or whatever?"

Suddenly, I was feeling a little like the guy in the hot seat during an interrogation. Shep must have felt the slightly hostile vibe too, because he stepped in. "I'm pretty sure they've had that discussion, they just never put a label on what they are for now since she's going through a divorce at the moment."

I tipped my head forward in agreement while eyeing Kent. "What's up with the divorce anyway? Why is it taking so long?"

I sighed deeply then. "I don't know. My ex is being a pain in the ass. At first I thought it was about the money, since he knows I'm selling my family's house and land. Now, I just think he's being a jerk. If he cared, he would have fixed things long ago, so it's not that."

"Sometimes, you don't realize what you had until its gone," Kent interjected.

"Sometimes, you never appreciated it to begin with so there isn't much to miss. Walker is just being difficult, and for the record, no, I don't want him back. No, the thought doesn't even cross my mind. Yes, I am pushing to expedite the divorce rather than continue dragging it out. Yes, I am serious about your brother. He's a good man, he shows that he cares, and I enjoy being around him. Where we will go from here is between us though, and I'm sure he'll let you know if and when things change."

Kent smiled then. "I like that. You aren't a pushover, and that's a good thing with the man and the club he's in."

"You don't approve of his lifestyle?"

"I don't understand why he does it." Kent glanced at Shep then. "Look at Shep. They have the same career, make decent money and benefits, and both enjoy motorcycles. Why be in a club that takes you away from your family even more?"

"They are his family," I answered simply. "I know you are too, but while he was raising you and your sister, who was taking care of him?" Kent looked startled for a moment. "I know about your past, and I know that the club filled a void that needed filling whether he realized it or not, and whether you agree or not. He needed that positive male role model to keep doing what he was doing for you guys. It benefitted everyone. It was also the driving force keeping him in line to become the man he is today with his job at the fire department. So, while you see a club that takes him away from the people he loves, you forget that he loves those people just as fiercely. It's probably not much different than you've felt for some of your teammates over the years."

Kent looked away, seemingly lost in thought for a minute. "I never thought of it that way," he spoke quietly. "Hell, I sometimes forget that we were a burden on his shoulders for a long while."

"I doubt you were ever a burden to him. Smoke wouldn't see it that way."

Kent huffed out a small laugh. "You're right about that. He wouldn't see it that way. I am lucky to have him as a brother, and I think he's lucky to have you in his life, too. I know my sister gave you some shit when you first met, but I see now why she changed her tune about you so quickly. You are definitely nothing like that conniving bitch he was hitched to for all those years."

"Why didn't you ever tell him about her coming on to

you? You might have saved him a few years with her if you had."

"I don't know. I figured I owed him my silence after all he sacrificed for me, you know? He seemed happy with her at first, and I didn't want to take away his happiness."

"You're a good brother too, you know?" I questioned him, but he didn't get a chance to say anything because Shep came back from the bathroom then.

"Why haven't you picked a movie yet?" He moved in closer and took the remote control from me. "Never mind, you lost your chance, now I get to pick." He turned toward the TV and started flipping through the channels, landing on one of the Thor movies as he did so. I wasn't going to complain about that choice so I settled in and allowed myself to get lost in another world for a time. At least I did until I fell asleep.

I awoke to someone wrapping their arms under my knees and behind my back, but the person didn't feel familiar at all so I startled and came awake immediately.

"It's okay, sweetheart," Shep's familiar voice soothed a bit of my initial panic. "I'm just moving you to Kent's guestroom so you'll be more comfortable and stop drooling on his butt ugly couch."

"What time is it?" I managed to ask through my gritty sleep-filled voice.

"It's late. Kent and I just finished up a second movie, but we both thought you'd be more comfortable in a bed."

"Have you heard from Smoke or Chief?"

"Not yet, sweetheart. We'll let you know as soon as we do, though."

"Okay," I managed to get out as he put me down on the fluffiest damn bed I had ever been on and then proceeded to take my boots off my feet for me. "Thank you," I managed to get out before I nodded right back off to dreamland.

By morning, none of us had heard from either of the guys and I began to worry. It wasn't out of the norm in the MC life to have them go silent on you, especially when things were going down, but it still sucked to be left sitting around wondering. The scenarios I was coming up with in my head were probably far worse than they were encountering, to be sure. Kent had just knocked on my door when my phone pinged with a message.

> Smoke: Sorry, babe. Caught up in club biz, asked Kent and Shep to make sure you get back home ok. Everyone is fine, just stuck doing this thing. I swear I will make this up to you!

"Come in," I offered in response to the knock at the door.

He glanced from me to the phone in my hand and tossed me a weak excuse for a smile. "I'm guessing he finally got a hold of you too?"

"Yeah, he did."

"Shep asked if you'd be okay riding on the back of his bike to get home. If not, I can lend you my truck."

"The bike's fine. I don't want to put you out and take your vehicle."

"It's not my only vehicle, Poppy. It won't be any kind of hardship, I promise. If you're not comfortable riding with Shep..." he let the words hang in the air and I knew what he was getting at.

"I'm no one's old lady right now, so it won't matter."

"Are you sure Smoke will see it that way?" he asked.

"I'm sure it doesn't matter since he left me here without the ride I arrived with," I spat back without meaning to.

"Shit, my brother is an idiot," Kent hissed out.

"No, he's doing what he's supposed to do. Just because the women know they might get left behind doesn't negate the fact that it sucks when it happens. Can you let Shep know I'll be ready in a few minutes? I just want to clean up a bit and then I'll be good to go."

"Yeah, I'll let him know. For what it's worth, my girl struggles with my schedule, too. Although, at least she knows well in advance what it's going to look like. I'm not sure I know a single woman who would stick by me in any kind of honest way if I had to run at a moment's notice. If you're willing to do that for my brother, then you have my utmost respect."

"Thanks for that," I told Kent before I turned my back to him and walked into the bathroom to go try to tame the rat's nest that my hair had become while I slept.

12. THE TEST

THE RIDE BACK TO CEDAR FALLS WAS MOSTLY UNEVENTFUL, APART from the queasiness I kept feeling in my belly. I had asked Shep to pull over twice, because I honestly didn't think I would be able to keep down the little bit of my breakfast I had eaten before we left.

We had parked in my driveway long enough for me to hop off and give Shep's spare helmet over to him when he took his own off and eyed me curiously. "I'm not really wanting to leave you here alone. Are you sure you're going to be all right?"

"I'm positive, honestly, it was probably something I ate, or nerves maybe." I pulled a face as I said the last, because I knew it wasn't that. I didn't feel nervous, just nauseous.

"Are you sure there's no one I can call to sit with you? If not me, I think someone should be here for a while just in case."

"No," I told him definitively. "I promise, I will be fine. I'm going to call Leanne, and have her drop Bubba off for me, so it's okay. She'll probably be here with my boy within the hour."

Shep didn't appear entirely certain, but a text coming through on his phone sealed the deal. "Damn it," he hissed out after glancing down. "I need to go deal with this. Promise me that you will text and let me know you're doing okay?"

"I promise I will update you periodically until Smoke is back even though I think it is entirely unnecessary."

He grinned at me then. "Good. If I don't hear from you, I will be back to check in on you, and I'll be mad enough not to leave until Smoke or Chief get back then." He grinned at me as he threw his long leg back over his bike. "And no, I'm not afraid of that beast you call a dog either. I'll win him over to my side when he sees I'm just worried about you."

"Good to know," I told him with a grin. "I promise to stay in touch and let you know if I start feeling worse. Now, get out of here to whatever emergency that text was, and focus on that for a bit." At that, Shep blanched a bit and looked guiltily down at his cell phone.

"Right, see you later, Poppy."

As I watched Shep pull his red and black Kawasaki Ninja out of my driveway, I couldn't help but compare him to Snake, my soon to be ex-husband's best friend. The man who still called to check in with me once in a while, making sure I was okay despite the fact that his best friend never did. I had learned, before moving to Cedar Falls, that Snake had a thing for me that he kept in check, and I had apparently been oblivious to for years. That was apparently why he cared so much and checked in so often. I did not think Shep was in the same category of holding a torch, but he cared about my wellbeing, because he cared about his buddy. It was endearing and spoke well of Smoke that he had friends both in and out of his club that felt that strongly for him that they would protect and care for what and whom they felt belonged to him.

Once I managed to get back inside, I thought maybe some soup would help settle my restless stomach. I shouldn't have attempted it. The minute I smelled the chicken in the chicken noodle soup heating, my stomach turned violent and I immediately had to run to the sink to throw up since it was the closest, easiest to clean spot to do it in. Hell, it had only been a few steps from the stove, and I still barely made it there.

"What is wrong with me?" I questioned out loud as I managed to wash the remnants of my sick down the drain and pull the pot off the hot burner before I heaved again.

I was laying on the couch, nursing my sick self when Leanne showed up with Bubba. "Oh honey, you don't look so good. What did those boys do to you on that Pittsburgh trip?"

"I don't know. I'm thinking I ate something that disagreed with me, but to be honest, I was already feeling a little off before I nibbled on my breakfast with Shep, so I think maybe I caught a bug?" I attempted a very defeated, weak looking shrug as Leanne kept eyeing me closely.

"Maybe I should take Bubba back home and come back to sit with you for a while?"

"No, really, I'm fine. I just think whatever it is needs to run its course, and I will be better."

She didn't look convinced. "I don't know, Sweetie. I think

if Chief or Smoke found out I knew you were sick and just left you like this they'd both have my ass hemmed up with Ghost." She huffed out a laugh. "Not that I couldn't turn that to my benefit, but seriously, I would also feel like shit for leaving you to it."

I waved away her concern. "Seriously, I lived basically on my own for five years in Georgia since Walker never would have bothered to check on me when I was sick. This is nothing, and I know how to use the phone if I get worse. Besides, Bubba will be here to keep me company, and I honestly just think whatever it is needs to run its course. I'm not running a fever or anything."

"True. I'd be more worried if you were. Okay, well, I'm going to go pick the girls up from school, and take them home, but if you get worse, do not hesitate to call me, okay? I mean it. If I find out you didn't call when you should have, I will be extremely mad at you!"

"I promise to call, just like I promised Shep. I will keep you both updated. Right now, I just want to take Bubba in the room and crash for a bit."

"Okay honey, just set an alarm so you can wake up in a while to text or call us. If I don't hear from you in a few hours I'll be pounding down that door of yours." She giggled at a thought she had. "Well, I'll have one of the prospects they left behind do that so he gets eaten by Bubba instead of me, but then I'll come right in and check on you while Bubba's using the prospect as a chew toy."

"You are not right," I told Leanne as she continued to chuckle while bending down to kiss her lips to my forehead. "Satisfied, mom? I told you there was no fever.

"You caught me." Leanne waved her dainty little hand my way as she walked out the door and shut and locked it behind her.

I ended up taking my nap right there on the couch instead of moving to the bedroom, because the thought of moving made me queasy. I was out for about two hours when Bubba nudged my arm. I tried to ignore him, but he wasn't having it. When the little nudge on my arm didn't work he immediately laid his big head across my neck and started a very low-level whining.

"What's the matter, boy?" I asked as I moved my hand up to rub the top of his head. As soon as I acknowledged him he moved back and wandered over to the backdoor off the kitchen. "Damn, nature calls, huh?" I asked as I slowly rose from the couch, hoping the nausea wouldn't reemerge.

Thankfully, it didn't. I was able to go stand outside and enjoy the crisp fall air while Bubba roamed around the back-yard looking for the perfect spot to do his business. It had seemed so urgent for him to get out here to do it, but the boy sure was being picky about where he finally went. When he was done, I managed to praise him for being a good boy and letting me know he had to go out, and then we were headed back inside just as a knock sounded on my door. Sadly, as I turned to get all the way inside my kitchen, I smacked my boob right into the doorframe, and the resounding tingling painful sensation took my focus off the front door and whoever was knocking and put it on the fact that both my boobs had a weird tingling sensation going on with them.

The knocking persisted and I went to answer my door before I could ponder that any further. "It's me, if you don't open up I'm calling a prospect over to break this door down!" Leanne was shouting at me as I approached the door. I unlocked it and opened it to a panic-stricken Leanne. "Thank God!"

"Sorry, Bubba had to go out, we were out back," I explained.

"You look better," she told me as she followed me inside. "Except for the fact that you're molesting your boob."

I glanced down and stopped what I was doing even though massaging it had given me some relief momentarily. "Sorry," I whispered sheepishly. "I just smacked it into the back door when I was trying to get out here."

"Oh, sorry honey." Leanne apologized while giggling at me so I wasn't certain her apology was all that heartfelt. I glanced down at my boobs then, realizing I hadn't even been massaging the one I hit with the doorway.

"It's so strange, because I bumped into this one, and the other feels almost worst somehow." Leanne was watching me oddly. Then her eyes rounded wider than I'd ever seen them before she reached out and grabbed hold of my hands and damn near pushed me down to a seated position on my couch.

"Sweetie, when is your period due?" At first, I thought she meant I was probably just sensitive because my period was coming, but then I thought about it, and truthfully I should have had a period already, about two weeks ago. I glanced up and saw a small smile on Leanne's face.

"No," I whispered. "I can't be," I started to say because I'd been trying for five years with no success, but then I remembered that I'd been trying with a different man. "Oh shit!"

Leanne sat back watching me work through everything in my head with curiosity, but she refused to interrupt until the tears started to fill my eyes. "I honestly don't know what you're thinking right now or if those are happy tears or not so happy ones," she finally admitted.

"I think they're confused tears," I told her honestly. "I tried for five years to have a baby with Walker. I'd give anything to be able to hold my own child in my arms, you know? I'm not just talking about biological children either. I just wanted my own family to raise."

Leanne smiled and I knew from our previous conversation about her deceased husband and their struggles that she knew exactly what that felt like. "But?" she finally asked.

"I don't know how Smoke is going to feel about this. We haven't been together long, and you know, things are so new and I'm still technically married to another man." I startled to hyperventilate as everything hit me at once. This was the absolute worst timing in the world for a pregnancy to occur.

"I don't think you need to worry about Smoke's reaction. If I know him the way I think I do, he'll be by your side every step of the way, and he'll do it gladly."

"I just don't want him to feel trapped. It's too soon for this."

"According to Ghost, the man has already claimed you with the club, so I don't think this will make him feel trapped at all, sweetie."

"I need to get a test. I need to know for sure."

"Come on, I'll take you," she reached her hand out and pulled me up off the couch before grabbing my purse and walking us both out the door.

13. THE ACCIDENT

THE TEST RESULTS WERE TWO PINK LINES. THE SECOND ONE boasted "pregnant" on it. The third had a blue plus sign on it. It was official, sort of. At least the home pregnancy tests all confirmed my suspicions. "How in the hell am I going to tell him?"

You will think of something, sweetie. You just need to decide if you're going to come right out with it or try to do one of the cute little surprise reveals."

"I think those are more for established couples that are hoping for positive test results," I informed her.

She waved off my information. "Nah, I think Smoke would appreciate it. Maybe you could get him a little teddy bear in firefighter gear that says 'my daddy is a firefighter' or something." She clapped her hands together. "That would be so darn adorable!"

I couldn't help but catch her infectious happiness. "Yeah, that would be cute. Now, if only he'd get back from wherever they went so I could do something like that."

Leanne screwed up her face in distaste. "I think the same assholes who burned down the warehouse are up to no good. I heard Ghost talking about it before he left. I'm worried about them."

As she said the words, her cell began ringing and she reached into her the purse at her feet to answer it. "Hey baby, everything okay?" She listened a moment, and while I could hear a male voice on the other end, I couldn't make out what he was saying. I knew it couldn't be anything good though, because Leanne's happy mood changed far too quickly to one of fear.

"I'm at Poppy's place with her. The kids are with Lydia right now." She listened a moment longer. "What? No, she's fine. Yeah, she just wasn't feeling' well and I wanted to check in on her." Leanne glanced up to me trying to let me know that my secret was mine to tell when I was ready. I appreciated that. "Okay, I'll make sure we get over there. Uh-huh. Love you, too. See you in a while, baby." She hung up and let out a sigh that made me feel the tension she was trying to alleviate.

"What's going on?"

"We need to get you packed up and over to the clubhouse. You can bring Bubba with you. Actually, I think we'll be glad to have him there."

"What's going on?"

"We're going into lockdown. Something happened, and Ghost wants all the families under one roof until the guys get back. The word is already out. I need to call Lydia and make sure she's bringing the girls over with her. Then I have to go pack some stuff up for them, too."

"How long will be there?"

"I don't know, better prepare for a few days at least."

"Okay." I got my butt up and moving, getting things that Bubba and I would need for a few days.

WHEN WE GOT to the clubhouse it was already somewhat crowded. I glanced around at all the women and children and wondered where everyone was going to go. I'd seen that there was a space about half the size of the place upstairs, but it didn't seem as though you could fit enough rooms up there for everyone. With that in mind I turned to Leanne. "Where is everyone going to stay?"

She grinned at me, and pulled at my elbow to get me to follow her. "I guess no one ever gave you the grand tour, huh?"

"I'm guessing not. Chief pointed out that he had a room up there if he needed it," I mentioned as I pointed to the stairs leading up. Leanne just shook her head.

"Those rooms are for club brothers only. The women, children, and families have rooms downstairs."

"Downstairs?" I hadn't seen a set of stairs leading down anywhere. Leanne kept moving us until we were beyond where the bar stretched across the back wall and then we went down a hallway that I hadn't ever noticed before. Once we were at the end there was a wooden door to the right. Leanne opened it and there were the other set of stairs that had been missing. "Why is it hidden like this?"

"It's hidden because the guys don't want their enemies finding out that we have a basement level, or that it's where they tuck their family members when shit is going down. If outsiders think the only rooms here are upstairs, then upstairs is a target. The hidden basement is not. Plus, there's a tunnel down here that leads out to a garage on another property in case we all need to escape."

"Wow, that's a lot of forethought. I know the club has been in some shit down in Georgia a few times, but they don't have a hidden bunker there or anything." Leanne gave me an odd look then, and my stomach absolutely sank. "Seriously?" I asked when her look inferred that they did indeed have a special hiding place for family members.

"What in the hell did that husband of yours do with you when all that shit was going down and they had to be on lockdown?"

I just shrugged my shoulders. "I stayed at the farm-house," I told her.

Leanne's eyes were rounded in surprise, but her nostrils flared in anger. "Does Chief know that?"

"I assumed he did," I stated.

"I'm thinking he did not," Leanne shot back. "Dear Lord, anything could have happened to you. What in the hell was that husband of yours thinking?"

"I'm guessing he was thinking I might have ran into a few of the club whores who might have spilled some of his secrets." I sighed then. "The more I learn about how sheltered I was from his life the more I wonder if he ever even really gave a shit about me or if I was just some trophy he collected. How could I have been so blind to it all?"

"Oh, sweetie, that's the bitch of life. Sometimes we see what we want. Other times, we see it and still just ignore it because we feel like we're supposed to for some stupid reason. I'm sure when you first got together with him, things were different. Then you went with what you thought was expected even if it wasn't what you hoped for. It became habit, and habits are hard to break. Don't beat yourself up over it."

"I do though, because now I feel like all that time was wasted."

She blew out a breath and then smiled brightly at me. "Sweetie, it was never wasted if it got you to where you are right now." She patted my tummy knowing there wasn't anyone around to see. "Blessings come when we least expect them sometimes, but they only come after the perfect storm gets us to a point where we can receive them." She had no way of knowing how her storm reference would affect me, or what it meant. So when I burst into tears Leanne panicked a bit. "I'm so sorry, what did I say?"

I tried waving her off. "Sorry, it's just my wakeup call came on the heels of a storm," I explained.

"The Lord works in mysterious ways then," she stated while nodding her head. "Let's go down so I can show you where everything is and where you'll be staying."

We walked down the carpeted stairway with Bubba trailing behind me carefully, never coming close enough that he might trip me up. He was such a good boy. When we got to the bottom, there was a small hallway that opened up into a large open room that looked like a giant living room with couches everywhere. There were a couple kids playing on a game station over in one corner, and there was an entire wall made of bookshelves. I breathed a sigh of relief knowing there would at least be something to keep me occupied besides Bubba.

We moved past the common area to where a hallway split down to the left and right. There were doors down either side, and Leanne explained that this was the hall for the people with children so that they were closer to the family room. Then we continued down the right side of the hallway until it turned and started a new one. "Down here is where you'll be. They like to keep the childless couples a little further away on account of the noise."

"Just because I don't have kids doesn't mean I don't mind hearing them once in a while."

Leanne laughed at that. "Oh, sweetie, I wasn't talking about the noise the kids make. I was talking about the noise that usually ends up with us needing more family space in nine months."

"Oh." I joined her laughter then. "Well, not quite nine months for me. Honestly though, I'm not sure how far along I am."

Once we were at the door to the room I would have, Leanne took us inside and shut it behind the two of us. "Sorry, didn't want anyone overhearing." All levity disappeared, and I knew whatever she was about to say probably wasn't going to make me happy. "Is it possible," she started and then bit her lip, seeming to second-guess her question. "Do you think it's Smokes, or is it possible that you're carrying your husband's baby?"

It was my turn to laugh. I laughed so hard tears began to

form in my eyes, and when they started to fall, my laughter stopped, and I just cried because my answer was so damn sad. "I'd be big as a house by now if it was Walker's. I've been here almost two months now. I kicked Walker out two months before that. It was another three before that since we'd slept together, because we were fighting so much about everything. He was refusing to come home to sleep with me when our chances were the best, and since he did that, I punished him by refusing to sleep with him any other time. Apparently, it wasn't punishment since he had backups for his needs." I rolled my watery eyes as I said the last. "My point is that I'd be about to pop already if it were Walker's baby. There's no way. Besides, I had a period a couple weeks before I moved here, and they were regular before that, too."

"I wasn't trying to be mean," Leanne added sadly.

"I know. I'm sure it's the same question a lot of other people will be asking, too."

"It's no one's business," she reminded me. "Mine included."

I gave her a watery smile then. "You are my friend, and you are trying to be there for me. That makes it your business." I finally took a moment to glance around the room. It was basically a large bedroom with a queen size bed, a small loveseat at the end of the bed, two tall chest of drawers on either side of a standard dresser on top of which sat a television. There was a door off to the far right of those pieces and upon further inspection it led to a small bathroom that had a sink, toilet, and a shower that was standing room only. No bathtub in sight, which I supposed wasn't a huge deal. "This place is nicer than a hotel," I commented.

Leanne grunted out a half-laugh, half pained sound. "It'll be nice for about 48 hours, and then cabin fever sets in and the walls will close in around you." Her shoulders shook with an involuntary shiver.

"Do you think we'll be here that long?"

"Who knows? The guys still aren't back and it's been a full day already now." I glanced down at the time on my phone and realized she was right. The guys had been gone for a full 24 hours at this point, and I was starting to get tired, and a tad queasy. Leanne and I left to go grab some food, take Bubba for a walk out back, and then I retreated to my room to get some sleep, because I was suddenly feeling exhausted, and worried about how to approach Smoke with my news. Leanne seemed to think he'd take it well, but I honestly didn't know him well enough yet to make that call. All signs pointed to him wanting to be in a committed relationship with me, but an unwanted pregnancy in the mix could change things. I couldn't believe I'd been so damn stupid that I hadn't even thought about using birth control. It had been five years since I'd been on anything. I fell asleep with all of those thoughts running through my mind.

WAKING up the next day left me disoriented, because I was a in a strange place and Bubba was whining to me while watching the door. I wasn't sure if that was a warning, the dog needing to go out, or what. It was hard to tell since there were so many people around the clubhouse. "You need to go out, buddy?" he whined a little louder then, so I assumed his answer was yes. "I hope you don't mind if I go first," I told him as I got up and hurried into the bathroom, suddenly feeling a bit sick with the movement. After doing my business and puking my guts up, I grabbed the small pack of crackers Leanne had ordered me to take back to my room with me the night before. I started gnawing on one as I took Bubba to go head out for a quick break in the backyard.

It took us a while to make it outside because every single child in the family room wanted to pet the dog, and then some of the women we ran into along the way as well. I was headed back inside when Leanne found me.

Her blond hair was swept up into a high ponytail and she had her girls trailing after her. "Have you eaten yet?"

"Just a pack of crackers."

"Come on, you can grab some breakfast with us, because I just got word the guys are on their way back, and it didn't sound like they bringing good news with them."

"What does that mean?"

"That's all I know," she stated. "These are the times when I doubt if I'm right for this life. Even after all the years I've been with Ghost and watched Angel Girl living it, too. I can tell by his voice that it won't be good news, and all I can do is wait to find out how bad, who it's about, and how it will affect us and everyone we care about."

I offered a small smile to the woman as we moved into a kitchen area where the smell of cooking breakfast meats turned my stomach in a violent way. I ran for the trashcan I saw, because I didn't have to time to ask where a bathroom was. Once I was done puking, Leanne hurriedly ushered me out of the kitchen. "I'm so sorry, I wasn't thinking."

"Me either, apparently. Chicken soup did that to me yesterday, too. I'm thinking I'll have to become vegetarian or something." I did not even attempt to hide the disgust in my voice. It wasn't that I had anything against being vegetarian or vegan or whatever, I just enjoyed and craved meat.

"If you're anything like I was, the smell is hateful, but the taste is wonderful. You'll figure it out in just enough time for the sickness to finally abate and then you'll have new, and interesting symptoms like having to pee every five minutes."

"You make it sound so wonderful," I teased then watched as she gazed at her darling twin girls.

"It really is, though. Every miserable part leads to that," she pointed at the girls who were lost in their own world playing with Bubba as we moved further away from the kitchen. "How about I bring you something, and you can go wait in the family room downstairs?"

"Sure," I agreed.

We were just finishing our food when we heard the commotion. It was faint, but the rumbling of motorcycle engines had me running Bubba down to my room and putting him inside before taking off to the upper level in search of all the other adults and news. The men started trailing in looking grim, and my stomach sank as each new face through the door wasn't my brother or my man.

Finally, Chief came through the door wearing an expression I hadn't seen since our family died. My stomach rolled, and there was no holding it back at that point. I ran for the bathroom, and emptied the breakfast I managed to get down into the toilet. Once I finished and was able to pull myself together, I found my way back out into the main lounge area where all the club parties and whatnot were held. I didn't see Chief once I reemerged, nor did I see Smoke. Instead I saw Leanne, crying into Ghost's shoulder. I started moving toward them when an arm snaked out around my waist and pulled me into a body that was most definitely not Smoke's. I turned to see my brother standing there, unshed tears dancing in his eyes.

"Smoke?" I questioned.

"Fine," my brother managed to get out. "He's at the hospital," he started and upon seeing the panic that must have flared in my eyes, he immediately shook his head. "It's not him. He's there with Brantley."

"Brantley? What happened to Brantley?"

"There was an accident, or fuck, I don't know exactly what happened yet. They were run off the road. Soph, Bender, and Brant were all in Soph's car." His shoulders began to shake and I had a horrible feeling I knew where this was going, because he'd only said Smoke was at the hospital with Brantley. I just stood and waited for confirmation that came too quickly, and I hated being right. "Soph and Bender didn't make it," the words were broken by him trying to choke back sobs. My brother was grieving for his other family right now. I threw my arms around him and held on tight as his whole body shook with his emotion.

"I need to go to Smoke," I whispered in his ear. He nodded his head.

"I know. I'll get a prospect to take you. I need to be here right now. There was," he started to say and then shut up. It made me curious about the accident. "There were people in near the scene that shouldn't have been there. We're looking into it. Not so sure it was an accident, Pop. Thinking it might be retaliation for what we did to help Shep out."

"No!" I sincerely hoped that wasn't the case, because if it was, Smoke was going to take his sister's death even harder than he already would. Guilt was a heavy burden to bear, and knowing Smoke, he would feel that even if he shouldn't. His little sister was gone, her husband – his club brother – also gone, and their child was in the hospital. There was no way the guilt wouldn't fall on his shoulders. "Does Shep know this?" Chief shook his head in the negative. "Someone might want to let him know." Chief looked as though he was about to protest, but I stopped him. "I know it's club business now, but it started with his family business that he dragged you guys into. He deserves to know, especially since Smoke may blame him, too."

Chief's shoulders sagged back down again as he realized what I was saying. Smoke wouldn't only blame Shep, he'd blame himself, and that wasn't something I knew him well enough to calculate what his reaction might be, but Chief did. I could see in his eyes and his stance that things might not turn out so well in that regard.

"Your sister's a pretty smart woman, I'm actually about to head out to go see Shep." Ghost stated quietly. I wasn't sure how long he'd been standing close enough to hear us, but he was apparently agreeing with me.

"I need you to go with your sister to the hospital. Don't send a prospect. I'm going to need someone I trust, someone Smoke trusts to be there when it all sinks in and hits him,"

Ghost directed my brother and then he turned to me. "I called Kent, and he's on his way. Brant is going to need someone for a while. Kent won't be able to take him, and I know for a fact that Soph and Bender's wishes were that he went to Smoke if anything happened to them. I'm just not sure Smoke's going to be up to the challenge at first." I nodded understanding completely what he was asking of me.

"I won't let them down," I assured him before Ghost pulled me into a tight hug and whispered in my ear. "I'm glad you're ours right now, Poppy. Take care of our boys for us." Tears stung the backs of my eyes as emotion swelled in my throat. Almost seamlessly, my body was transferred from Ghost's embrace to that of my brother who also hugged me before pulling me along behind him to the parking lot where he got on his bike and I took my car, following him to the hospital to figure out what the damage was there and how my boys were going to need me.

We were guided into a private room within the emergency room once we arrived and the sight that greeted me was just heartbreaking. Smoke was sitting in a chair beside a bed, holding Brantley's little hand in his own while his head rested on the mattress beside it. Brantley appeared banged up with bruises on one half of his face, and probably elsewhere though I couldn't see anything else due to the covers and Smoke's body hiding the rest. He was only hooked up to what looked like a heart monitor, no tubes, or anything that seemed to indicate things were dire. I moved quietly into the room, closer to Smoke, and before I could announce my presence, he stirred and glanced up at me. It took him a moment to get his bearings as sleepiness sloughed off of him like a blanket he was shedding in the morning. I watched as awareness of reality overtook and heartbreak melted into his features before his body shook and he broke right there in front of me.

I didn't hesitate and went straight to him, pulling his head into my midsection and holding him there, rocking back and forth, giving my strength to him as best I could. "Shh," I cooed. "I'm here. Chief's here. Whatever you need, we are here for you, Love, I promise." The endearment just slipped out, but I felt his arms tighten around my thighs as it did. I wasn't sure if it was from that, the assertion that we were there for him, or just the fact that he needed someone to hold on to. It didn't really matter in the big scheme of things. I had grown to love the man, and I was there for him in whatever capacity he needed me.

"I need to get ahold of Kent," Smoke finally stated as he released me and swiped at his eyes with his shirtsleeves.

"I already did, Brother." Chief moved forward and came to stand beside us so he could speak quietly. "They were already in the air headed to Anaheim to play the Ducks. The team is sending him back the minute they land."

"That's good then." Smoke spoke as if he were far away from the situation, the room, and was looking in as an observer. It was so detached that I began to worry until he snapped out of it. "Do they know yet?"

Chief shook his head in answer. "Ghost has people working on it now. It won't take long."

Smoke nodded. "I need to get in touch with Shep and let him know, just in case."

"Ghost went to loop him in," Chief explained as Smoke eyed him warily. Chief's lips tipped up in a somber smile as he lifted his chin to indicate me. "She was telling me that Shep should be made aware just in case, and Ghost overheard. He assured us that Poppy was right and he was headed over to do just that so we could be here for you and Brant."

Smoke's hand found its way to my thigh again, and he squeezed lightly. I just kept an arm around his shoulder and continued rubbing small circles on his back. I didn't know what else to do. "I need to talk to Chief a minute. Could you sit with Brant?"

"Of course, but um, what if he wakes?"

"Just distract him as best you can until I get back. I won't be long." Smoke stood, leaned in and kissed the top of my head as he helped me into the chair he'd just vacated, and then he left the room with my brother in tow. I glanced down at Brantley lying there so still and peaceful, and wondered what he would think of his world when his sleep ended and he learned the horrible truth. How did you tell a toddler that he just lost his whole world? My heart ached for him, as my belly rolled, reminding me that I had my own little one growing inside me. It hurt to think that I might somehow end up not being there to see him or her grow up. My heart broke for Sophie and Bender then, because they were going to miss just as much as their boy would. I promised them right then and there that so long as I was able to be in his life I would make sure he didn't miss out on a single experience, because hopefully they'd be watching down on their boy from heaven. I remembered back to the barbecue when I'd first met Brant and Sophie. The pride in Bender's eyes as he listened to his son saying naughty words and telling his momma she was going to get a spankin'. I remembered the protective way Sophie's eyes trailed the little boy everywhere he went. They loved him fiercely, and now he was going to need every adult in his life doing the same to make up for that kind of loss.

I was holding Brant's tiny little hand in my own and making a huge list of promises to two dead people that I hardly knew when a little voice called out to me. "Pop-wee?" It was scratchy with sleep, and when I looked up into his sweet face, it was scrunched in pain. "Popwee I feels owie."

I hit the button for the nurse immediately, and moved a little closer to Brant as I did. "I know, sweetie. I just called for the nurse to come in, okay?"

"Popwee, where my momma?"

Oh God! I was not equipped to answer this. "Hey, sweetie, let's get you checked out by the nurse first, then we'll talk about your momma, okay?" He nodded his head and winced as he did so. Poor baby.

"The car went boomed, Popwee."

"I know, sweetie." I told him and felt my heart drop right down into my stomach. Where was the damn nurse?

"Momma screamed weal loud," he told me quietly. "She was scawed. She yelled my name. Then she didn't yell no mowe." His little lip poked out and began to tremble. I had a feeling he already knew what we were going to tell him even though he was far too little to be able to comprehend. "Pop-wee, why da big truck crunch us?"

"Hey little guy, how are you?" The nurse interrupted, finally.

"He says he's owie, and looked to be in a lot of pain," I explained. The nurse nodded.

"I bet you are, honey. We're going to fix the owie right up, okay?"

"Otay," Brantley told her as I looked around hoping to see Chief or Smoke. I remembered my phone in my pocket and texted both of them the same message.

Brant is awake. He asked why the big truck crunched them. He's asking for his momma, and I don't know what to tell him.

I didn't get a response, but I didn't have to wait long either. Before the nurse was finished giving Brant some medicine, the guys were moving into the room quickly. Chief came over and gave me a side hug as Smoke moved to the side of his nephew's bed.

"Hey, little man, you hangin' in there?"

"Unc Moke," the boy offered sluggishly. "My gots owies."

"I know you have owies, Brant. The doctors are fixing you up as quick as they can so you can be even stronger when you leave here."

"Me Batman?" It was a question, but a sleepy one.

"Yeah, Bud, just like Batman." He couldn't have picked a worse or better superhero to identify with could he? The boy who lost both his parents to what was shaping up to be a horrible crime. My heart clenched in response to that realization.

"I gave him a little something for the pain, but unfortunately it will make him super sleepy," the nurse explained when everyone just sat there quietly watching the little boy fall back asleep. "Probably for the best, considering." With that, she turned back to me and added. "Just hit the button and call again if you need anything. I'm not sure if they'll be moving him upstairs to the pediatric wing or not. I do know they want to keep him here for at least 24 hours to watch and make sure there weren't any internal injuries didn't present right away."

"Thank you," I told her and she left quickly. I wasn't sure if the guys' overly large presence, or maybe their kuttes, unnerved her, but she was not able to get out of the room quickly enough.

Once she was gone, Smoke turned to me. "What exactly did he say?"

I really didn't want to tell him the first part, because it made me think that maybe Soph had suffered a bit before she died. I couldn't hold it back though, because no doubt Brant would repeat himself later. "He told me his momma was screaming and then she wasn't. Then he asked why the big truck crunched them. He was in a lot of pain. That's really all he said other than to tell me he hurt."

Not even thirty minutes later Shep, Ghost, and Leanne came through the door in a hurry. It appeared that Ghost and Leanne were just trying to follow in after Shep, who was white as self-condemnation poured from him in waves. "No!" he choked out. "Tell me this isn't my doing," I could feel the guilt and heartache in every word he spoke. It hadn't occurred to me that Shep would take on the burden of what happened as if it was his.

Smoke turned to him, watching warily a moment, and

then he stood and moved to the man that was drowning in his emotion in the doorway. Smoke pulled him into a fierce hug and whispered something in his ear that I couldn't hear. His words caused Shep to tremble and then cry as he just kept repeating over and over, "I'm so sorry. I'm so sorry."

"This isn't on you," I finally heard Smoke tell him. "This is not on you. This is on the fuckers who thought it was okay to run my sister and her family off the road. We will get them. They will die for this. All I need you to do is make sure your mom and sister are somewhere safe until we do. Send them away if you can. If you cannot let us know, and we'll see if one of the other chapters can house them for a while."

Shep was shaking his head back and forth. "No, look what happened when I got your guys involved before. I can't. I won't let you take on anything else."

"They killed my sister," Smoke hissed. "This is out of your hands now. Take care of your family so they don't end up dead, too. We will get the bastards who did it."

"Jesus, I can't believe I did this."

"You did not do this!" Smoke wasn't taking no for an argument. "No one in this damn room is responsible for this happening. You hear me? Any one of us would choose to help you out all over again if you called, even knowing what might happen. It's the life we live, man. We don't let family down, and you are my family. So, let go of the guilt, and just worry about getting the women out of town."

"What about your woman?" Shep finally asked when he noticed me watching them.

"We've got her, and all the rest handled. Everyone's on lockdown for now. They'll be plenty safe. Don't worry about us. Worry about your family, and if we need to get them out of town we will. The Dakotas will take them for sure, probably Sierra High too, maybe they can even stay with the girls of S.H.E. down there?" Smoke asked as he glanced over his shoulder at Ghost.

"Already put in a call. Angel Girl said they'd take them in, no problem. They also volunteered some people if we need them."

"See, we have this covered," Smoke reassured Shep once more.

Shep stopped talking and just watched Brantley as he lie there asleep. "What's going to happen with little man now?"

"He's going to stay with me," Smoke confirmed.

"Does he know?"

"Not yet." Smoke moved away from his friend and came to join me back over by the bedside. "Gonna have to tell him when he wakes up again. Not sure how the hell to do that, though." Smoke ran his hands across his tired face. "How the hell is a someone so small supposed to comprehend that his family is gone?"

"He'll get through, because not all of his family is gone," I told him. "He has you, Kent, and the club at his back. He won't want for anything."

"Except his parents," Smoke muttered.

"There's no helping that part, but we'll get him through it."

14. THE KID

THREE DAYS LATER, WE WERE PREPARING FOR THE GRAVESIDE
service for Smoke's sister and club brother. The entire club
was there, along with members from several other chapters
who came to pay their respects and say their farewells to
Bender and his old lady, Sophie. When Sweet and Angel Girl
showed up, I was happy to see they did not have Walker with
them. Before the service Angel Girl approached me.

"Can I have a word?" Angel Girl asked as I was trying to
get Brantley's shoe tied. Leanne came over to help.

"Go ahead, I've got him for a minute."

"No, Popwee, don't weave me," Brant whined, and it
broke my heart in two, because I knew he was feeling left
behind by his parents even though he didn't understand that
they didn't want to go without him.

"I'll be right over there, and you'll still be able to see me,
okay, buddy?"

He nodded and Angel Girl trailed me to where I told
Brant I would be standing.

"What can I do for you?"

Angel Girl released a humorless chuckle. "No, sweetheart, I think the question is what can I do for you? It's been brought to my attention that I didn't do enough, we didn't do enough, when you were going through your shit back down in Georgia, and for that I apologize."

"It wasn't your problem," I stated simply.

She shook her head. "That's where you're wrong. If it wasn't for others stepping in and making sure I was okay when I first got back together with Sweet, and we had our rough patch, we might not have made it together. If I'd stepped in," she started to say.

"Stop. I didn't need anyone to step in. My marriage didn't need to be saved. I'm much happier now, despite the sad circumstances we're in at the moment."

She smiled at me then. "I get that, but you probably could have used a shoulder to cry on at the very least." She shook her head, and then pulled me into a hug. "You also probably could have used a round or five hundred in our boxing ring beating the shit out of someone and wishing it was Walk. Lord knows if it had been Sweet and I'd heard the rumors of what he was doing while we were separated, that's where I would have been."

"Actually, that would have been pretty useful," I agreed.

"So, I dropped the ball. The women who should be taking care of the old ladies down there have a lot on our plates with our own club, but that's no excuse for us forgetting you. If there's anything I can do to make things up to you, just let me know."

"I think you're already doing it. Smoke said you took in

Shep's family for the time being until they can straighten this mess out."

"We did, and we're using our resources to make sure we track down the people who need to pay as well, but that's club business and you don't know anything about that." She winked at me then before walking away when Sweet called out to her from across the room. I moved back over to Brandt and Leanne stood and gave me a hug.

"How are you feeling, sweetie?"

I swished my hand back and forth in front of me indicating I was iffy about everything. "I've still been getting sick, but I've learned to control it a bit with eating the crackers throughout the day."

"Good, and have you mentioned anything to Smoke yet?"

I shook my head. "There hasn't been a good time. He's been away most of the last three days making arrangements and you know dealing with club business. I've barely seen him."

"What about Kent? I thought he'd be handling the arrangements since Smoke was working on the club side of things."

"Kent and Smoke have been arguing over everything. Kent didn't want the club involved, because he blames them for his sister's death. He even offered to spirit me away from here so that I would be safe. It's really sad watching them interact, Leanne. I'm worried for them, because they were so close, and now there's this rift."

"I know it's tough now, but they'll come around. Kent will come around when he realizes what everything was about, and why this all happened."

"He knows already. He won't even look at Shep, let alone talk to him."

"Kent needs time, sweetie. That's all. I promise, with some time, he'll change how he feels about the lot of it. He doesn't strike me as the type of man who would turn a blind eye to a person in need, especially when he's offering to spirit you away from here so that you don't suffer the same fate his sister did. Someone just needs to point out the fact that doing what he wants to do is exactly what Smoke did for Shep's family. It'll click eventually."

"Popwee?" Brant called out to me and I looked down, bending at the knees so I'd be at his level.

"What's up, little man?"

"I have to piss!" He exclaimed it loudly even though I was on eye level with him, and I couldn't help my reaction. I burst out laughing, as did a few of the people around us.

"Okay, baby, let's take you to the bathroom then."

"Mens piss outswide. That's what my daddy told me."

"You know what?" I asked and he shook his head no, letting the little brown wispy hairs float back and forth across his forehead as he did.

"No, what?"

"I think you're right. Big boys and men should piss outside on days like today." That put a smile on his face, and he put his hand in mine so I could walk him out back to go piss outside like his dad used to do. I couldn't help giggling thinking about how he was probably remembering an over-heard conversation between his parents about how men pissed outside. I would do anything to keep those memories alive for him as long as I could. Too soon, they would be forgotten and only a remembered story he heard other people tell. I knew this, because I was an adult when my family died. There were plenty of memories I kept, but I couldn't imagine Brant would have that same luxury as he grew older.

When we got to the door, he turned to me and crooked a finger so I would bend back down closer to him. "Popwee, you not s'posed-ta see me weiner." I sucked my lips into my mouth and bit down to keep from laughing as I nodded to him. A hand on my shoulder made me glance up and see that my brother was standing there.

"I've got him. This is man's business," he stated much to Brant's delight as he took the little boy's hand and walked him out back.

"You're doing a good job with him," Wren said to me as I stood again and swiped at a rogue tear that fell there.

"Thanks," I whispered before Wren pulled me into a hug.

"No need to thank me. You need to hear it. We all appreciate the way you stepped in and have helped out. Can't tell you what a relief it's been on Smoke that he can seek revenge for his sister and our brother without having to worry about his nephew. He'll be there for him when all is said and done, I promise. He just doesn't need anything else added to his plate until then." If that wasn't a reminder that I had things to tell Smoke that I simply couldn't tell him right now, I didn't know what was. I couldn't add to his burden no matter how sad it made me that I couldn't share my news with anyone else either. I loved Leanne to death, but I wanted to be able to talk to my brother about the baby. Most importantly, I wanted to be able to talk to Smoke about it so that I could stop worrying about how he'd react. Wren's reminder that he had too much going on just made it harder to do any of that.

I HADN'T SEEN Smoke at all that morning. I wondered if he'd even bother showing up to his sister's graveside service by the time we all got there. Luckily, I had plenty of people around me to help distract Brant every time he asked where his Unc Moke was. I was beginning to wonder if Smoke had forgotten that his priorities lie with the living and not with avenging the dead. I hated feeling that way too, because I knew he was also doing what he was doing to make sure we were all safe, and yet it made me wonder if I was going to be left behind yet again. Tears started forming in my eyes as I thought about that and while The Reverend Thompson spoke of life being cut short far too soon.

Brant started getting fidgety and antsy, not understanding why everyone had to stand still so long. I took him by the hand and pulled him off to the side, deciding that walking him around was to burn off some energy was something I could do. As I rounded the last of the mourners there to pay their respects I caught a glimpse of Smoke off in the distance. He was standing quite far away and was wrapped in the arms of a tall, blond woman who was wearing a thigh bearing tight black mini-dress and heels so high I had no clue how she hadn't twisted an ankle on all this soft ground.

I watched as Smoke attempted to dislodge her a few times while the woman just clung even harder to him each time.

"Why Jew-wee attacks Unc Moke?" Brant asked, apparently having seen the same thing. Funny how a three year old ended up answering the question of who the woman was for me. Apparently that was Julie. The ex-girlfriend. The one who was clinging to Smoke like she was the one who had just lost her sister and she couldn't live a minute more without his arms wrapped around her.

"Don't know, kiddo," I answered honestly. I would also like to know why Julie was attacking Uncle Smoke. Better yet, I'd like to know why Smoke hadn't been with us during the service when he was clearly here and had plenty of time for Julie. I was about to turn away and head back toward the crowd of people who were tossing flowers onto the caskets now when Brantley made certain that didn't happen.

"Unc Moke!" He yelled, not only calling everyone's attention to the fact that Smoke was there with another woman, but that I'd witnessed it, and he hadn't been with me. With us. Smoke's head shot around and he managed to dislodge Julie long enough this time to turn and head in our direction. He did not look pleased either. I wasn't waiting for him to get to us. I grabbed Brant up and settled him on my hip so that I could easily carry him back to where we were supposed to be. Before I could get very far, my brother was by my side glaring back over my shoulder where Smoke had been standing in Julie's embrace.

I knew that my past would influence how I perceived things. I knew that it would color questionable interactions with a haze of red anger and betrayal like I'd felt when I found out about Walker and what he had been doing behind my back. I didn't know if I should be feeling it in this situation, but I couldn't help wondering if that was truly where Smoke had been spending his time. With her. With his ex, because maybe it was too painful to be around me since I had Brantley with me all the time. The fact of the matter was I didn't know, because I wasn't in the loop, and it all felt a little similar to me. He hadn't even really said more than five words to me each day since Brant left the hospital. "How's Brant doing?" Was pretty much of the extent of our conversations, because even though I answered, I don't think he actually heard the words I spoke before he was gone again.

"I really don't think it's what you're thinking," Chief finally said to me in a quiet tone that only I could hear. I just shrugged my shoulders as if I was indifferent even though I wasn't. I kept walking away from the people still gathered around the twin coffins and towards my car. I had refused to come in a limo that had been organized by Kent for 'family use' because I didn't want to be stuck there if Brantley became ill tempered or too sad to deal with everything. Brant had his head resting on my shoulder as I walked.

"Poppy!" I heard him call my name, but continued to walk towards my car. I was just reaching for the door when a hand clamped down on my elbow.

"You might want to back off a minute, Brother," Chief informed him.

"Seriously?" Smoke's question came out as if he was truly shocked by the order.

"Seriously," Chief agreed and Smoke's hand dropped off of me just like that while he took a solid step back, giving me space to open the back door so I could get Brant into the new car seat I'd had installed.

"What's going on?"

Once I was finished buckling Brant in the car, I closed the door and turned to face Smoke. Chief just stood there watching with interest, but it was clear he wasn't going to interfere unless it was necessary. "I'm taking Brant home, because he's tired, and I think he's had enough today. I've been answering questions all day for him about why we were saying goodbye to the boxes when his mom and dad are in heaven. Why can't we go to heaven to see them? Why can't they come visit? Why didn't they take him with them? It's been nonstop. Frankly, I'm not even sure I'm telling him the right things, but you haven't been around to ask. Kent is angry with me for some reason and won't speak to me. You've been God knows where with Lord only knows who, and I just can't help thinking I'm the last person your sister would have wanted answering these questions for her son. She only met me the one time, and she didn't have a high opinion of me for at least half of that time." I blew out a frustrated breath and just stood there while both men took me in.

"You look tired," Chief finally said before moving forward and wrapping his arms around me. "I'll come back with you and watch Brant so you can get a nap, okay?"

"There's no need for that. I was planning on heading out with them when they went," Smoke informed Chief.

"Really? Up until they spotted you with your ex hanging all over you, Poppy wasn't even aware you had shown up for the funeral. She didn't know if she'd see you there at all before she left. I get that you have a lot going on right now, man, but that kid ain't hers. It isn't her responsibility to do all the tough stuff with him, and have you come in once the dust has settled and finally decide that you have time for him. My sister isn't your damn nanny, and you need to remember that. She's already had one man treat her like she was only good for keeping his house when he wanted to be there. She doesn't need a repeat performance with extra responsibilities thrown in for fun."

"Jesus, Chief!" Smoke yelled out at him. "You know where I've been! I've been hunting down the maniacs who took my fucking sister. You'd be doing the same goddamn thing!" He shook his head and stepped back again, apparently trying to calm himself. "Look," he started then glanced between Chief and myself before sighing and starting again. "I don't know how to do this. He's my nephew, and I've watched him before, but I've never had to prioritize him before like this. I don't know what to do here, because I can't let Soph and Bender's deaths go unanswered for. I can't exactly take Brant with me when I do those things. I'll find someone else who can help with him for the time being if it's a problem. I didn't mean to put the burden on Poppy." He turned completely to me then. "I didn't mean to leave you holding my family's bag, I swear."

"Brant is not a burden. Not knowing what you expect me to say to him or do with him is, though. I can't be the one making the decision about what to tell him about his parents, or how to cope, or God, any of it. I can't because I didn't know how to do those things for myself when I lost my family and I was an adult."

"Plus, she hasn't been feeling well. Not that she'd tell anyone and admit she's not perfect."

"What?" I asked my brother, eyes rounding in shock as I did.

"Saw you get sick this morning," he stated coolly while eyeing me in an assessing way. Damn. I hadn't realized he'd noticed.

"Probably just something I ate," I told him.

"You were sick?" Smoke asked as he started taking note of what were probably dark circles under my eyes and my overly pale skin.

"Yeah, something you may have noticed if you'd even checked in with her for more than two minutes a day," my brother grumbled out.

"Shit," Smoke huffed again. "How about we get you guys home, and then we'll figure everything out where you can relax." I glanced around and noticed that the blond woman from earlier was standing a few cars down watching our interaction. Again, my doubts reared their ugly little heads and started spitting ideas into my mind about how it was odd timing that he wanted to get out of here all of a sudden when she was there to witness the drama he was having with another woman. He saw where my attention was pulled and shook his head. "No," was all he said before he pointed to the car. "Get in, drive home, and I'll meet you there."

When I left, Chief and Smoke were still standing there talking. When I got home, I took Brantley inside, put him down for a nap in my second bedroom that had become his over the past few days, and I took Bubba out back to do his business. While I was out back with my dog, I heard the pipes roaring up the road. That wasn't unusual since Chief lived just down the road. Instead one continued on down the road and one sounded as if it pulled into the driveway and then the engine was killed. I knew who would be here just as well as who wouldn't. Smoke was a lot of things right now, grieving, looking for retribution, confused, heartsick; but I also knew he wasn't Walker. He hadn't left me to my own devices this whole time because he didn't care. He left it all to me because he thought I could handle it while he handled his stuff.

I heard the knock on the front door, but that small, petty part of me refused to go answer it until Bubba was done and ready to go inside. It turned out I did not have to worry about that when after a couple minutes, the side gate opened, and Smoke sauntered into the back yard. "Figured you were out here when you didn't answer."

"What if I just wasn't up for company and ignoring you?"

He gave me a half-hearted smile then launched right in to where it seemed we had left off in the cemetery. "I haven't seen or spoken to Julie in six months until this morning. She heard about Soph and showed up, caught up to me as I heading to the," he choked on the words and couldn't say them. I knew how that felt. It was the final acknowledgment that the person you loved is gone. "What you saw wasn't..."

I cut him off by throwing my hand up in the air as if to wave off the rest of his words. "Stop. It doesn't matter, because the only reason I entertained doubts was because of your behavior over the past few days. Had you been around at all, helping with Brantley, I would have never thought..." I sighed then as I watched his face crumple.

"I couldn't stop. I couldn't sit still. In the brief minutes when I do, everything is real and she's never coming back. She was my little sister, but I raised her, too. After my dad left, when my mom had to work so much, it was me looking after them. They're like my kids in a way, and now," he swallowed thickly. "She's gone and Kent won't speak to me, because he thinks it's my fault. I don't know what to do with all that."

"I understand. I really, honestly do understand what you're going through. That doesn't make it easier when I have a past that clouds everything in muck. I know that shouldn't fall on you, but I can't help the way I feel or that I'm questioning everything now, because I didn't question enough before."

Smoke stepped forward then, moving closer, before pulling me into his embrace. "I'm sorry, Poppy." His shoulders began to shake as his head dipped into my hair and I just held onto him while he let go of some of his grief. Bubba stood there beside us waiting to see if he was needed for this moment or not. When he decided he wasn't necessary he loped off across the yard.

"Will they come for us, too?" I finally asked the question that had been on my mind as I was left here alone with Brantley for days.

"No!" He answered vehemently. "I've had Gray watching out for you."

"Surfer-dude?"

He grinned then. "Yeah, surfer-dude. He's been watching the house when I haven't been here."

"I haven't seen a bike out there the past few days."

"That's because he's been incognito in a fucking cage. Listen, Poppy, I know what you were thinking and I just need you to understand that you weren't forgotten. You haven't been far from my mind, in fact, I've been gone so much to make sure you don't end up like Soph. I want you and Brant safe even if that means I can't be here while I'm hunting for the assholes who destroyed my family." He whistled for Bubba who just looked at him from across the lawn like he was an idiot.

"Bubba, Heir," I called out and the dog immediately responded. Smoke chuckled.

"I don't even know how to feel about that shit," he admitted. I grinned up at him.

"Just go with it. He knows who is boss."

"Come on, let's get you inside. I remember someone other than Brant was in need of a nap, too." As if on command, I yawned and couldn't seem to stop myself from doing it three more times before we even got turned around and inside the house.

15. THE EX

I AWOKE TO THE SOUND OF LITTLE BOY GIGGLES AND SMOKE'S laughter. Unfortunately, I didn't get a chance to lie there and enjoy it, because my stomach turned the minute I moved and I had to run for the bathroom. Judging by the sun coming in through the bathroom window, I'd apparently managed to sleep the rest of the evening and the entire night away while Smoke took care of Brantley.

"Poppy?" I heard Smoke call my name, but slammed the door shut behind me anyway in order to get to the toilet as quickly, and with as much privacy, as possible. Once my stomach was emptied of the little-to-nothing I actually had sitting on it, I brushed my teeth and made my way to the kitchen where I could still here the boys laughing and joking.

"Hey!" My voice sounded a little rough to my own ears as I glanced around and noted that Bubba was sitting right beside Brantley's chair looking for all the world like his guard dog.

"Hey babe, we were just making pancakes for breakfast. Want some?"

"Sure."

"You were out of pretty much every breakfast meat," he offered with a pout. I made eggs too, though."

"I see that, thank you." I was out of the sausage and bacon because the smell of them cooking literally made me sick. I still hadn't been given an opportunity to tell Smoke my news. I figured now was as good as ever, but his cell rang, and he glanced down at it with a frown. It didn't take long to know that he'd be heading out to deal with whatever the call was about. I was looking into his apologetic eyes as he spoke into the phone, and before I could let him see my disappointment, I glanced away and started asking Brantley about his pancakes. They were shaped like little footballs, which seemed to thrill him.

"Unc Moke told me no frowing deez balls."

I laughed at him. "He's right. That would make a mess, and Bubba might eat them.

"Bubbsba likes cancakes, Popwee."

"Bubba likes pancakes?" I asked while trying not to laugh at the way he butchered the English language. He just shook his little head vigorously in agreement. "How do you know Bubba likes pancakes?"

"I gibbed hims some." He shrugged his shoulders all the way up to his ears and then back down in an exaggerated gesture as if he were calling me out for being stupid. Of course he thought I should know that he'd fed Bubba pancakes.

"You know Bubba shouldn't get people food."

"Why?"

"Because it's not good for him," I attempted to explain and then watched in horror as Brantley spit his own mouthful of syrupy pancake out of his mouth and onto his plate.

"Cancakes bad?" He glared at his Uncle Smoke then, as if he'd betrayed the little boy.

"Pancakes aren't bad for little boys, just doggies," I told him.

"Why?"

"I don't know why. They just are."

Brantley looked at Bubba then before turning back to me. "He wikes dem."

"Okay, well how about we don't feed him anymore. I think he has had enough since he already ate his doggy food, too."

"Otay, Popwee."

"Hey babe," Smoke cut in, and I turned to see that he had been watching my exchange with Brantley.

"You have to go?"

"Yeah, I do. I want to talk with you, but it's going to have to wait awhile. Are you okay with that?"

I sighed. "Yeah, go do what you have to do."

"Pop, I don't want to go. This is important, though."

"I get it, Smoke, really. Go; take care of your crap. We'll be fine."

"I'll send someone in a bit to grab Brant for a bit if I'm going to be too long. You need to be able to get your stuff done too, and I know that's not easy with a little one running around."

"It's fine. I'll let you know if I ever need help."

"I'll call you later and see how things are going." Smoke moved to where I was sitting and put a plate in front of me loaded down with pancakes and eggs. Then he kissed the top of my head and did the same to Brant. "I'll be back later, lil man, you listen to Poppy, and be a good boy for me okay?"

"Otay, Unc Moke. Bye" He waved his sticky fingers in the air and Smoke just did manage to dodge them before getting syrup all over his kutte.

Once he was gone, I managed to get everything cleaned up, including an incredibly sticky Brant. While he played with Bubba and watched cartoons, I managed to get a little work done. By the time lunch was ready to roll around, Brant and I had taken Bubba for a walk around the neighborhood and ran into my brother who offered to go get some food for us.

"When we eats?" Brant asked for the third time since we came back from our walk.

"We eat when Chief gets here with the food," I explained.

"Popwee, why you got no food?"

"I have food, but Chief is bringing us special food, okay?"

"Otay," he sighed indignantly. He turned around to play with Bubba who was large enough that Brantley could have ridden him like a small pony. "Bubbsba, sit!" The boy commanded and the dog listened, making Brantley clap with glee. I ruffled his hair as someone knocked on the door.

"I bet that's Chief with our special food," I called out to Brantley as I moved to the door and opened it without thinking. I don't know what made me do it, because I knew better than to not check. I opened the door to see the same tall, blond woman from the cemetery the day before standing there in a pencil skirt, a rumpled looking dress shirt, and four inch peep-toe heels. She gave me a look of moderately disguised disgust and then smiled sweetly over my shoulder.

"Brant, it's time to go, sweetie."

"Excuse me?" I growled out. Bubba moved himself in between the door and Brantley so he couldn't get any closer. Smart dog.

"Smoke sent me to get Brantley. I'll be taking over care of him from here on out so he won't need you."

"Like hell he did," I seethed. There was only the tiniest part of me that thought for the briefest second that she might be telling the truth, and only because Smoke had mentioned sending someone to help with Brandt. I knew deep down though that Smoke would never send this woman, especially if the first time he'd spoken to her in six months had been the previous day.

"It's great that you're taking your babysitting duties for Smoke seriously, but I'm his girlfriend," she started saying.

I laughed in her face then. "Really? That's the road you want to take with this? You're his girlfriend?" Her pinched face didn't appear to be too happy with me. "You do realize he sleeps here every night right?" I asked. That made her grow more agitated.

"We were split up for a while, but he needs me to be there for Brantley now, and for him. I'm not letting them down."

"You need to leave!"

"No, you need to hand Brantley over, right now. I know

this is what Smoke wants. We talked about it yesterday at the cemetery."

My jaw dropped, because clearly this woman was delusional. It didn't matter though; because I could tell by the sound of pipes that backup had just arrived. I wasn't wrong either. In less than two minutes my brother was in the driveway and jumping off his bike like the thing was on fire. Then, he was up in Julie's face.

"What in the fuck are you doing at my sister's house?"

Julie appeared shocked, whether by something he said or his demeanor towards her I wasn't certain. "Your sister?" she questioned. "There's no way that woman is your sister. You two look nothing alike."

"As interesting as that news is, there's no way you're taking Brantley anywhere so you can get the hell out of here like I just told you to do," I explained to her.

"Julie, I don't know what kind of shit you're trying to pull, but you seriously need to get gone now. Smoke is on his way."

"Good, then he clear this up so that woman gives my boy to me."

I growled at her. Brant was still standing there stroking Bubba's fur and watching what he could see, which wasn't much since I was blocking his view in the doorway. Call me petty, but I didn't even want that woman to get a glimpse of Brant. Three minutes later, Smoke was pulling up on his bike. He jumped off almost as quickly as Chief had done.

"What in the hell are you doing at this house?" he yelled as he moved closer. Julie jumped at the tone in his voice, but then smiled brightly at him.

"Hey baby, I came by to pick up Brant. We talked about me taking care of him yesterday, remember."

"What the fuck kinds of drugs are you on? I told you my woman would be the one caring for Brant when you asked."

She shook her head, still watching him with something like awe in her eyes. It was clear this woman still had it bad for Smoke whether they'd been apart or not. I wasn't sure if this woman was straight delusional or just seeing and hearing what she wanted, because she was hopeful, and unwilling to give that up.

"Why are you here?" he asked her again, and then the foggy look in her eyes dissipated somewhat and she cocked her head to the side.

"You told me I would be taking care of him."

"I fuckin' said my woman would be takin' care of him." He pointed back to me. "Poppy being that woman." He gestured his hand back and forth between the two of them then. You and I haven't been together in six months, why in the hell would you be the one caring for him?"

"You and Poppy?" she questioned softly, then glanced back at me before returning her attention to Smoke. "You're with her?"

"Yeah, like I told you yesterday."

"I thought you just meant you had brought her with you to the cemetery, because she was caring for Brant temporarily. How is it possible you moved on so quickly?" The hurt in both her voice and features was palpable.

"Julie, I told you when it was over that I meant it. Hell, you knew I'd been with other women since," he stated making me wonder how exactly she knew if he hadn't talked to her in all that time.

"I thought Jewel was just telling me those things to make me jealous. I thought you just needed to get some things out of your system, because you were mad at me. You were supposed to come back to me. She said she'd help make sure you came back," the woman whined then. "Yesterday, I thought you were talking about…"

"How the hell did you know where to find Brant?" Chief asked, obviously more concerned with the fact that this woman was off her rocker and still managed to find herself on my doorstep.

"I followed you here yesterday. At first I thought you got a new house, but then I saw the car she got into yesterday too, and figured it was your babysitter's house."

"Not my babysitter. She's my woman. You hear me? You are nothing to me. We are history, and it's a lesson I don't miss. You need to get that through your head and move the hell on. I catch you near Poppy, Brantley, my work, home, the club, or anywhere else, I will be forced to take action. The club will take action, you feel what I'm telling you?"

Tears began to drip down her face so there was no doubt she was grasping the concept. "I'm s-sorry. I really thought, um…"

"IF I wanted you here I would have fuckin told you where to go. I didn't. You followed me like a stalker to get that information, and that's concerning as hell."

Her eyes bugged out and she jerked back with the implication. "No! I'm not, I wasn't. I just… I'm sorry, it won't happen again." With that promise, she turned and all but ran across the street to the Mustang that had been parked out there when Brant and I got back from our walk with Bubba.

We all watched as the woman lost inches on her regal height as she slunk into herself on the walk back to her car. It took no time at all before she had it started up and was peeling down my road. I turned to Smoke then. "That was not okay." I didn't wait for his response; instead I turned on my heels, and moved so I could shut the door behind me. Then I threw the lock, too. I knew it wasn't his fault. I knew he had no control over other people's crazy, but damn it, I was angry that his ex-hand presumed to come to MY house and demand the child I was caring for, and call herself his girlfriend. Not that I was his girlfriend, since we hadn't discussed it, but like I'd told her, he'd been sleeping at my house more than not so it felt like it. Maybe I was just as delusional as that woman.

I heard Chief chuckling outside, and a growl from Smoke. "Popwee, where da foods?" Shoot. I was going to have to unlock the door and lean out to get the food now, ruining my gesture of shutting him out. Jesus needed to take the wheel, because apparently I couldn't drive my life for crap. I reopened the door and glanced out at the two men who turned to look at me, Chief with amusement dancing in his eyes and Smoke looking pissed as hell.

"You brought food?" I questioned my brother while ignoring the angry bull to his right. Chief just grinned at me and held up the two bags I hadn't noticed during all the commotion. I probably hadn't noticed them because they were still in his saddled bags at the time, but he'd retrieved them at some point since I shut the door on him.

"You going to invite me in to eat with you guys or slam the door in my face again?" Chief was teasing me so I just glared at him as I held the door open wider. He moved inside and laughed again as I shut it behind him, leaving Smoke on the other side of the door. "You do realize that scene wasn't exactly his fault, right?"

"That doesn't help me get over my anger that it happened. I need a minute. We didn't even get to talk things through completely yesterday, because I was so tired. So, I don't even know where I stand with that man. She told me she was his girlfriend, and I couldn't say something asinine like, 'no you aren't because I am' since I don't know what I am."

"He clarified that for you out there, Poppy. He told her you're his woman."

"Yeah? What does that even mean? I'm his woman, but in what respect? I was Walker's wife, and you see how we were on two separate pages about what that was supposed to mean and how he was supposed to behave when I wasn't around."

"You can't punish Smoke for Walker's bullshit."

"I know that, but also can't make the same mistakes and overlook the same issues I did with Walk, because that didn't turn out so well for me."

"Didn't it though?"

I was taken aback by his question. "What?"

"You're here. You have me, you have a club that stands behind you, supports you, and you have a man standing outside being pissed off and refusing to leave until you talk to him. He is here, even though you're probably pissing him off right now with your bullshit, in order to make sure you're okay and that his past life bleeding into yours didn't kill what you have started here."

I glanced away, suddenly ashamed of my actions. "Let him in," I told my brother in a whisper.

"Nope. That's for you to do. I'm taking little man there into the kitchen, and we're going to eat while you work your shit out." With that, he took Brant's hand and disappeared into my kitchen while I was left standing there staring at the front door and wondering how I got to this place in my life. I knew part of my problem was that I was pregnant and overly emotional, but no one else knew that was an issue, and I couldn't explain it without revealing that.

I opened my front door again, and glanced out to find Smoke sitting on my bottom step. He turned to peer at me over his shoulder, and stood before I could say anything. "You're right to be mad. My shit hit your doorstep, and that is not okay. You have to understand that I agree with you. It is abso-fuckin-lutely not okay. I will deal with Julie to make sure this never happens again."

"I think you already did that," I informed him. Smoke grunted in my general direction and just watched me, waiting. "I'm sorry. I know you couldn't help the fact that she just showed up with all of her assumptions. That doesn't mean I don't feel the things I do. I needed a moment to get myself together."

"I know," he stated simply and then he was hugging me tightly to his body. "I promise, we'll get everything figured out and this won't be an issue moving forward, ever. If someone comes to your doorstep claiming I sent them, I'm a phone call away or you call someone from the club immediately, okay?"

I nodded my head. I already knew this, and the only reason I hadn't called before was because Chief was there. The problem really boiled down to the fact that I had a secret to share with him, but wasn't sure if this was the right time. He made the decision for me, though.

"I don't have long. I came running when Chief called, but I'm still in the middle of shit." I could see the apology there in his eyes, and I just smiled up at him and nodded my head to let him know I understood, and that it was okay. I felt like timing was against us, and we only had to wait to see if it would do damage or if it would all turn out okay in the end.

"Go, get back to what you're doing. I've got Brant, and neither of us is going anywhere."

It was then that Smoke leaned in and kissed me fiercely, all but devouring my lips with his own. The gesture sent tingles racing through my body and made me ache with a want so deep I wasn't sure what to do with it, because he didn't have time to even attempt to satisfy it. When he broke away it was with a promise. "We're finishing this later, Poppy, and I'm not just talking about where that kiss was going."

16. THE TALK

NOT LONG AFTER CHIEF FED BRANTLEY, I WAS ABLE TO GET HIM down for a nap. My brother hung around for a while anyway. I think he was nervous that Smoke's ex might attempt to show up again, but I saw her face and her body language when she left. She was devastated, heartbroken, and more than a little embarrassed that she'd had it all wrong. I honestly didn't think we'd see or hear from her again. I felt bad for her, but at the same time, she'd played one brother for the other. What did she think would come of that?

"You want to talk about it?" My brother asked me once I was able to plop my booty down on the couch and relax a bit.

"About what exactly?"

"All of it," he stated as if that was helpful. "Julie showing up at the cemetery, here at your house, Smoke being gone so much, having the responsibility of a toddler dropped in your lap," he shrugged then. "I don't know, take your pick. I imagine you need someone to vent to at this point. I don't want to be left out of your life like I was when you lived in

Georgia still. I want you to be able to come to me with your problems, frustrations, and whatever. If I can help, I will. If I can't, then at least maybe it will just help you get it all off your chest instead of letting things sit and fester."

Tears welled in my eyes as he spoke. I was so grateful to have my brother nearby again, because that was exactly what I needed. "The entire Julie situation was regretful, but not really Smoke's fault." When Chief gave me a dubious look, I felt the need to clarify my feelings for him. "I had my doubts in the cemetery, seeing her clinging to him the way she was. I wondered if maybe she was the reason he was gone so much even though I knew what he was doing with his time. It's not even an idea I would have entertained had things not come out about Walker when we were together, you know? So, that was strange for me to be second-guessing my gut, and then wondering if my second-guessing was wrong. It was all confusing, and having her show up here just reiterated the fact that part of my confusion is because I don't honestly know where I stand with Smoke."

"Where do you think you stand?"

"I don't know. The last time we really discussed it, we were going to take things slow and see how it all played out. Now, I just don't know. I think we're exclusive. He says I'm his all the time, and I know what that means to most guys in and around the club, but I don't know if it's the same for Smoke. They all seem to have their own level of commitment that goes with those words."

"I'm guessing you'll be discussing that one together fairly soon considering what went down today. What about Brant? How are you feeling about that situation?"

"Well, if I'm serious and committed to Smoke, then that means Brant comes with him now. He would have come with him before too, just in a different way. I love the little man. He's a sweetheart."

"That's what I'm worried about."

"What do you mean?"

"You have feelings already developing, and strong ones, for that little boy. I'm guessing you do for his uncle too, no doubt?" I gestured that I agreed with a tip of my head and he continued on. "You aren't even clear where you stand with Smoke, but you're basically being forced to build this family at the same time. I don't know if that's a healthy place for you to be right now, Poppy. After trying so hard to have a kid with Walk, and then everything that happened, plus it wasn't that long ago. Now, you have a kid landing in your lap who you're crazy about, and what happens if Smoke decides he doesn't want this with you?"

"What happens if he decides he does and another accident happens that takes either Smoke, Brant, or both away from me? Life has no guarantees, Chief. You either jump in and hope for the best, or you live in fear. I've let the fear paralyze me in a life I shouldn't have stayed in as long as I did. I won't live that way anymore. If he takes Brant away from me, then I'll have to grieve, and move on. I don't think he'd ever do that to me or to Brant, though."

"I don't either, Sis. I'm just wondering out loud if you've thought about all the possible ways this could go."

"Of course I have, but when you love someone, it's really easy." His eyebrows rose high on his forehead and I realized what I had just said. "Oh!" I huffed out as I collected myself.

Chief grinned big then and stood from where he'd been perched on the edge of the chair across from where I'd plopped down on the couch. "I think I've heard all I need to. I can already see how he feels about you. I just wanted to know how you felt. Just know that if you ever need me, I'm here. That includes if Smoke fucks up in any way. You were my sister first, long before he was my brother. You feel me?"

I stood and wrapped my arms around my brother's waist and pulled him in for a hug. "I get you," I told him with a sniffle, because damn these hormones and my brother for making me a giant sap!

17. THE HUSBAND

THE NEXT DAY, CHIEF CAME BANGING ON THE DOOR OF MY HOUSE first thing in the morning. Smoke hadn't come home the night before, and I also hadn't heard from him so when I saw Chief's face as I opened the door I started to panic.

"Please, tell me you don't have bad news," I whined. He didn't deny it, and I nearly fell right there before my brother grabbed my arms to steady me.

"Whoa, Poppy, it's not like that."

"Smoke?" I questioned him, but damn it, he should have already known what I was talking about.

"Shit! I forgot he was held up last night. No, it's not Smoke. Last I heard, he's fine, just out of communication for a bit. I came to get you, because there's someone at the club-house demanding to see you."

"Who?" I asked, because other than Leanne, I wasn't really on 'summoning terms' with anyone in the Cedar Falls clubhouse.

"Walker is there, and he's demanding to see you." The

minute he said Walker's name, I think my jaw hit the floor. "Ghost asked that I come get you. He'll be there to arbitrate anything Walker wants to talk to you about if you need him."

"What in the world could he want to talk to me about?"

Chief shrugged his shoulders. "Gee, I don't know, maybe the dumbass finally realized what he lost out on when he was stupid enough to fuck up and let you go."

"Well, it's way too late for that now," I shouted.

Chief grinned at me. "I know that and you know that, but now you need to come with me and make sure Walker knows that. I've got your back and so does Ghost, so you don't have to worry about him."

"I'm not worried about him, but I'm also not dragging Brantley to the clubhouse to witness my drama."

"Leanne's going to meet us in the parking lot and take Brant to play out back for a while until we give her the all clear," he informed me.

"You guys planned it all out well, I see."

"Well, after I told Ghost I thought you'd refuse to bring Brant around Walk, he suggested it. You know he is club president for a reason."

"Yeah, I know. Let me go put some actual clothes on, and get Brant ready then," I stated as I moved through the house. "Can you walk Bubba out back for me while I do that?"

"Sure," my brother shouted back at me. "Bubba, heir," he called out. Bubba hesitated in my bedroom door where he'd follow me.

"Go on Bubba, go with Chief," I told him and he looked back at me one more time before trotting off to my brother.

"I really hate the fact that you listen to her before you'll listen to me," he grumbled to the dog before I couldn't hear them anymore. Then I proceeded to get ready and finally to get Brant woken up and ready. That little boy was not a morning person.

TRUE TO THE plan that Ghost and Chief had concocted, Leanne met us in the clubhouse parking lot and took Brantley around back to go play outside on the swing set the guys had built in the grassy area beyond the multilevel decks. Instead of following them, like I really wanted to, I trailed behind Chief as he made his way inside. It didn't take long to find Walker. He was standing by the bar talking to a woman – go figure – and she was trailing her bright red talon-like nails across his forearm.

"What a dumbass," my brother hissed out as he began stalking across the floor at a much quicker pace. I couldn't disagree. Not that Walker ever had a chance in hell of rekindling anything with me, but still. If he thought he did, why in God's name would he be here letting some club slut touch him?

"Walker?" I called out, as we got closer. He immediately shifted away from the woman causing her to drop her arm when he pulled his away. He stood and quickly erased the distance between us only to be stopped by Chief's stiff-arm against his shoulder.

"Close enough, Walk."

"What the hell, Chief? You're acting like I used to beat her something. I've never hurt Poppy!"

"I wouldn't go that far. You might have never laid a violent hand on her, but you sure as fuck hurt and betrayed my sister. So, that's close enough."

Walker ignored my brother, imploring me with a look instead. "Do we really need a chaperone?"

I cocked my head to the side and took him in. I was left with an odd realization that while he seemed familiar he also felt like a stranger, or someone I might know in passing. It was strange to think I was still technically married to the man before me, or that I'd spent the past 10 years of my life with him, because now I felt nothing. It was obvious, though, from the look on his face that the feeling was not mutual.

"What exactly do you want, Walker? Did you bring signed divorce papers?"

"What? No, Poppy, I don't want the damn divorce. I understand you were mad, but you've had time to cool off and realize how hard things were on me. Yeah, I should have handled things differently, but I was under a lot of stress and you..." he stopped talking when I turned around and started walking away.

"Wait, where are you going? We're in the middle of talking."

"No, we aren't." I turned again so I was facing him and he could see every bit of what was playing out on my face. "You have the audacity to come here, demand to see me, and then tell me about how hard your life was and how the stress you were under caused you to fall dick first into every whore at the clubhouse, never check on your wife, or do any goddamn thing for her either. You had it so hard because you couldn't do simple tasks the doctors asked you to do in order to get your sperm count up like wear different underwear. Yeah, I can see how that demand made you run straight to other pussy to prove what a man you are. Don't you dare stand here and try to trivialize this shit. You are a grown ass man, who made dumbass decisions, and now, as a result, the woman who once loved you with everything she had, does not want you anymore. Guess what? It's time to suck it up, and reap what you sowed, because I'm done. I've been done, and I don't ever want to go backwards."

"Poppy, I know you were mad. I get it. I fucked up. I know I did, but I'm here now. I pulled my head out of my ass, and..."

"Stop right there. Even if you had managed to pull your head out of your ass – which I highly doubt considering the first thing I saw when I walked in here was some other woman touching you and you doing nothing to stop it – you're still forgetting the part where I said I'm done."

"You don't have to be done. We can work through this. We still love one another. I'll find a way to give you the baby you want, I swear it!"

I growled out a ferocious, fed up noise that quieted the whole clubhouse, or at least the parts in close proximity to us. "I do not still love you. I love someone else. I already have my own baby on the way, and it's not yours!" I was yelling at this point. "You gonna raise another man's baby?" I laughed then. "Never mind, that's a moot point, because even if you were man enough to agree to that, I don't want you to. I can't count on you to be there for me during a goddamn storm, I sure as hell couldn't count on you to be there for sleepless nights, teething, vomiting, and any other thing that might inconvenience your life. I am happy here. I am in love with someone, and that someone isn't you. He's the father of my baby. Now, do you understand? There's nothing left of us. It's all gone, and what little bit had been left before I moved here, you trashed and threw away with your actions."

"You're pregnant?" It was only at his reiteration of my words that I realized what I'd just done. In my anger and frustration with Walker, I'd let my secret out of the bag. I felt warm hands wrap around my waist from behind me, and then whispered words found my ear.

"We'll talk about that revelation later at home, but honey, I need you to know, I love you, too." His hands dipped low on my belly and settled there protectively. Walker started to get pissed.

"You're my brother!" He yelled out. "You knocked my wife up?"

"Ex-wife," Smoke corrected.

"Those papers aren't signed yet," Walker argued.

Smoke made a tsking noise in the back of his throat before he responded to that. "She just told you all the ways you screwed up, all the reasons she didn't want you back, and that she was happy, finally. She signed the papers already. In her eyes, in her mind, you two aren't together. She's just waiting for you and the law to catch up with everything.

"Club first," Walker called out.

"Yeah, we all know you put the club first, every aspect of

it, including catering to the whores. That seemed to be your problem. I don't regret making Poppy mine, or anything that resulted from that decision. Best damn woman I've ever met, and I'd be a fool to let her go. You didn't hang on to a good thing, and now you're seeing that, but it's too late. I suggest you get gone back to Georgia, and do something for someone other than yourself for a change, and sign those damn papers.

Walk just stood there digesting everything Smoke had just put out there for him. Then he turned to me. "I wouldn't care," he finally told me.

I just laughed, but there was no humor in it. "Yes, you would. The thing is, that part doesn't even matter, because I'm happy right now. I wasn't before. I meant it when I said I wasn't willing to go backwards for anyone, Walk. Not even you."

"Poppy, I promise you I'll get it right this time," he pleaded. It made me sick to think where I'd be right now if he had done this right away after I kicked him out. If he had come to me with promises and pretty words, would I have stayed there stuck in the middle of his bullshit games and lies again?

"How long, Walk?"

He frowned at me before asking the question he couldn't help asking. "What do you mean? How long? I plan on loving you forever, just like I said when we got married."

"No, how long were you fucking other people?" I asked the question point blank, even though phrasing it like that was not something I'd normally do. I couldn't consider him having sex with other women in any other terms. It hurt too much.

Walker looked extremely uncomfortable as he watched me standing there waiting for his answer. He fidgeted and glanced away eventually.

"You won't even answer her?" Smoke finally stated. "You can't come clean, but you expect her to believe you care enough to stick with her now?"

"Four years," he spat out at Smoke. Then his guilty eyes found mine. We'd been trying to have a baby together for five years. We didn't even seriously start until four years ago.

"We were trying to have a baby then, and you were off fucking other people?"

"Sex was becoming a chore with you, Pop. It was so important to get the baby as a result, but there was no fun in it anymore, because it was like going to work. You know? Something you have to do and not necessarily something you like doing."

That hurt. It didn't matter if I didn't want him anymore, it still hurt to hear that your ex felt like sex was nothing more than a chore they didn't want to do with you so they went looking for excitement elsewhere.

"You do realize that you having sex with other people was probably why you kept failing to get me pregnant in the first place, so you literally perpetuated your own problem and made the situation worse?"

"I didn't," he started to say, and then it sank in. There were reasons the doctors told us to wait in between having sex, because he needed time to build up a high enough sperm count. Instead he was blowing his load with whomever else and leaving nothing behind in the batter.

Smoke scoffed. "Like I said, you're an idiot."

"Well, I think we're done here," I said as I turned to move toward the back door so I could go find Leanne and Brant.

"Poppy," he called out, voice sounding as though it was being affected by emotion, but I didn't bother to turn and look. I was done with Walker Smithson. There was no fixing what he'd broken between us, especially after that admission. I couldn't even wrap my head around the fact that he'd been unfaithful all that time. Had I run into any of the women who were sleeping my husband? Just the thought threatened to make me sick. I'd gone to the doctor and asked to be tested just in case after the storm that opened my eyes to everything – or what I thought was everything at the time. I had, thankfully, been clean. To think I was trying to make a baby while he could have been passing me diseases was an awful feeling. I really needed to get away from the man.

"No!" I heard Smoke say, and I still wasn't interested enough to turn around and look at Walker again. I couldn't look at him. It hurt too much to know how long he had been lying, betraying and cheating on me. "If you hadn't fucked up bad enough before, you have to know that there's no coming back from that. You don't come back from that kind of bullshit with a woman like Poppy." Chief was at my side by the time I reached the back door, and he whispered into my ear, cutting me off from hearing whatever response Walker gave.

"Sis, I need to know you're okay."

"I'm fine," I stated as I waved off his concern. "Obviously, it hurts to know how far back it all went, but I'm in a better place now, I'm happy, I'm healthy, and..."

"Pregnant?" he questioned with a hurt tone.

"Yeah, that too," I turned to look him in the eye then. "I wanted to tell Smoke first, but every time I tried something happened. I found out when I got home from Pittsburgh, and then everything happened with Smoke's family."

"Jesus, talk about bad timing."

"Exactly. Then every time I've attempted to tell him, he's had to run off or something has happened to make me put it on the back burner," I explained.

"We're going to talk about that when we get somewhere private," Smoke's voice trailed over my skin, leaving goose bumps in its wake.

"Smoke," I started to say, but he cut me off.

"Let's get Brantley, and get back to your house before we talk about anything else, okay?"

"Okay," I agreed, because what else could I do?

18. THE PROMISE

I thought he would be leaving the clubhouse at the same time I was, but I had been wrong. Chief had texted me to let me know they were having a chat and then Smoke would be on his way. I had a feeling big brother was attempting to make sure that Smoke wasn't going to be angry with me. I wished he wouldn't, though. I didn't want to get a filtered response to my news. I wanted to know exactly, honestly, what he thought and how he felt about the news.

It was about an hour later when I heard the telltale rumble of a bike in the distance. As it moved closer, my stomach started to flip-flop a bit thinking about what Smoke's reaction might be. It didn't seem as though he took the news poorly in the clubhouse, but that was in front of a whole lot of other people. I almost felt the rumble of his bike as he pulled in next to the house and then the absence of noise when he killed the engine. I had given him a key when Brantley started staying in my spare room so he was able to let himself in. Bubba didn't even flinch at the intrusion now since he was used to Smoke, his sounds, and scent. Brantley was sitting in front of me, with Bubba by his side, playing with his building blocks. Unlike the dog, Brant actually reacted to his presence.

"Unc Moke, wook what I made."

"That's really cool, little man!" Smoke's enthusiastic response put a smile on the boy's face immediately. Smoke leaned down and kissed the top of his head, ruffling his hair as he moved away. Then he started for me. His expression was blank, holding no clues as to how this was going to go for me. So, I waited. He sat next to me, reached over and pulled my legs across his, and turned slightly so he could look me in the eye.

"I'm getting that I have failed to make myself clear with you," he stated with zero emotion as I gulped down my apprehension that was attempting to bubble up from somewhere deep inside me. "I thought I was clear, but according to your brother you're still confused so I'm going to lay it out for you and I need you to hear me." I tipped my head ever so slightly in a nod of agreement before he continued. "I'm with you. Only you. I don't want anyone else, Poppy. I am committed and I honestly don't know how else to say that except that I thought it was straight forward that you were my old lady." I huffed out a shocked breath and he just waved it away.

"Don't care that you're still married to some other fool who was too stupid to hang onto the best thing he'd ever get." He scoffed at that. "Better than he deserved, the idiot. You're my old lady, I don't see you any other way."

"Sophie told me you never told anyone that Julie was your old lady. I just thought," he stopped me by squeezing my thigh.

"Julie never was. The difference is I've already told every single man in the clubhouse and the firehouse that you're mine. They understand that. Now, I need you to understand that I should have made that perfectly clear to you, and I'm sorry I didn't do better." I couldn't even reply to him then because the words and the overwhelming emotions all seemed to get stuck inside me. Honestly, about all I was able to manage were some tears welling up in my eyes, and I damned those bastards, because they didn't convey enough.

"Now, tell me our news, because I don't want to think about the way I found out. I want to hear from your lips to my ears like it was meant to be."

"I'm so sorry about that. I got so frustrated earlier, and I just blurted it out. I hadn't even told anyone. Well, Leanne, but that's because she was worried I was getting sick a lot."

"See, that's something we're going to discuss, because I feel like a real asshole right now since I didn't know you were even getting sick."

I reached up and smoothed out the crinkled up lines of concern on his face. "I didn't want you to know." Clearly, my words did not make anything better so I hurried to explain. "I didn't want you to think there was something wrong until after I knew for sure what was going on. At the same time you had things going on with your family, and when I found out I wanted to tell you right away, but that was the day you guys walked into the clubhouse with bad news."

He thought for a few minutes and then he blew out a

frustrated breath. "Then I was constantly running out every time you wanted us to talk." He shook his head back and forth. "I really fucked that up, didn't I?"

"No, you didn't. This hasn't exactly been an easy week for anyone, but especially not for you. I understand. I'm just sorry you found out that way. I'm sorry you weren't the first one I told, because that was how I planned on it happening. I hadn't even told Chief, because I wanted you to know first. I guess everything just hit me all at once and I really wanted it to sink in for Walker that I am never coming back to him."

"You said you were happy. Earlier, when you were talking to him," he clarified before I could agree.

I smiled at him then. "I am the happiest I've ever been, which makes me feel horrible at times, because this is such an incredibly inappropriate time for me to feel that way considering your loss, and Brant's loss. I know he doesn't really understand yet, and maybe he won't until many years from now. Still, it's crap timing for me to find my happiness and you to be so lost in grief and driven by revenge."

"Poppy, it's not revenge driving me. I want that too, but mostly I want to make sure that you and Brant are safe, even more so now that I know it's not just the two of you I have to worry about." He leaned in then and placed his hand gently on my belly. "In case I forgot to say it, I am so damn excited about this." He leaned over then and kissed my belly just above where his hand was splayed out. "I will take good care of all of you, I swear. I will never step out on you. I will never take you for granted. Poppy, you are everything, and if I ever don't treat you like that's exactly what you, you will kick me in the ass and set me straight, because I can't lose you. Your idiot ex still doesn't realize. Obviously, he thinks he does, but one night soon he's going to be sitting there with some cheap imitation of you, he'll hear about how wonderful your life is, and then it's going to click for him that he could have been part of that. I think it's starting to set in for him now, otherwise I doubt seriously he would have offered to raise another man's kid today."

"I don't care what he's going through. He brought it on himself."

"I know that, honey. I'm just saying, you and me, we are never going to get to that point, because I know exactly what I've got right here." He smiled up at me and then kissed my belly one more time. "When do you need to go see the doctor?"

"Soon. I haven't made an appointment yet, because of the timing of everything else."

"Don't do that. You take care of yourself and our baby above everything, you hear? There are plenty of people who can keep an eye on Brantley while you go to an appointment, and as long as you schedule it for a day I'm not with the fire-house, I'll be there, too." He leaned in and kissed me on the lips then. "Make no mistake, I want to be there. I want to be there for everything."

I couldn't stop the grin from spreading across my face. "That's good because I want you to be there for everything," I told him just before a little boy decided to climb into my lap.

"I be der for tings?" Brantley asked looking worried.

"You will always be there for things, lil' man," I answered.

His smile rivaled my own then. "Good. Me likes tings."

Smoke chuckled at that. "Wonder what he's actually thinking of?"

"Who knows, but if I have anything to say about it, he'll get everything he dreams of."

"You have everything to say about it now," Smoke told me solemnly. I knew there was one thing I'd never be able to grant for Brantley. I couldn't bring his parents back, but I could make sure Smoke and I did our best to stand in for them. It was my promise to them both.

19. THE FEVER

WE SPENT THE NEXT TWO DAYS TOGETHER AS A FAMILY. THAT WAS so weird to say in my head, let alone to experience. It was just Smoke, Brantley, and me. I wondered briefly if Smoke had threatened everyone, because even my brother stayed away. Leanne had worked some of her special brand of magic and got me in quickly to see her doctor. I will never, as long as I live, forget the look on Smoke's face when we were able to hear the heartbeat.

"That's our baby," he'd choked out on a breath so full of reverence and awe that it brought tears to my eyes faster than the heartbeat had.

"Yeah," was all I was able to manage to get out before the doctor was saying things that I just wasn't hearing. He must have figured that out, because he stopped momentarily and just smiled at us while allowing us a few extra seconds to hear that precious sound. "It looks like you are measuring about 8 weeks along, and from what you've told us about your menstrual cycle, I'd say that matches with your estimated due date just fine."

"She's already two months along?" Smoke questioned, coming out of his shocked state. He turned to me then and just grinned. "I guess it's a good thing we like each other, huh? That means we managed to get this done the very first time."

I choked on a laugh as I watched the doctor's eyes round out in surprise. "Well, I'm going to give you a prescription for prenatal vitamins, and get the ladies to set you up with another appointment a month from now. We'll be doing a couple tests then to check on your sugar levels and whatnot, so Amy will let you know what to do and what not to do prior to that appointment."

"Thank you," I told him before glancing over at Nurse Amy whose eyes were laser-locked onto Smoke. Not that I blamed her, because he was a beautiful man, but I suddenly liked Amy a whole lot less.

The doctor noticed my narrowed eyes and turned to see what I saw. He cleared his throat, and Amy seemed to come out of her Smoke-induced haze. She blushed, and then all but ran from the room to gather all the necessary information I would need.

"Sorry about that," my doctor mumbled, and Smoke – who hadn't been paying a bit of attention to Nurse Amy – looked confused. "I'll make sure it's in your records that she doesn't work with you anymore, if I need to."

I waved him off. "It's fine. I can't blame her really, I get lost looking at him too sometimes."

Understanding started dawning on Smoke then as he

chuckled. "If it makes you uncomfortable, get someone else, honey. Though, you know you have nothing to worry about."

The doctor laughed at that. "That was just about as obvious as my nurse," he stated with a chuckle. We both had to laugh at that even while a secret thrill fluttered my tummy, because the fact that Smoke hadn't noticed the woman's obvious attention was something I hadn't experienced in my past. Being someone's world felt amazing.

FIVE DAYS LATER, I wasn't feeling so amazing. I had caught some sort of bug and felt like death. Smoke had been on at the fire department for 24 hours after our doctor appointment to confirm the pregnancy. Then he was called away on club business that I believed involved his sister's killers. It had to be that, because I didn't think anything else could tear him away for that long. On day three, I started with the sniffles and a sore throat that escalated pretty quickly into a full-blown cold, or possibly the flu. Then the vomiting started, just when I'd stopped having issues with morning sickness. I still managed to keep going despite how gross I felt inside and out. Finally though, I had to give up and call someone for help when I realized I didn't have the strength to get up and make Brant breakfast.

"Popwee, I maked you soups, you feelz better. K?"

"What? Brant, no. You don't make soup," I muttered as I used the last of my reserves to text Leanne.

Please help Brant, too sick.

Sure, it was vague, but it was all I could manage, and then, sadly, I don't remember anything after that text message went through and the phone dropped from my hands.

My nose itched with the funny, sterile smell assaulting it. That was the first thing I noticed before hearing the voice that had apparently been speaking to me for some time. There was also the guitar being strummed in the background that made me wonder if I had left the television on, but I didn't remember. That's when panic set in, because I couldn't remember leaving the TV on and now I worried for Brant. "No," the word pushed through my lips on a puff of air, but I didn't think it made an audible sound. The voice I'd been hearing was still a rough timbre against the side of my face, as if someone were lying next to me and whispering in my ear.

"As soon as you're better we'll work out a date to go get it done. I'm not waiting anymore on what everyone else thinks is appropriate. Screw them! I already know everything I need to. You're my woman, you're carrying my baby, and we're already a family so nothing else matters. We'll just be making it official."

What in the world? I glanced to my right and Smoke was there, sitting in a chair beside the bed I was in, and he had his head lying on the bed beside my own. He had stopped talking when I turned my head to look at him and raised his hand up to gently push some of the hair out of my face that had been displaced with my movement. He smiled at me in such a tentative way that I wondered if he had been about to tell me that I was dying until I heard the scrape of something across the floor from the other side of the room. That's when I actually looked around and finally realized I was in a hospital room and it was full of people.

I reached up to push my own hair back in an attempt to smooth out the unkempt, slept on mess, but then it snagged on something and Smoke stopped me from tugging my hand away. He untangled the hair from the object and as he slid my hand back down the sparkle on my finger caught my attention. My eyes widened as the ring came into focus. I glanced around at everyone who all smiled at my reaction and then back to Smoke who sat waiting patiently for my reaction.

"Brant?" I asked, forgetting the ring as it dawned on me that the little guy was not amongst the people in the room. My brother was here, as was Leanne, so who the hell had Brant? Panic set in and the machine to my left started beeping like crazy before a nurse came in to shut it off. Smoke was cooing to me. "Shh, calm down, honey. He's fine." It took a few minutes for his words to register. "He's okay. He's with Kent right now. He's taking care of Bubba too, honey. They're both fine. Leanne got there not long after your text." He appeared to want to say more about that, but stopped himself on a slight growl.

I looked around the room again, finally registering that aside from Smoke, my brother, and Leanne, there were others in the room, too. Wren and his old lady were there, along with Ghost, who most definitely had better things to be doing than sitting in this room with me. Which made wonder how long I'd been here. "The baby?"

"Just fine. They brought an ultrasound in, and we all got to see the heart beat and everything." While I was a bit saddened that I had not been able to see my little baby's heartbeat, I could not deny how happy I was to know that he or she was doing okay.

"How long have I been here?"

"Two days. Leanne was here with you until we got back. Everyone just stopped in to check on you at the perfect time though since you finally decided to stay awake."

I didn't remember ever waking up before now. "I'm so sorry," I stated as tears began to well in my eyes.

"You couldn't help getting sick," he scoffed.

"But Brant..."

"Stop! You let Leanne know, and you did your best. Nobody is blaming you for anything. Brant was obviously worried about you, but he was fine. He just sat there with you until Leanne got there. He wasn't harmed, and it's not like you neglected him. You got sick and passed out. That is more my fault for leaving you with him so long with no help."

"Enough of that shit from both of you," my brother called out as he put down the guitar he'd been holding. Apparently I hadn't been delirious when I heard someone playing. "Neither of you are at fault. It is what it is. Shit happens, and then we get over it and move on. I'm glad you're getting better, Sis. You had us all worried! Don't ever do it again though!" He stood and came to the opposite side of the bed that

Smoke was on and leaned in to give me a kiss on the forehead. "Maybe you should try to get up and get a shower sometime soon though, you stink!

I weakly swatted at him for that comment as Smoke chuckled. He probably wasn't wrong. I felt funky, and was sure all the sweating I'd done while the fever was raging through my body hadn't done me any favors. It was then that Smoke stood too, and turned to everyone.

"Chief is right, Poppy stinks!" Everyone laughed but me, because I was too busy being mortified and trying to hide my reddened face under a pillow. "I think maybe you should give us some time to get her cleaned up and back home, and then you can all stop in see her."

Leanne spoke then. "Don't listen to these brutes, sweetie! You look fabulous, even in your sweat-soaked state. I'll be around to check in on you as soon as you're back home, okay?" I nodded my head after lifting the pillow off of my face long enough for her to see. "I'm really happy to see you're feeling better. You scared the daylights out of me when I showed up and saw Snake was pounding on the door."

"Snake?" I questioned. It was the first time I'd heard about him being there. "What do you mean Snake was pounding on the door?"

As if he'd been summoned by the sound of his own name, the door to my hospital room opened and the man himself walked in. He glanced over and smiled immediately. "Ah, she's finally awake, I see." He wasted no time in walking over to the side of the bed my brother had only vacated moments ago and then he leaned in to give me a kiss on my cheek.

"Hey, sweet girl, how you feeling?" I heard a grumbly, low-level growl coming from my other side indicating Smoke was not thrilled with Snake's interaction with me. Snake just grinned over at him before leaning back.

"I see you didn't waste time moving on from Walker," he stated. I glared at him, which caused him to raise his hands in mock surrender. "I'm not judging, you know that. I just didn't realize you had gotten so serious so fast."

"Didn't Walk tell you about his trip here last week?"

Snake visibly bristled then. "No, he did not." The man turned to get clarification from Smoke then. "He showed up in town?"

Smoke nodded his head. "Confronted Poppy before I could make it there. Seemed pretty sure of himself that he was going to sweep in, apologize, and carry her home with him on the back of his bike."

Snake laughed at that. "No wonder he came back from his trip and sank into the bottom of a bottle."

"You knew about his trip, and no one sent a heads up?" Smoke chastised.

"Nah, man. We knew he was going on a trip, only he was supposed to be headed south to see family in Tallahassee. Thought maybe his ma took a turn for the worse when he showed up drowning his sorrows."

"Is she not doing well?" I asked, genuinely concerned. After all, the man's sins were not his mothers. She had only ever been kind to me.

"Cancer's back from what I hear. Though, I don't hear much from directly these days since he seems to think I picked sides between you and him."

"I'm sorry," I started to apologize to Snake for coming between him and his friend.

He waved my apology off before I could fully make it, though. "Nah, don't you go worrying about that. I just did the right thing when he wouldn't, and he's mad about that. One day he'll realize he's mad at himself and not me."

"You came to my house and found me?" I finally asked after we sat in silence a moment.

"I did. I had to run up here to help with support while the guys were out, and then I figured I'd stop in and let you know I was around if you needed anything, but no one answered the door even though I could hear the dog barking and a kid crying. I took a look in the window and saw you on the floor." He put a hand over his chest rubbed where his heart was. "Took a year off my life to see that, at least." Another growl came from just beyond my shoulder. Snake turned to look at Smoke then. "I know she's your woman, I got that. She's been my friend for a long damn time now though, so calm down with that growling bullshit. I'm not a threat. She's never looked at me the way she does you. There's not a damn thing for you to worry over."

I snickered then, which turned to full blown laughter when Smoke glared in my general direction. He stood then. "I'm going to grab a coffee then find the nurse to hunt down the doctor to see when we can spring you from this joint. You two catch up until then."

We sat quietly just watching each other for a few minutes after Smoke left. Finally, Snake spoke after I moved my hair out of my face again.

"I see he put a ring on your finger already." I glanced

down at the ring that hadn't been there when I passed out and laughed.

"I woke up with this on, and it wasn't there before, so I guess he was making his claim when I couldn't deny it. Not that I would," I hurried to add.

Snake offered up a sad smile. "I'm really happy for you that you're getting what you've wanted all this time, Poppy. I can't say I haven't wished a time or two that things had been different. Hell, I hated Walk for a while after he swooped in and won your heart, because I liked you even back when I first met you. I always wondered what if, you know?"

"Snake," I started to tell him that I didn't feel that way about him, but he waved away my words before I could form them.

"I know I was never on your mind that way, believe me. That's why I'm happy for you. It does my heart good to see that Smoke knows what he has in you, and will cherish that the way Walk never did."

"Thank you, that means a lot. One day, you're going to find that woman who lights up your world and sets it on fire. What you feel for me will be a dim memory in retrospect, I promise." He nodded his head at that, and stood.

"I'll stay until Smoke gets back, but then I need to head out. Sweet's already called me back now that the boys here are back at their clubhouse."

"It was good of him to send you," I told him.

"Yeah, that was a tactful decision on his part. He didn't want anyone hanging around that might make you uncomfortable in any way. Besides, I volunteered so I could see for myself that you were doing okay." Smoke stepped in the room then and Snake turned to leave. "Take care of her," he told Smoke as he clapped him on the back. "Congrats man, you got the best of them right there, don't ever forget it!"

"Don't worry, I won't!"

We both watched as Snake left the room and closed the door behind himself before Smoke over to sit on the side of the bed with me. "He's a little bit in love with you," Smoke mentioned as he absently toyed with the ring on my finger.

"He thinks he is, but maybe now he'll let go of that and be able to find someone who is perfect for him."

"I think you're perfect for me," Smoke stated clearly as he leaned in to look me in the eye.

"That's a good thing since you went and put a ring on my finger while I was basically in a coma for two days." He grinned at me then, and I couldn't help my answering smile. "It's beautiful, by the way."

"I'm glad you like it. I got it while we were away, and then I thought I'd missed the opportunity to give it to you when I was told to get to the hospital."

"Did you think I'd been hurt by the people who..."

"No, we took care of them. There's nothing to worry about any more, honey. That is a chapter of our lives we'll be closing forever now."

"Good." We both sat quietly a moment just breathing each other in before spoke up again. "What about our future chapter? What does that look like?"

"It looks like us being together as a family with our boy and this little one," he stated as he ran his hand across my blanket-covered belly. "I talked to a lawyer about having you adopt Brant with me, and he said he didn't see any reason that couldn't go forward unless Kent were to step in and object. He's not planning to do that, though."

"He was pretty upset with you and this lifestyle last I saw him."

"Yeah, and then his girlfriend apparently pointed out that horrible things happen to people all the time, and it doesn't matter what kind of life they live. Her twin sister was raped and killed when they were young. It was a man from their church who did it. She said she hadn't told anyone about that in years, but she thought Kent needed to hear it so he didn't end up missing out on the living family he still had."

"I'm sorry to hear about her sister, but thankful she shared that with him if it helped."

"It did. We've already spoken about it." He scooted me over a bit and stretched out beside me on the tiny hospital bed, taking up the majority of the space with his large frame. The entire time his hand stayed cradled around my belly. "I can't believe I was gone so long that I didn't even know you were sick, let alone bad enough to end up in here."

"Stop. You heard Chief earlier. Things happen. Please, don't beat yourself up about it. I didn't tell you I was sick because I didn't want you to worry if you were in any danger out there. I just wanted you to stay focused on what you had to do so that you came home safe to Brant and me."

"I love you, Poppy!"

"I love you too, Jared Lewis!" He grunted at my use of his given name, causing me to giggle.

"I hope you like that, because before long you're going to be Mrs. Jared Lewis. There's no way in hell you're bringing our baby into this world while you're still wearing another man's name."

I sighed then. "I think it has a nice ring to it," I offered wistfully, at which point he kissed the side of my head and tucked himself around me, giving me his heat and his strength so I could get better and get the hell out of the hospital sooner.

20. THE HAPPY

I WAS SIX MONTHS PREGNANT BY THE TIME I WAS SUMMONED TO appear in court for my divorce proceedings. Heading down to Georgia with my burgeoning stomach and Brant on my heels wasn't exactly an easy trip, but Smoke did his best to make it pleasant even though what should have been a five-hour trip took nearly eight thanks to all the bathroom stops between Brant and me.

I still didn't understand why I was being made to go all the way back to get this done, but once we were there, the truth would be revealed, or I supposed I should say Walker's fabrications were revealed. I had been forced to attend this mediation farce and it was not making my cranky, needing-to-pee every five minutes, tired-of-traveling self very happy.

"I don't understand why I have to attend mediation. I didn't think Georgia made couples do that," I stated out loud again to my lawyer just as the judge finally walked into the room.

"It is something that we like to encourage when there's a baby on the way."

"Why would my pregnancy matter in any way for me staying with Walker?"

"Well, man, we like to try to keep families together." My jaw dropped.

"He's not my family," I huffed out.

"Ma'am, you're having his baby. Even if your divorce is granted you will still have to deal with one another for the rest of your lives since you share a child together," the judge informed me.

I glared across the table at Walker, who was squirming in his seat, because he knew I was about to hand him his ass.

"Your honor, I would have to be about 15 months pregnant to be having this man's baby. That got the attention of everyone in the room. "I am six months along. I kicked Walker out of my house two months before I left Georgia to go live in West Virginia. I certainly wasn't going to be sleeping with him during those two months, because he was too busy screwing every woman in our town to come check to make sure I was even still alive, let alone possibly in the mood for sex. For a few months prior to that, I couldn't get him to sleep with me either, because sex was a chore for him since we'd been trying to get pregnant for a few years at that point. Let me rephrase, I'd been trying to get pregnant while my husband was cheating on me left, right, and center. He was doing so for four years prior to our split, and he admitted it in front of an entire room full of witnesses who gladly sent their signed statements along to help me out here.

"I did not ever step out on my husband until after I was confronted with the fact that he had been cheating, I kicked him out, and then I filed for divorce and moved to another state to get away from him and all the bad memories. That is when I found the love of my life and the father of my baby. He's right outside in the hallway if we need to bring him in."

"What do you have to say to this?" The judge asked a very uncomfortable looking Walker.

"She had talked to me before about IVF or adopting. I figured we could raise the baby together, like we planned in the beginning anyway."

"Did you not just hear her state that the love of her life is the father of her baby?" The judge glanced between us. "It doesn't seem like that is news to you."

"I was the love of her life!" Walker argued.

"Son," the judge started, "you probably were once upon a time, before she found out you had been betraying her in such a way, and in a repeated fashion. That kind of behavior tends to kill a person's love." He then turned to me. "Mrs. Smithson, I will grant your divorce."

"I would like a name change as well, Smithson belongs to him, and I don't want any part of him in my life any longer."

"Understandable," the judge concurred as Walker choked on emotion I hadn't seen in him in years.

"Poppy, don't do this," he sobbed out as he wept openly.

"Mr. Smithson, I suggest you take this hard-learned lesson into the future with you, and remember what it was like to love someone and mess it up so bad that the outcome is a woman who no longer wants to remember you."

The judge turned back to me then and started to tell me

that my attorney would have the finalized papers to me within a week. Walker stood to leave and the judge cleared his throat. "Mr. Smithson, you should have a seat."

"I thought we were done here."

"I am done with Mrs. Smithson, but you, your lawyer, and I need to have a discussion about the false pretenses I was brought here under today. That type of thing comes with penalties, sir."

I didn't wait around to hear what happened to Walker, or what kind of penalties he was about to suffer. Instead, I left and ran straight into the arms of the man I loved while the little boy we were now responsible for came and clung to my legs like a little spider monkey.

I gave Smoke the abbreviated version of what happened as we walked outside to my car, and he just laughed. "I can't believe that idiot tried to tell them the baby was his." He shook his head. "He'd better be glad the judge is in there reaming his ass for it, because if he'd walked out here with you I wouldn't have been able to hold back this time."

"It doesn't matter," I told him. "He's my past now, officially. They said I'd have the papers this week."

"Good, the day after you get those papers, be prepared, because you're about to be my wife."

"I'm looking forward to it," I told him, and I meant every single word. There was a time when I didn't think I'd ever be able to marry again. Hell, I had actually mourned the loss of being able to have children too, because I thought there was no way I'd ever trust another man after Walker. I was so darn happy to know that I had been wrong, and that there were good guys out there still. The kind of guys who were actual men, and knew what it meant to care for someone completely. I'd finally found that in Smoke, and I wouldn't give up the opportunity to tie myself to him officially for anything.

TWO DAYS after my divorce papers came in the mail, Smoke managed to throw together the quickest wedding in the world. Ghost was ordained already, as he'd apparently married Wren and his old lady the previous year. I wore a simple buttercup yellow sundress and white ballet flats to my wedding. I wanted something bright and cheery, and thankfully we had an unseasonably warm, spring day full of sunshine and bright blessings for our union. My brother stood ready to walk me down the makeshift aisle on the outside decks behind the clubhouse. The clubwomen had worked hard turning the decks into a gorgeous space filled with yellow ribbons and white and yellow flowers. The entire space was pleasantly peaceful and jubilant all at once. My soul smiled on the space as my brother tucked my arm through the crook of his elbow.

"I know you would rather have dad here, but I have to tell you, Poppy, I'm glad I'm the one getting to walk you down this aisle, because I know this is your forever. I can feel it all the way to my bones."

Oh man, the tears started to well up in my eyes with his words. I leaned in and placed a quick kiss on his cheek and patted his arm with the hand I had resting there. "Then get me down that aisle to my future, big Brother."

That was how my brother ended up marching me down the aisle to the man of my dreams and the little man standing there with him who had also stolen my heart. Brant stood there looking sleek in his black, little boy suit with his hair slicked back and smile plastered to his face. He waved at me, causing me to grin even bigger as the tears continued to pool and threaten to spill from my eyes in joyous rivulets.

Brant glanced away from me long enough to look up at his uncle then. "Unc Moke, we maweeying Popwee?"

"Yeah, lil man, we're marrying Poppy." Smoke told him as they both glanced back over at me.

"Yes!" The little boy announced loudly and added to his enthusiasm with a solid fist pump, too.

"Yeah, buddy, I feel the same," Smoke agreed with him, much to the entertainment of those gathered to witness our union. Speaking of, I hadn't even noticed a single other person. My boys were all I could see as I moved closer to them. I knew that Kent was there standing in as best man for his brother and Leanne was there standing up for me where my sister, Layla, would have been. Then there was Ghost in the middle of everything waiting to officiate and pronounce us man and wife.

My life was on a crash course with perfect, and there were moments where I couldn't believe I wasn't dreaming. This was one of them. Smoke stood there wearing a matching suit to Brant's. It was dark, and he still had his kutte on over top of the thing, which was perfect in my opinion. He also wore his riding boots, because unless he was running or at work, that was it for him. I didn't mind, because he looked damn sexy as I finally made my way there and realized Ghost was already speaking.

"I do," my brother told him as he placed my hand into Smoke's. "Be good to her," my brother commanded.

"Always," Smoke returned before shifting his attention back to me.

"Me too," Brant yelled before taking my other hand. I smiled down at him and watched as he beamed back up at me. "We gettin' mawweed Popwee," he told me quietly.

"I know, baby," was all I could say before the emotion choked me up. We managed to say our "I dos" with Brant joining in, and I hoped that someone was recording this, because there was no way I wouldn't want to show this to Brant one day. I was already picturing playing this video for him at his own wedding!

Once our vows were spoken, we received congratulations from everyone, and had some cake, Smoke swept me away to points unknown. We hadn't planned a honeymoon since I was pregnant and we had Brant, too. I was curious as to where we were going, but not one single person would give me a hint. They just sent us off with well wishes and promises to keep Brant safe and entertained for the night.

We drove passed the house I was currently renting, and a few blocks further before Smoke turned down a tree-lined drive. We followed the drive for a bit before it opened up into a gorgeous and well-maintained lawn. Beyond that stood a beautiful farmhouse complete with wrap-around porch. The siding on the house was a pale yellow with white trim, shutters, and door. There was also a porch swing hanging there along with white flower baskets that had yellow daisies planted in them. I figured it was some sort of bed and breakfast place, though there were no cars there, so that couldn't be right.

As soon as Smoke killed the engine and came around to open my door, I heard the telltale sound of barking. A very specific bark, too. "Bubba's here?" I asked.

Smoke just grinned at me then pulled me to stand in front of him while we gazed out at the house in front of us. "Welcome home, Poppy!"

"Welcome? What?" I asked, not fully understanding what he was saying.

"This is our new home, and my wedding present to you."

I turned in his arms then so I could see his face. "Are you serious? This is ours?"

"Yeah, honey, it's ours. I thought it would remind you of the house you grew up in. Chief said it's a lot like it on the inside, and we'll have plenty of room for the kids."

I shut him up with a kiss that could have melted the damn house down. "I love you!" The words were muttered into his lips before he returned my heated kiss tenfold. I honestly didn't get to see much of the house as Smoke swept me up in his arms, moved through the door, and each of the rooms until we were in the back of the house and walking into a first floor master suite.

"There's furniture in here already," I stated dumbly, because obviously there was furniture when he sat me gently on top of king sized bed with the fluffiest down comforter beneath me.

"We can get new furniture if you like. This is my stuff from the condo."

"What are you doing with your condo?"

"Selling it," he told me with a shrug of his shoulder. "Actually, Ghost made mention that the club may think of taking it over that way we have a place for anyone who might need it that's not inside the clubhouse. Besides, Gray's still staying there for now, but I honestly don't think it will be long before he..." I shut him up with another kiss.

"Don't want to talk about Gray or the club right now," I murmured against his lips. I felt them turn up into a grin only moments before he moved in, and laid me flat on my back, hovering over my body, and kissing me senseless. At least, I would have been kissed senseless if it weren't so damn uncomfortable. Being pregnant definitely had draw-backs and losing the ability to lie comfortably on my back was one of them. I squirmed beneath him, drawing his attention, and he quickly retreated, backing away until I had room to turn onto my side. I let out a contented sigh as soon as I got comfortable.

"Sorry, honey, I wasn't thinking." His hand flew to my belly, rubbing it gently as he watched my face for clues that I was mad. I wasn't. I had been just as swept up in us.

"It's fine, Smoke. It's just really uncomfortable like that." He moved further away, and my emotions heightened with the impending onslaught of rejection only to be turned on their heads as the man stood before me, removing every stitch of clothing he had been wearing. Then he came to me, sat me up, and gently lifted my yellow dress over my head, and off my body to join his clothing in painting our new bedroom floor.

Once I was divested of my panties and bra too, Smoke climbed in the bed behind me and gently lifted my hair up and off my neck only to replace it with his kisses and warm breath which was torture, because my nerve endings seemed to be a million times more sensitive throughout my entire body. I would blame the pregnancy hormones, but honestly, I think it was just the Smoke effect. His hands glided down my body from my shoulders, fingers teasing down my arms, and launching shivery gooseflesh on in their wake. Then he moved one to cradle my belly and the other to cup my breast as his mouth continued to worship my hairline at the nape of neck and down to the juncture of shoulder and neck where I was super sensitive these days.

Another shiver followed the movement of his mouth and the hand that he'd had wrapped around my belly disappeared momentarily from its position as he moved to test that I was ready for him. I was always ready for him, though. He nipped my shoulder playfully with his teeth before sinking himself into me from behind, and then his arm was back around my mid-section gently cradling my belly as he made love to me like that. We didn't have to be face to face for it to be the most intimate position I'd ever been in. His love wrapped around me in a cocoon just as his body did. His gentle reverence and care for my comfort would have brought me to my knees were I still standing. Instead, they brought me to a blissful release as his hand sunk down and deft fingers toyed with my clit as he continued his slow, languorous thrusting in conjunction with the movement of his fingers.

It didn't take long to tip me over the edge, and when I went, he fell over that cliff into oblivion with me.

21. THE BIRTH

Contractions were the devil's work. I was certain of it. There could be no other reason why they felt as though my entire mid-section was on fire and being ripped open all at once. "Ow! It fucking hurts!"

"I can tell, honey." Smoke stated, looking pained as well.

"How can you tell?"

"You mean besides the fact that you're dropping f-bombs left and right and damn near ripping my arm off with each..." he stopped mid-way through his speech as another contraction rocked through my body, leaving me panting for breath and squeezing the absolute crap out of Smoke's arm.

"Damn, dude, that looks like it hurts," my brother called out from somewhere in the room.

"Why is he still here?" I asked on a whine as the contraction released me from its grasp for a moment.

"I was just dropping off your bag since you two were out of the house so fast you forgot it."

"Hi, everyone! How is our patient doing today?" The

bubbly blond nurse asked as she came skipping into the room. I kid you not she was skipping.

"I'm doing," I said flatly and then the mother of all contractions hit and the exorcist-level demon inside me took over speaking. "FUCK THIS SHIT, I'm not doing just fine at all! Get this baby out of me!

"Oh dear, that sounds like it was a bad one," the nurse offered in a patronizing tone. I wanted to throat punch her on principle for the skipping, and that just wasn't like me, but her words were like blades stabbing me in the back, and I wanted to return the gesture. At the thought, I wondered what the hell was wrong with me. It had to be a demon. I was going to give birth to a demon. I just knew it.

"Honey, you're doing just fine. You use as many f-bombs as you need. I'm sure they won't be our child's first word," he told me at the end, which caused me to roll my eyes just before another contraction ripped through my body.

"Oh, God, something's happening down there," I told the nurse through gritted teeth.

She just smiled at me and waved off my words. "It's a bit too early for all that. I'll be checking you in just a few minutes when the doctor comes in. She glanced down at the little tablet in her hand and nodded her head as if she needed to agree with herself. "Yep, it says here that your nurse prior to shift change just checked you about 45 minutes ago."

I screeched words out through pain level 20-gazillion. "There is a head coming out of my body, and it burns like a motherfucker."

Smoke moved over some and went to take a look between

my legs only to get a knee to the face when I jerked in reaction the excruciating pain that was burning through me. As soon as he shook off the blow, he continued with what he was doing as if nothing happened and glanced down between my spread-wide legs. "There's a head, get the goddamn doctor in here, now!"

The nurse jumped into action, running to the bottom of the bed, and dropping the end portion out from under my feet. She caught one and Smoke caught the other, bringing them up to perch on the edge, while my legs stayed splayed apart, gifting everyone in the room a clear shot at my poor vagina being stretched by the demon child who couldn't wait to be born.

"Shit! I did not need to see that!" Chief yelled before running from the room. I heard him calling out to someone. "I just saw the head, someone better get my sister's doctor in there now!" There was a clanging sound as someone came running through the door, and before the man could bend down and take a look between my legs I heard my brother yell from the hallway again. "Anyone have some whiskey? Jesus, I can't un-see that shit."

Great! I'd never hear the end of his trauma after this. Never mind that I'm the one pushing a baby out of my body. "Oh-dear-lord-sweet-baby-jesus-take-the-wheel!" I screamed out in a jumble of nonsense as the burning sensation in my poor lady parts had me nearly coming off the bed. I bared down and pushed for all I was worth, despite the nurse frantically yelling at me not to push. Screw that. I wasn't on her time frame and neither was this baby. Obviously.

"Please, you have to stop pushing, because the doctor isn't here yet."

"Are you fucking insane?" I screamed at her. "Get out! Get the hell out of here. My husband can deliver our baby, because it isn't waiting!"

"Whoa, now, honey. We'll get you there. If you need to push, you push."

Just then the doctor came bounding into the room, took one look at the scene, and jumped into the action pushing the shell-shocked nurse out of the way. "Get her out!" I yelled again.

The nurse sputtered a moment before the doctor quickly turned an evil eye on her. "You heard the patient. Send someone else in, right now."

She took off in a flurry, tears noticeable, and I did not give one single fuck, because "Ahhhh!" I was pushing again, and this time, both Smoke and the doctor were cheering me on and telling me what a good job I was doing. For one fleeting moment, I couldn't believe I had been trying to do this on purpose for years. What had I been thinking? Who signed up for this kind of torture? No one, that's who! Not a single damn person who knows what's coming signs up to do this all over again!

"One more good push, and we'll be handing your baby over to you, Poppy!" The doctor ordered, and I gladly made it happen. I felt the instant relief when the baby finally came out and was placed bloody and squirming on my chest. The new nurse reached in immediately and suctioned, then the most beautiful noise I'd ever heard erupted throughout the room. My sweet baby was screaming..."

"It's a girl!" The doctor called out.

My sweet baby girl was screaming her head off and I couldn't be any happier than I was in that moment. I didn't care that there was still a strange man doing things between my legs. I'll be honest, I probably didn't want to know what he was still doing down there. I shivered at the thought and then finally realized Smoke was now beside me again, looking down at our daughter with the most elated expression on his handsome face.

"A baby girl," he spoke in an awed hush as our daughter stilled and seemed to attempt to turn in the direction of her father's voice.

"You want to do the honors and cut the cord?" The doctor asked him, breaking Smoke's trance momentarily. He shook his head, 'no' while placing his finger in our little girl's hand and watching as she clamped down on it, holding him right back. Tears welled up in his eyes at that moment and it was all I could do to keep my heart inside my chest. I knew it was too full in that moment to be contained.

"Do you have a name for her?" The nurse asked.

"Sophie," Smoke spoke on an emotion-filled rasp.

"Layla," I said a moment later.

"Lewis," he finished for us.

"Sophie Layla Lewis?" The nurse confirmed the name, and we both agreed while watching our daughter. "That's a beautiful name." She continued about her business, writing things down, and then came to us with a blanket in her hand. "I need to get this little one cleaned up for you real quick. I promise I'll bring her back quickly."

Panic ensued, and Smoke stood straight, looking suddenly angry with the nurse.

"Calm down, daddy. You can come and watch her get her first bath. She never has to leave your sight." Smoke looked equal parts relieved and conflicted at having to leave me behind.

"I'd rather you stay with her," I told him. He nodded and followed the nurse out into the hall. My brother came back into the room then. I was now covered up and whatever the doctor had been doing while I was lost in my family had been finished.

"Sophie Layla Lewis, huh?" he asked as he swiped at a tear that went rolling down his cheek.

"Yeah," I started to say, wondering if I'd overstepped by not asking how he'd feel about me using our sister's name.

"I think that's the most beautiful thing I've heard all day, next to that little girl screaming when she came into this world. Our sister and his will always be looking over her, they'll be a part of her, forever." My brother leaned in then and hugged me gently before placing a kiss on my forehead. "Proud of you, Sis."

"Thank you for coming to get me, Chief." If it hadn't been for my brother coming to take me away from Sierra High, I would still be there wallowing in my own misery instead of living my dream. I yawned, suddenly tired beyond anything I'd ever felt before. That didn't stop me from hearing my brother's response, though.

"I will always be there for you, Sis. Always!"

WE TOOK a week to get used to our new family dynamic before we allowed anyone to come over. It was a week full of blessings, because it gave us all time to bond as a family. Brant was taking his big brother duties seriously, even disposing of dirty diapers while gagging, and telling Sophie how pretty she was the entire time. That kid was born to be a big brother. Smoke was heaven-sent too though, so it must have been in their genes. It didn't matter that Smoke would argue that fact since his own father had walked out on his family, but he was bound and determined not to be the same man his own father was. If I was up at night feeding Sophie, then so was he. He would sit there, talking to me while stroking the fine little reddish brown hairs on our daughter's head.

My world had come full circle from a place where I used to dread getting up in the morning straight into the dreams I'd once had for how I saw my life going. I had the best of men by my side, the sweetest little boy, and the most darling baby girl ever. My life was complete here in Cedar Falls.

A knocking on the door was about to reiterate just how complete my life actually was. Bubba moved himself to stand in front of the bassinet we had set up in the living room. The one that currently held a sweetly sleeping baby girl and where a big brother stood watch, waiting for her to wake. I moved to answer the door, but Smoke came down the stairs and beat me to it. Dear, sweet lord, he was trying his best to get me to make another baby with him already. He was still somewhat dripping from his shower, shirt off, and jeans on but not buttoned up yet, and bare feet padding across the wooden floors. I licked my lips, and the fool caught me, giving me his sexy-beast grin that told me he knew exactly where my naughty mind had just gone. Straight to the baby making process that I had foresworn only a week ago. So that was how women ended up going through the fresh hell that was childbirth again and again. Damn our hormones and the sexy men in the world who incited a riot inside our bodies!

When Smoke finally opened the door it was to my brother's disgruntled ass fussing at him. "Go put some damn clothes on. No one wants to see that shit!"

"I do," I stated loudly. I definitely didn't want my man covering up all that perfection when I was finally awake enough to appreciate it. Again, Smoke just grinned at me as the house started filling up with people. My brother dove to the head of the line, waiting to get some sweet baby love, only to be stopped in his tracks by a growl from Bubba.

"Good boy, Bubba!" I praised my dog and then turned to my brother. "Go wash your damn hands, and do not even think of kissing my baby on her face, no matter how cute she is. That goes for all of you!" Maybe I was being neurotic or overprotective, but I didn't want my baby girl exposed to any more germs than necessary while she was still so tiny. My brother's eyes were saucer wide, but he still listened and went to the kitchen to wash his hands. Suddenly, a line formed behind him with all the women who had come in waiting to do the same thing.

Ghost chuckled. "You sound like Leanne did after the girls were born. Jesus, times have changed. I remember when Jamie was born, we didn't even think about things like that." Jamie was Ghost's adult daughter, Angel Girl, the one who ran Sierra High Evermore MC back in my hometown in Georgia. Since she was into her thirties now, I figured he had a point. Times had changed, but that's because someone learned the hard way so the rest of us could be more careful.

My brother was the first back to the baby, and of course he had her cradled in his arms in no time flat. This time Bubba allowed the invasion into his little human's space. I swear that dog knew things no dog should be capable of.

"How are you doing?" Leanna asked as she moved in beside me to watch my brother coo at the baby in his arms.

"I'm doing well. Tired, but otherwise I feel fine." Then I glanced down at the sweat pants and t-shirt I was wearing. "I'll be glad when this jelly-belly thing goes away. I never knew!"

Leanne laughed. "It is definitely a weird feeling until it goes back to normal, that's for certain." She glanced over at Smoke who was in the middle of pulling a shirt over his head while Brant clung to his legs. "How's he handling daddy duty?"

I beamed over at her, which was probably answer enough. "He's perfect. If I'm up with Sophie, so is Smoke. He gets Brant up, makes him breakfast, and then makes sure I get something to eat too while he takes care of getting her ready for the day." I turned to face Leanne. "He's perfect and there are moments where I don't think this is all real. Like, maybe I cracked all to pieces back in that house in Georgia, and I'm sitting there locked inside this fantasy, you know?"

Her sweet smile came just before her arms wrapped around my middle. "Welcome to your life, Poppy! It's fabulous now, and you deserve nothing less."

THE END - EPILOGUE

July 12, 2018

I can't believe this is happening!" I breathed the words out through clenched teeth as another contraction hit me. "They still have a couple weeks before they're due. It's storming. Not on this day..."

"Calm down, babe, everything will be just fine." Smoke was the epitome of a calm in the storm. He literally put my mind at ease, if not my body. There was no putting that at ease until our boys made their way into this world. Even if my water hadn't just broken, I would know that there was no stopping them now. They were going to be relentless, just like their dad.

"But, this day?" I whined out the semi-question. "Why this day? Why during a storm? You know what this has meant to me in the past."

"Shh," Smoke offered up on a whisper against the side of my head as he buckled me into my car. "We're going to the hospital so you can deliver our boys, and everything is going to be just fine, I promise." He turned to look over his shoulder then at my brother who stood there with grim concern written all over his chiseled features. "You got them?"

He meant our boy Brantley and our daughter Sophie, of course. Chief nodded his head, then allowed himself to smile. "I'll bring them by to meet their brothers as soon as you give me a heads up."

"See you soon," Smoke called to my brother as he tucked himself into my car. "Fuckin' cages," he mumbled, making me chuckle before the next contraction hit me full force and I had to grab on to the oh-shit handle on the side of the door. "Easy, baby. Breathe through it, you can do it."

"Shut up and drive!" I grumbled through the pain. He did just that, and had us at the hospital in no time, despite the horrid weather slowing us down a bit.

We managed to get inside, have me changed into a hospital gown, wired up with monitors, and settled into a room about five minutes before the doctor came by to check on me. "Looks like those kiddos didn't want to wait around another couple weeks after all, huh?" he announced as he came through the door grinning at me like a loon. Smoke stiffened a bit, because he wasn't fond of the doctor we had this time around. That probably had something to do with the fact that he was in his early thirties and very handsome. Not that he held a candle to Smoke, but who was I to judge why men became territorial?

"Nope," I stated quickly just before another contraction sent pain wrapping around my waistline. "Ouch," I managed to whimper out as I felt a tear slip free of my eye and fall down my cheek.

"Okay, let's get you laid back so I can check your progress." As the doctor peered between my legs Smoke grabbed hold of my hand and started smoothing my hair back from my hairline with his other. He was attempting to comfort me, but I thought maybe he was doing it a little for himself at that moment, too. "Hmm," Doc's voice caught my attention immediately.

"Hmm? What is hmmm?" I asked in a panicky state.

"Hmm means these boys are ready to get the show on the road. You're at a solid nine centimeters already. I'm going to have Libby start breaking down the bottom half of the bed so we can get you closer to the edge. You remember the drill from last time, I presume?"

Last time I had a horrible nurse and a no-show doctor until the baby was almost out of me. It had been a nightmare. This time, I was happy to hear my doctor talking me through things. "I'm not sure I can do this. Last time I was so exhausted after Sophie," I lamented. "This time, I have to keep going for baby number two."

"That's the plan, and you will do just fine, I have no doubts."

"Well, that's good, because one of us should be sure of things," I stated simply before attempting to breathe through the jolting pain in my belly.

"I believe in you too, honey. You've got this. I'll be here to help you through it, just like last time."

"Last time, you ended up with a black eye," I reminded him. Smoke just chuckled.

"That's how I know you'll do just fine this time too, honey. You're a fighter, and our boys are impatient. So, let's do this. The sooner you get them here, the better you'll feel."

I sighed at that, because I remembered how much better I did feel once Sophie had been placed in my arms. The difference between labor and holding my little nugget in my arms had been night and day.

"Okay, but what if... there's the storm, and this is the day..." I started to say before Smoke cut me off.

"Babe, no. This day is different. This is redemption weather, come to wipe the slate clean and set things right. Those storms took too much from you before, now it's time to give back. Your family is giving over our boys to us, and this storm is their way of blessing them. Don't ever allow yourself to think any different."

Tears trailed down my face, and this time it had nothing to do with the physical pain and everything to do with my heart, the man standing before me, reassuring me, and all I could do was believe every word he uttered as the doctor yelled for me to push. That push and all the others to follow gave way for the birth of our boys, Decker and Devon Lewis. I may have lost a lot to the storms, but I had gained so much more in Brantley, Sophie, the twins, and the man who loved me so well I never had to question anything. I just knew. His love surrounded all of us – day in and day out – without fail. I couldn't have asked for more. He was right. This was our time, and our growing family was blessed beyond measure.

THANKS FOR READING REDEMPTION WEATHER, book #1 in the Aces High MC - Cedar Falls Series

Please read/review the book, as this is how other readers find the books you love.

Don't forget to check out the other books in the Aces High MC - Cedar Falls Series.

- Smoke and the Flame
- Proven

ACKNOWLEDGMENTS

This book was brought to you by coffee – thank you especially to Bones Coffee Co. – and Strawberry Twizzlers! No, seriously, I think I have an addiction, okay several addictions! Whatever. Don't judge me! ;)

Keeping this short and sweet because no one reads them anyway. 😌

Thank you to the readers who have always been so supportive!

ALSO BY CHRISTINE MICHELLE

Angel Girl · JoJo · Keys

Robeson Family Novels (standalones)

The Forgotten Wife · When the Last Petal Falls · A Different Husband

Standalone Novels

The Groupie Journal

Letters to Lily

His Bittersweet Regret

Bad at Love

TFO

The Fortunate Ones

T.I.E. Series

The Infinite Something · The Infinite Beat

Valhalla Rising

Revived

Dark Leopards MC (paranormal)

Ridden by Darkness · The B Team

Mirage Island Mates

Into the Grasslands · Beyond the Grasslands

Seasons Pack Series

Winter Wolves

The Ancients Series

Shadows of the Ancients · Falling into the White · Branches of the Willow
· Bound by the Moon

Vukodlak Brew Series

Entwined · Enraged

The Awakening Series

Birthrights · Revelations · Incarnations

Death Viewers

Breathless

Upper YA Titles

The Voodoo Follies (PNR)

Catch a Falling Star (Dystopian Romance)

ANNE STORM

Savage Vipers MC

Wait For Me · Devastate Me · Surprise Me · Baby Me

Loved for the Holidays

Cupid Broke My Heart · Ghosted by Texas · Resolving Rumors

Cheating Hearts Series

The Homewrecker's Fate · The Regrettable Mistake

ABOUT THE AUTHOR

Christine Michelle runs on coffee and giggles as she writes her angst-fueled romance stories (motorcycle club, rockstar, paranormal, college, & other contemporary as well as women's fiction and marriage in trouble novels).
She is a mom to four humans (2 girls, 2 boys – all grown now).
When she's not writing books, she enjoys reading, drawing, hiking, or feeding her soul with live music at concerts.
Christine is a traveler and has lived all over the USA (and other parts of the world). She currently lives in San Antonio, TX with her two fur babies.

Universal links to everything

(website, social media, book links, and more)
https://linktr.ee/christinemichelle

facebook.com/M00nlitDreams

instagram.com/christinemichelle_annestorm

tiktok.com/@christine.michelle.books